Now You
See Me

CHRIS McGEORGE

ORION

An Orion paperback

First published in Great Britain in 2019 by Orion Fiction,
an imprint of The Orion Publishing Group Ltd
Carmelite House, 50 Victoria Embankment
London EC4Y 0DZ

An Hachette UK Company

1 3 5 7 9 10 8 6 4 2

A CIP catalogue record for this book
is available from the British Library.

ISBN 978 1 4091 7810 1

Typeset by Input Data Services Ltd, Somerset

Printed and bound in Great Britain by Clays Ltd, Elcograf S.p.A.

MIX
Paper from
responsible sources
FSC® C104740

www.orionbooks.co.uk

for the lost and
for the found . . .

1

Robin's phone buzzed on the table and he looked up at the man standing over him apologetically. The man didn't even seem to notice – he just kept staring at Robin with a blank expression, waiting for Robin to do his thing.

Robin signed the book to a 'Vivian', writing his standard message and signing it with a quick flick of the wrist. He closed the hardback, sliding it back over to the man who picked it up, grunted in something that resembled approval and made a break for the cashier. Robin hoped Vivian would appreciate his scrawl a little more.

Suppressing a sigh, Robin looked down at his phone at the exact second it stopped buzzing. A bubble popped up on his locked screen indicating he had a missed call from an unknown number just before the display went to sleep. Probably just his sister using the surgery phone.

He looked around. The signing event wasn't going particularly well. Robin was sitting precisely in the centre of Waterstones Angel Islington at a round table piled up with copies of *Without Her*. When he had first got there, thirty minutes previously, the stack had been ridiculously high. Now it was more realistic, but not because of sales. Robin had hidden most of the copies under the table, to make the pile seem less daunting. Still though, people seemed to dispel when they saw him like paperclips flying away from the wrong side of a magnet.

A plucky young Waterstones employee, who had introduced herself as Wren, came over with an enthusiastic bounce. She was full of energy, genuinely excited at the prospect of matching a good book with its owner. Robin wished he could summon up even half as much energy as her, but these days, his bones had started to creak, the grey flecks in his hair had turned into patches and he found himself out of breath with the mere prospect of a walk. Wrinkles had burrowed into his face in all the usual places and any spark of youth in his eyes had dimmed a long time ago.

Often he wondered if Samantha would even recognise him anymore – if she walked into their flat tomorrow, she would shriek at the sight of the old man sitting on the sofa. Sometimes that thought made him laugh, sometimes it made him cry.

'How's it going?' Wren said, looking at the pile of books with delight. Robin shifted his body so the stack under the table wasn't visible. He didn't care about his own image, he just didn't want Wren to feel bad. It wasn't Wren's fault that *Without Her* was a hard sell.

'It's fine,' Robin said, not able to summon up a more positive adjective. His phone buzzed and without looking away from Wren, he reached and declined it.

'Right,' Wren said, her eyes flitting from him to the phone and back, losing some of her smile, 'well, if you need anything, you know where I am. I'll try and direct some people over if they look the type.'

'Thank you,' Robin said, making up for Wren's fading smile with one of his own. 'That would be great.' As Wren turned away and made her way to the front of the shop, he wondered how she would pitch his book to any unfortunate passer-by. It wasn't exactly a rip-roaring tale. Robin knew that when he wrote it, and had been ready to deem the whole project a therapy exercise and lock it in a drawer never to see it again. He still wished he had done that. But his twin sister Emma had persuaded him to give it to an agent and it had gone from there. 'It's so good, Robin. You just don't see it. It's the pain. The real, genuine pain of it. It's sumptuous,' Stan Barrows said, when they had first met at his high-rise agency office. He had never heard pain described as sumptuous before, as though the old, smart gentleman was going to take his heartbreak and carve it up like a steak before his eyes.

Robin didn't like Barrows but the man had got him a good deal. And his freelance journalism had hit a brick wall. A new wave of journalists were coming to take all the articles away from older guys like him – kids who couldn't remember a time without the Internet, and could bash out an article and sell it on before Robin could even fire up his word processor. He needed something. So he signed the contract for the book, trying to think Sam would approve.

And eighteen months later, here Robin was, still not knowing if it had been the right thing to do. He picked up one of the hardbacks and looked at it. The cover was a pale tinge of blue, with four photos of Sam – Polaroid-style – scattered across the background almost as though someone had thrown them. They overlapped, and in the spaces between, the title and his name were embossed in black letters. The topmost photo was of Samantha as a baby, six months old sitting on a playmat with a toy Thomas the Tank Engine in her hands. The second was a photo of her in her school uniform on her first day of secondary school, looking apprehensive. The third photo was her graduation photo when she graduated from Edinburgh University – MSc in Psychology, top of her class. The last photo was of their wedding day – Robin and Samantha Ferringham, till death they do part. Robin didn't like looking at the book but he wouldn't have no matter the cover – the photos had been picked by the publisher and he had gladly relinquished that duty. He'd just sent them all the photos he had and they had obviously chosen the most heart-wrenching ones – the ones that would sell.

To say Robin resented the book was too strong – he still felt a certain pride for writing it – but he didn't ever want to look at it. It would always be a physical representation of pain, his pain, the pain of—

That familiar sound. The buzzing. His phone again. He looked at it to see the familiar 'UNKNOWN NUMBER'. What was this – the third time? If it was his sister, she wouldn't be ringing without cause – she knew he was working. And if it wasn't Emma, then someone really wanted to get hold of him. He let the phone buzz a few more times, looked around to see that the store was still quiet and picked up.

'Hello,' he said, as soon as the phone got to his ear.

He expected Emma to answer him, but instead a harsh robotic female voice crackled into life. 'You are receiving a pre-paid telephone call from . . .' a young man's voice cut in, 'Matthew,' before returning to the robot, 'a resident of Her Majesty's Prison New Hall. If you are on a mobile device, there may still be charges associated with accepting this call. In accepting this call, you are accepting that this call will be monitored and may be recorded. If you accept these terms, please press 1.'

Robin's mind scattered in many directions. Someone – some 'Matthew' – calling him from a prison? He didn't know anyone in prison – hadn't ever known anyone who had gone to prison, hell, he hadn't even known anyone who had worked in one.

His first thought was that it was a mistake. But then he remembered this person had rung him three times, one after the other. And by the sound of the robot, he had paid for it. Whoever this Matthew was, he really wanted to talk to him. But then maybe poor Matthew had just gotten the number wrong?

The robot lady started up again – 'You are receiving a pre-paid . . .' but Robin cut her off by pressing 1. And he waited.

Any pretence that this was a mistake was shattered when the same small voice on the other end said, 'Is this Mr Ferringham? Mr Robin Ferringham?'

Robin looked around suddenly in shock, as though

5

he might catch the perpetrator of this weird call in his sightline. But no – the store was almost empty as before, and of course no one was watching him.

This was wrong. Robin had been very careful to safeguard his mobile number. It had been one of the most beneficial suggestions Stan Barrows had ever offered, when Robin had submitted his draft of *Without Her* with a plea for information at the end that included his phone number. 'No,' he had said simply, not elaborating until he was asked. 'People, sick people, will play with you. They'll have some fun. They'll call you and call you, trying to get a rise out of you. And they won't stop until they do.' Robin argued at first and then Barrows said something he would always remember. 'Don't be the kind of person, Robin, who thinks everyone's moral compass is as configured as theirs.' Ever since then he hadn't put his personal number on anything – no online profiles, no contracts, not even take away orders.

'I've been calling,' the voice said, almost as if he were reminding Robin he was there.

'Who gave you this number?' Robin said, so pointedly that one of the only customers in the shop – an old woman perusing the Ms of the crime section – looked around. Robin met her gaze for a split second before turning away. 'Who?'

'I've been calling.' The young man was fumbling for his words. 'I didn't think you were going to pick up.'

Maybe I shouldn't have, Robin thought, but instead said, 'Tell me who gave you this number or I'm going to hang up.'

Robin felt something in his gut, a hot rage that he hadn't felt in a long time, and he wasn't sure exactly why, until the speaker said, 'She did. She said her name was Samantha.'

Robin gripped the phone so hard the sides cut into his hand and his fingers went white. Sam. Sam had given some guy in a prison his number? When? Why? Wait, NO – this was a troll attempt, pure and simple. This Matthew was playing around with him. Maybe he wasn't even calling from a prison – maybe that robotic voice was just part of some stupid prank, made to lower his guard.

Robin's finger moved to the red button, even as he still held the phone to his ear. It hovered there. Something was holding him back. The number – how had Matthew got the number? And then he remembered what his contact at the police had told him. To write everything down, to detail every interaction no matter how small because maybe the police could track down the idiot responsible for the harassment and stir up some trouble. Although the last time he'd talked with his contact was eighteen months ago and now he wasn't returning Robin's emails.

Robin tapped his pockets with his free hand, finding his signing pen but no paper to write on. He looked around, searching, and his eyes fell on the book he had been looking at. With barely a thought, he opened the book, rifled through the opening pages, finding the page he usually signed his name on. He put the pen to paper, wrote 'HMP New Hall' and 'Matthew' and added a question mark.

'Who is this?' Robin said, trying to keep his emotions in check.

'Did it not . . .? I'm Matthew.' Matthew was close to tears. He didn't sound like he was enjoying this, but then Robin didn't know the mind of someone so sick as to do something like this.

'Full name.'

And at that, Matthew did sob. He sounded like a wounded animal. Robin's edge softened slightly. What was happening?

So he tried a different question. 'How have you rang me three times?'

This worked. 'What?'

'If you're in prison, how have you rang me three times? You only get one phone call.'

Matthew sniffed loudly. 'I . . . my lawyer sorted it out. I haven't just been arrested – that's when you're—. That doesn't matter right now.'

'It does,' Robin said.

'No, what matters is – I didn't do it, Mr Ferringham. You have to believe me. I didn't kill them.'

'What?' Robin said, before he could stop himself. 'What are you talking about?'

'They think I did it. But I couldn't. My friends.'

'I . . .' Robin trailed off – there was something in the young man's voice. Something so . . . familiar to him.

'We went through. All six of us. And only I came out.' Matthew said, through sobs. 'Only I came out.'

What was this?

'How do you know Samantha?'

'You have to help me, Mr Ferringham. Please, I just . . . I need you to say you'll help me.' Matthew was openly crying now.

Robin shivered. He wasn't feeling angry any more, he was unsettled. He felt as though he were communicating with a spectre, having a conversation that was not possible. 'I . . . I'm sorry but I don't know you, and whoever gave you this number was not who you say it was, so I'm going to hang up now.' He stopped and then added, 'I'm sorry.' And he was surprised to find that he was.

Robin took the phone from his ear, and was about to terminate the call when Matthew shouted so loudly that it sounded as if it were on speaker. 'Clatteridges. Um . . . 7.30 p.m. 18 August . . . 1996.'

Robin froze. The single shiver had turned into a cavalcade coursing through his body. He looked down at the phone in his hand, and then past it, at the open book on the table. Something plopped onto the page, and it took a moment for him to realise it was a tear.

Shut the pain away. And then the anger was back. He put the phone back to his ear. 'Where the hell did you hear that?' That wasn't even in the book, he'd omitted it purposefully. He'd wanted something to keep for himself.

'That's what she said. She said you wouldn't believe me. So she said to say those words, exactly. Clatteridges. 18 August 1996. 7.30 p.m.'

Robin couldn't think. He had boxed his hope up and put it to the back of the cupboard of his mind. Hope was the worst emotion that people in his position, the ones left behind, could ever feel. And now this Matthew was rifling through the cupboard trying to find it.

He closed his eyes, and breathed in and out slowly, trying to gain some perspective. This could all be explained away – a coincidence or something like that. That's all. Because it couldn't . . .

'She rang me,' Matthew said, his voice steadier now as though he were stating facts. 'In the dead of night. A few years back. I didn't know who she was or why she was calling me or anything. I couldn't even understand her at first. Thought she was either drunk or on some kind of drugs. She seemed flustered, confused. But as she talked, she started to make some sense. She told me her name. Then she said yours. She said "Robin Ferringham is the greatest man I've ever known". The only man to trust. And she said that Robin Ferringham would never let anyone down.'

This isn't real. It's a trick. Just a stupid trick.

'I didn't remember the call for ages – I think I might have even convinced myself it was a dream. And then I get put in this place, and you're given nothing but time to think. And I remembered. I remembered her. And I remembered you.'

A call in the middle of the night. Years ago. Clatteridges. Was it possible – really? 'I don't believe you,' Robin whispered harshly, although a more accurate sentence would have been, 'I can't believe you.'

'Can't you just ask her?' Matthew said.

Robin's breath hitched. 'Samantha has been missing for three years.'

10

Silence on the other end. And then a small 'What? No. No. That's not . . . Please, Mr Ferringham. You have to . . .' The call began to break up.

Robin looked at the phone. He had one bar of signal. He muttered an expletive under his breath and heard a slight tut. He looked up, suddenly remembering where he was. The same old woman who had been looking at the crime shelf was standing over him with a copy of *Without Her* clutched in her hands. It looked rather ragged and well-read, clearly her own copy. The woman went to open her mouth but Robin put the phone back to his ear.

'Matthew,' Robin said. There had to be something else. He had to know for sure. 'Matthew.'

'If you don't . . .' The voice was cutting in and out.

Robin got up. The old woman was saying something. 'I've been plucking up the courage to come and talk to you,' she was saying, but Robin couldn't focus on her.

Robin mouthed a sorry to the woman, who was still talking and he pushed past her. 'Matthew, are you there?'

'Please,' the old woman said, behind him, 'your book changed my life. It made me find peace when my daughter . . . Please, can you just sign it?'

'Please just search . . . Standedge.' And then the line went dead.

'Matthew,' Robin said, but knew it was no use. He looked at the phone to see the call had disconnected. He looked around, lost.

'Are you alright?' the old woman said.

Robin put his phone back in his pocket, sniffling himself. 'I'm sorry. That was rude. Of course I'll sign your book.' Sam would've approved. And he talked with the old woman for almost half an hour about her missing daughter, and how to cope, and when she was gone, he wrote 'Standedge' down on his copy, and underlined it twice.

2

Robin found his way to the sushi parlour in somewhat of a fog. Emma was already waiting for him. When he sat down and put the carrier bag on the table, she raised an eyebrow. 'Thought you didn't read anymore.'

Robin pulled out the copy of *Without Her* that he had written his notes in. Wren said that he could take it for free, but he bought it, not wanting to get her into trouble.

'Haven't you got enough of them?' she laughed. She was right – the hallway of his flat was littered with proof copies, hardbacks and foreign versions all stacked up with nowhere to go.

'I wrote in it.'

'Isn't that the general idea?' Emma said, and smiled. 'How'd it go?'

'Fine,' Robin said, trying to keep his mind from what Matthew had said and thinking of nothing else. 'The usual, you know. Slow. But I met some nice people. Have you ordered?'

They ate in relative silence. Emma talked a little about her day – complete now, as there were only morning appointments on a Saturday – although she never went into too much detail about her patients. The most she elaborated was about the rise of hypochondriacs having absolutely nothing wrong with them. The rise of Web MD had been the bane of Emma's existence.

Robin stayed silent, only half listening to her, and picking at his food. He managed some salmon but that was about all he could stomach. And then – was Emma talking to him?

'What's wrong?' she said, staring at him with the intensity of a general practitioner and a sister all in one.

'Nothing,' Robin said, knowing that wouldn't work, but doomed to try.

'Uh-huh.'

Robin looked around and then back to her. 'Have you ever heard of Standedge?'

She thought for a moment. 'No, what is that – a band?'

'I don't know,' Robin said.

She stared at Robin. She was only four minutes older than him – but caught in the path of one of those stares, it felt like four minutes made all the difference. 'What happened?'

Robin looked away, rebuking the challenge. 'Nothing.'

'Ah good,' she said, her demeanour changing, 'do you want coffee or shall we get the bill?' which was subtext and reverse psychology all at the same time. Sometimes Robin thought Emma would give even a clairvoyant a headache.

Robin caved. He opened up the hardback and showed her the notes he'd made, guiding her through the conversation with Matthew. Ending on Sam.

She listened closely, not betraying her feelings until she had heard the full story. When Robin was done, she was quiet for a moment, thinking. After a beat, she said, 'And this is what's got you all . . .' she waved a hand at him, 'whatever this is?'

Robin was a little taken aback. 'Did you hear . . . he said Sam. He said he'd talked to Sam.'

She sighed and looked at him sadly. 'It was just a stupid prank, Robin. Your first impressions were correct. He was having you on. Somehow – who knows how – he got your number and thought he'd have a bit of fun with you. And it sounds like he had a great time.'

'You didn't hear him talk about this thing. This Standedge. And his friends. He sounded . . . He sounded like he'd lost something. Someone.' Robin stumbled over what he was trying to say, and didn't want to say what was next, as though it would make it real. 'He sounded like me.'

'Robin . . .' Emma started.

But Robin interrupted. 'You remember that day you came to my flat with the laptop and told me to write it down. The day I started writing *Without Her*.'

'You were sitting at the kitchen table staring at a bottle of Jack Daniels,' Emma said.

'Yes,' Robin said, 'I was lost. And you helped me. You helped me find a way through it. Matthew sounded like me that day. He sounded lost too.'

'And what?' Emma said, almost flippantly. 'Sam has led him to you.'

Robin threw up his hands. 'I don't know – maybe. I . . . I don't know.'

Emma's phone rang, and she looked at it before declining the call. 'I have to go but we're talking about this later. Don't let this open old wounds, Robin. It was just some idiot getting some jollies at your expense. Don't play his game. Focus on other things. Don't you have a meeting on Monday with your publisher?'

Robin wasn't even thinking about that. The publisher wanted to talk 'Book Two' and so did Barrows. The *Without Her* money was running out. They were moving on to the next project – they had the luxury.

Emma got up. 'Are you going to be okay?'

'Sure,' Robin said. And as Emma turned to go, he called after her, 'One more thing.' She turned back. 'Did I ever tell you about Clatteridges?'

Emma shrugged. 'No. No, you didn't.' And then she was gone.

Robin turned back to his plate and looked down at the notes he'd made. Emma's arguments were in his head – a stupid joke, just a prank, just a load of rubbish.

But what if Emma was wrong?

3

Robin got home a little after 1 p.m., his head still buzzing with Matthew's words. Emma's had faded into the background, and the hardback he was carrying seemed to pulse with the secrets he had written down.

He threw his keys on the kitchen table. The room wasn't a total mess, but it wasn't exactly clean either. There was an organised stack of dirty dishes on the draining board, which Sam would never have accepted. Robin, on the other hand, had let standards slip since she had gone. He only really tidied up when he was expecting company, and besides Emma no one came around anymore. His friends had been Sam's friends as well, and meeting them felt wrong without her. Evidently they felt the same way because he hadn't talked to most of them in a year.

He put the kettle on and turned to find his laptop on the kitchen table. He looked at it for a few seconds before sitting down in front of it. He opened it up and logged in. Emma's voice was in the back of his head telling him not to but he went to Google and typed the one word that had been swirling around in his head for hours: Standedge. He clicked 'Search' and was absorbed.

Standedge was the name of a canal tunnel in Marsden, Huddersfield.

Huddersfield.

That couldn't be a coincidence.

The last time he saw Sam was in this very room. He was sitting in this very chair, poring over a laptop just as he was now. It was 8.15 a.m. on 28 August 2016, and he had been up all night, trying to make an article slightly more interesting. Sam came into the room with her suitcase, and he didn't even look up.

He did now. The kitchen was empty, but he could almost see the ghost of her standing there in the doorway. She was going to the station. She made her money as a travelling lecturer, always on the move. Robin didn't like her being away but was proud of her for being so proactive. And she was good at her job. Universities were always fighting over her.

That day . . . she was going to Huddersfield University. She kissed him – he didn't savour it enough – and she told him again how to look after her cacti, after he had somehow managed to kill the last batch.

He looked away from the empty doorway to the kitchen windowsill. Her cacti were lined up on it. The same ones from that day. Alive and kicking. Waiting for her to come back.

Huddersfield.

What did it mean? Did it mean anything? He didn't know. But it was another piece of the puzzle. There was no way the number, the nickname and Huddersfield could be a coincidence.

He pressed on.

The first website he clicked on was the Standedge Visitor Centre. Standedge was the longest canal tunnel in England and looked like it was a fairly successful tourist spot, with guided tours in the summer on canal boats. Was this what Matthew was talking about – going through?

The second website he visited detailed the history of the tunnel, which he skimmed. It seemed to have an extensive past – built over a period of sixteen years from 1795 to 1811, costing around £16,000, being the deepest and the longest canal tunnel in Britain connecting a village called Marsden to one named Diggle. Any other time, he probably would have been quite happy to peruse these details with interest, but it wasn't what he was looking for.

Scrolling through the rest of the results, he found nothing really relevant.

So he searched 'Matthew Standedge'. This came up with mostly the same results.

He searched 'Matthew Standedge disappearances,' and he finally found what he was searching for on the third result.

It was an article from a Huddersfield regional paper. The more he read, the closer he got to the screen.

This was it. He opened the copy of *Without Her* and ripped out the marked-up page, clicking his pen top.

The Mystery of the Standedge Five
by Jane Hargreaves

Police are baffled as five local young people go missing inside Britain's longest canal tunnel. At 2.31 p.m. on 26 June 2018, six local university students and a Bedlington Terrier entered Standedge canal tunnel from the Marsden end, on a traditional narrowboat. Two hours and twelve minutes later, the boat emerged on the other side (the Diggle end) with only one of the students, knocked unconscious on the deck, and the terrier. Five of the students, Tim Claypath (21), Rachel Claypath (21), Edmund Sunderland (20), Prudence Pack (21) and Robert Frost (20) disappeared without a trace inside Standedge. The survivor, Matthew McConnell (21), claims to have no knowledge of what happened to his fellow students.

The disappearance of the Claypath twins is of personal importance to the Chief of local police, their father DCI Roger Claypath, who issued this statement earlier today: 'My wife and I are devastated by the disappearances of our children and we are actively seeking to bring the right party to justice. We are pursuing a number of leads, but it seems that Matthew McConnell who we thought of as our childrens' friend, had the means and the knowledge to carry out a horrific act of deception and murder. As is public knowledge, McConnell was employed by the Canals and Rivers Trust to give tours inside the tunnel, which is why the students were allowed to pass unattended.

Given his station, he knew of the various ways out of Standedge from the inside. Timing is still an issue and we are still trying to create a timeline of what exactly happened. We ask that the press respect the families of those dealing with this tremendous loss, including my own.'

McConnell is currently recovering from a head injury (that the police believe was self-inflicted) in Anderson Hospital. He will be transported to a holding cell when he recovers while the investigation team finalises the case against him.

The bodies of the five missing young people have yet to be recovered. A source said, 'The bodies are not in the tunnel, as the police have sent divers into the canal. They seem increasingly frustrated in trying to find out what happened to the five students. DCI Claypath has people working around the clock to try and bring this story to an end, no matter how tragic it may be.'

Huddersfield Press reached out to the Canals and Rivers Trust for comments on the situation. They refused to comment, other than to give sympathies to the families affected by this tragedy.

Robin stopped reading and looked down at his notes. He'd been writing without knowing it. He'd listed the names: Tim Claypath, Rachel Claypath, Edmund Sunderland, Robert Frost and Prudence Pack. And he'd circled McConnell. Matthew McConnell. Everything he read lined up with what Matthew said. Five kids, students, went missing inside the tunnel, but Matthew was left behind.

But this supposedly happened on 26 June this year? Less than two months ago. How the hell had he not heard about this? This should have been national news, this should have been in every newspaper in the country. But he hadn't heard a thing about it – hadn't even known what Standedge was.

And leaving the paper's website, he found that the other results were irrelevant. Only one result about this mass disappearance – it didn't make sense.

He searched 'Matthew McConnell Claypath Standedge Tunnel 26 June 2018'. This only brought up one page of results. In addition to the newspaper article, there were a number of articles, all from one other website. He clicked on the first link and went to a site that seemed like it was from the early days of the Internet. At the top of the site in big red text was the masthead, THE RED DOOR. Robin was immediately suspicious (it felt like a site that housed a million viruses) but as he read the first article it did seem to have useful information.

McConnell Pleads Innocence in the
Crime of the Century
by **The Red Door** 17/07/18 16.44 p.m.

Matthew McConnell, the lone survivor of the Standedge Incident, has once again pleaded his innocence, as he was transferred from Anderson hospital to HMP New Hall. The Red Door (the only outlet to witness his arrival at New Hall [*Ed: What's up with that?*]) heard McConnell's shouts that he was innocent and didn't remember anything after entering the tunnel on 26 June 2018.

You guys know I love a good mystery but the deck is stacked against McConnell on this one. There are just too many factors that go against him. You see, Standedge is, actually, a set of four tunnels. The left two are abandoned (basically one), the right one is a working two-track railway, and the 'middle' one is the canal. McConnell worked as a tour guide, meaning he would know this and be able to navigate the abandoned tunnel with ease. What's more, he'd have the keys to be able to unlock the large gates blocking the tunnel entrance. And furthermore, a couple of McConnell's acquaintances (you know, the ones that weren't spirited away) said that the guy had beef with the guys he went on his swansong voyage with.

Now, this is still crazy. How McConnell pulled off this crime is insane. He killed everyone, transported the bodies to a secret location, got back to the boat and cleaned up after himself, all in time to bonk himself on the head and collapse on the deck before the boat reappeared at the other end. That's seriously wacky!

Unless . . . Maybe McConnell's innocent. Maybe Tim Claypath, Rachel Claypath, Pru Pack, Edmund Sunderland and Robert Frost just simply disappeared. And whatever force evaporated them also knocked out McConnell in the process. Food for thought.

Maybe I should investigate some more! God, I love this job!

What do you guys think? Comment down below and be sure to subscribe to The Red Door feed to keep up to date with all the weird news you can handle. Peace!

The article was far less eloquent than the one from the paper, but the information still lined up. And it said that Matthew had been moved to New Hall. The same place Matthew was calling from – there was no way this wasn't real.

The only thing Robin didn't (and no doubt, wouldn't) find among the articles was Matthew's link to Sam. If Matthew was telling the truth about Sam, she had called him out of the blue. He didn't know her. He had said she was 'flustered'. Why hadn't Sam called Robin? If she was in trouble, why hadn't she called him?

Robin spent the rest of the day and evening on the Internet. When Emma rang him, he ignored it. He started to print out the important articles he found and opened a folder to put them in. The Standedge Incident seemed to be somewhat of an anomaly – an unusual crime that was not covered by the national news. Most of the information he found was on The Red Door, a site that only got weirder the longer he spent on it. Why were no official outlets covering this? When he did find a more official article – newspapers and websites – the snippets were always short and vague.

Robin found a group picture of the missing students

with one of The Red Door articles. They were standing by Standedge canal tunnel – Robin recognised it from the Visitor Centre website. In the foreground stood Tim Claypath, a dominant force in the picture with everyone else seemingly gravitating towards him. He was youthful, attractive, alive. His eyes seemed to glint even on the screen. Next to him was his sister, Rachel. Robin could tell, even without the caption. She shared the same eyes as her brother, the same fire, the same beauty. Beside the Claypath twins were three more young people. Edmund Sunderland, sandy haired and tall, stood close to Tim, looking into the camera with a strong intensity that made Robin feel his slight smile was deliberate. On Rachel's side, two people stood, slightly turned into each other as though in conversation just before the photo was taken. This was Pru Pack and Robert Frost, and their beaming smiles indicated their sheer joy at just being there. If Robin had to guess, Pru and Robert were in a relationship, and weren't exactly hiding it. At the front of them all, jumping up to fit in the frame and therefore being immortalised a little fuzzily, was a grey Bedlington Terrier. The caption said: 'Amygdala (Amy)'. The date of the picture was 26 June 2018. The day of the voyage, and the day these people (minus the dog) vanished.

Robin stared at the faces of the Standedge Five, his eyes sliding across the picture, and then he noticed that someone else was in the picture. If the caption hadn't pointed him out, Robin may have missed him. Behind Edmund Sunderland, a few steps away, standing next to the canal and looking over it and not into the camera,

25

was another young man. He was dressed in a T-shirt and jeans, in comparison to the others' smarter shirts and trousers and dresses, and he had his hands in his pockets. He wasn't smiling – he had an entirely blank expression, as though he were thinking absolutely nothing. He obviously wasn't aware of the picture being taken. The caption said that this was 'Matthew McConnell'.

Robin peered at him, getting closer to the picture, turning it, as though that would help him to better see past Edmund Sunderland. Something in one of the articles nagged at him, and he looked at the expanding mess of printed articles scattered across the table. A few minutes and he found what he was looking for. The Red Door article that said Matthew may have had something against the rest of the group. This picture seemed to illustrate that, and what was more, maybe the rest of the group had something against him. But Matthew hadn't mentioned anything to indicate that? But seeing as he was in prison charged with their murders, Robin guessed it wouldn't be the first thing he'd talk about.

Robin scratched his chin, feeling the stubble that had appeared since the morning. The natural light in the kitchen was dying, and he got up to turn on the light. From his new vantage point, he looked down at the table. It was a mess. And it didn't really amount to anything.

All Robin knew was that it was real. Matthew was telling the truth about Standedge. His friends were gone. And he was left. He'd left out the dog, but that hardly seemed important. His friends vanished – they were gone. They went into the tunnel and they didn't come out.

It was definitely a mystery — a rather tantalising one. One of the articles had detailed how long the journey took — two hours and twelve minutes. Two hours and twelve minutes of untracked, unseen and unknowable events. And the only lifeline into that world, that chunk of missing time, was Matthew McConnell, unless the dog started talking any time soon.

Of course the police would suspect Matthew. Of course they would arrest him. Because, with all the facts Robin had, there was no possibility other than Matthew killing his friends. The puzzle for the police would be where the bodies were, and they would lean on Matthew until he told all the truths he had to give.

Did Robin think Matthew was guilty? Or innocent? He didn't have enough to go on. But he was intrigued. Even without the fact that he had questions for Matthew. About Sam.

'Are you leading me somewhere, Sam?' Robin muttered, under his breath.

There was no answer. Except from the traffic noise on the street and a whoop from a passerby who was no doubt enjoying the benefits (and not yet suffering the drawbacks) of alcohol on a Saturday night.

Robin turned the light off again and decided to go to bed.

After a quick shower, he climbed into bed, lying on the right side of the double. Three years later and he still kept to his side, even when he was fast asleep and not consciously thinking.

He thought of Matthew McConnell and he thought

27

about what he had said to him, and more importantly, how he'd said it. Taking everything Matthew said as true, Sam had told him that he, Robin, was someone to trust.

Why had she told that to a total stranger? Why had she called Matthew?

He lay in bed for half an hour – sleep nowhere to be found. One question swirled around in his head: how could six people go into a canal tunnel and only one come out?

Robin thought for a moment of the voice on the phone that morning, the young man asking for his help, realising he had known what he would say for hours now.

Yes.

4

'I don't know, Robin. This sounds very odd,' she said, on the other end of the line. 'I think this guy is manipulating you. I don't know why you can't see that – maybe you just don't want to. But he's using Sam to get you to do stupid things.'

'You'd never heard of Standedge. You said that yourself. I spent six hours researching the case. It's real. Matthew is real. What happened is real.' Robin shifted the phone into his other hand so he could hike up the strap of the backpack onto his shoulder.

'Then why have I never heard of it?'

'I don't know. I think maybe someone stopped it getting out to the wider media.'

'This isn't the 90s, Robin,' she said with an icy tone that reminded Robin of their mother. She and Emma had never got along – probably because they were so similar. They were both pragmatic – seeing the world in front of them as a problem to solve. He loved his sister, but sometimes she looked at him more as a project than a brother. 'Things get out on the Internet – every single hour, every single minute. I don't see how we can't have heard of this before.'

'I think this Red Door website is run by some kind of whistleblower. Do you want me to send you the link?'

'No,' Emma said quickly, 'I don't want any part of this. Look, why don't I come over? I can be there soon. We'll just talk this through together.'

'You can't come over,' Robin said bluntly.

There was a long silence. '. . . Why?' Emma said, in their mother's voice.

Robin opened his mouth, but at that moment an announcement came over the loudspeaker saying that a train was boarding. King's Cross was the busiest he had ever seen it. The fast food places, the restaurants, the bars, they were all overflowing with commuters. Robin was amidst the sea of people looking up at the departure boards. At the announcement, about twenty people headed towards the platforms. Robin didn't have to say anything – he knew Emma had heard.

'You're going today? You're going now?'

'Yes,' Robin said.

'What about your meeting with your publisher?'

'I cancelled.'

'Robin, what are you doing? Really?'

'I'm doing what I feel I need to do. Can you just support me in this?'

Emma sighed. And was quiet for about a minute. He knew what she was thinking – that he was crazy, and that this was a fool's errand. 'Of course,' she said, 'but please be careful, Robin. If what you said – if what you found – is really true, this guy could be dangerous.'

'I know how to handle myself,' Robin said with a smile. 'I'll see you soon.'

He hung up, wondering if Emma was right — if he was making a terrible mistake.

But the wondering wasn't enough to stop him going through the ticket barrier, finding his train and getting on.

5

Samantha had been due to call him when she got into Huddersfield. And she did. But Robin didn't pick up. He was still so absorbed with his stupid article, about planning permission for a new multi-storey in Camden right next to residential land, which had somehow escalated into the political battle of the century. At least it had seemed so at the time. That multi-storey never got built, and was never talked of again.

He should have picked up the phone.

When a thirty-three-year-old woman, perfectly capable, mobile and mature, goes missing, it takes a lot to get someone to listen. But the moment he called back and she didn't answer – in fact, didn't even ring and went straight to voicemail – Robin knew, somehow, that she was in trouble. And having to wait seventy-two hours to report her missing killed him.

At the police station, he was shuffled between four different police officers, each more bored than the last. He repeated the story over and over and each time he uttered it, it became more real to him. He answered their inane questions – what time was the phone call from the university to say Samantha hadn't arrived? when did you first realise there was something wrong? did Samantha act any differently before she left? – even though they had all been addressed already. They wrote notes in countless black notepads. And alluded to things like a secret lover, or the even more heartbreaking prospect that maybe she just ran away?

Their blunt monotone responses were what Robin thought of when he first spoke to Terrance Loamfield, Matthew's appointed barrister.

'You have been put on Mr McConnell's approved visitor list, just give your name and identification at the gates. You will have to complete some paperwork when you arrive at New Hall, but should be good to go from there.'

Robin was on the phone again, in a packed carriage heading for his connection at Leeds Central. He was standing – he had a seat reservation, but the train didn't happen to have the carriage his seat was in.

'Thank you, Mr Loamfield.' He wanted to ask Loamfield so many questions, but he didn't really think he was in the right environment for it.

'Mr McConnell has not requested my presence at your meetings. May I ask what your relation is to Mr McConnell?'

Robin didn't know what to say. He wasn't really anything to Matthew – hadn't even known of his existence for a full twenty-four hours yet. And Matthew hadn't told the lawyer either – meaning he probably didn't want Loamfield to know. Robin assessed, from the five minutes he had been talking to the man, that Loamfield seemed to be a very closed person, spouting protocol instead of emotion, fact instead of opinion. It was clear he really didn't have a personal stake in seeing Matthew go free, or indeed be convicted. But in spite of this, Robin thought it wise not to tell Loamfield he was going to be sniffing around. 'I'm a . . . friend.'

'Well, you appear to be the only friend Mr McConnell has,' said Loamfield, not showing a hint of emotion.

'No one else has visited him?'

'No.'

'Not his parents?'

'Mr McConnell is an orphan. His parents died in a traffic pile-up in 1996. He lived with his aunt, who has since disowned him and left the county. I'm surprised you don't know this?'

'Ah yes, quite,' Robin said, squishing himself against the wall of the train as the snacks trolley passed. 'I'm sorry, sometimes I forget.'

Loamfield paused for a long time. Robin would have thought the call had disconnected, if he didn't hear the man's short, sharp breaths. 'You know Mr Ferringham, if this were any other case, I'd be asking if you were a journalist, but I guess it doesn't really matter. There's only a matter of days before McConnell's court date.'

'And when is that?'

'This Friday. He goes before the court to receive a date for his trial, and to decide conditions, if any, for bail.'

Friday. Today was Sunday. Five days. Five days until what was probably the best chance of helping Matthew. And five days to get answers about Sam.

34

'And do you think he's likely to get bail?'

'Not a chance in hell,' Loamfield said, almost like he was smiling on the other end. It was the first time he'd shown anything even vaguely akin to a personality, and Robin far preferred the emotionless android he had been mere seconds ago.

'Thank you, Mr Loamfield,' Robin said closing out the conversation.

'Not at all Mr Ferringham. And if you have any questions, please don't hesitate to call.'

Robin put the phone down. It wasn't until he changed trains at Leeds and was on his way to Marsden that he realised Mr Loamfield hadn't offered up his number. He went into his call history and noted it down.

6

Marsden station was merely a free-standing train platform with no buildings – only a ticket machine placed haphazardly against a board with a chart of train times pinned to it. Robin was the only one to get off, and he watched as the train left him there in solitude.

He looked to his surroundings to see that he had been dropped by a small car park and a pub called The Train-Car, which stood just over a small stone bridge. Past that, there was a steady hill lined with residential houses looking to lead down into what he would guess was Marsden proper.

He started to make his way over the bridge, and looked down to see a body of water. The Huddersfield Narrow. He had seen it on Google Maps, when he had sought out a map of Standedge and the surroundings. The Narrow snaked its way through Marsden until it disappeared into the tunnel. This section ran almost parallel to the train line, segmenting it off from the rest of Marsden.

From the map he'd seen on his phone screen, Standedge lay off to the right. He wanted to go there and see the tunnel for himself, but first he decided he should really find somewhere to stay.

The Train-Car, a very traditional British pub with green lacquered awnings, weathered benches outside, and a sign depicting three train-cars on a track and the name in gold lettering, appeared to be open. The door stood ajar, but no noise came from within. Although it did have a sign saying rooms available, Robin decided against it, opting instead to walk into town.

He started to walk down the hill, seeing a cut-through to the left, between two houses that seemed to lead off to a wooded area. As Robin looked through the gap between buildings, a loud 'baa' cut through the relative silence.

Robin started and looked around. Behind him, standing a few metres away, and looking unimpressed, were two rather fat and woolly sheep. They both had scarves on – one blue and one pink – making Robin think they weren't likely to be anyone's meal, but rather pets. They stared at him with their black marble eyes, and Robin stared back, locked in a battle over who seemed more out-of-place here. Robin was the first to look away.

The sheep with the pink scarf seemed to take this as its cue, and trotted past Robin, followed by the blue scarved sheep. They disappeared down the cut-through and Robin watched as they ducked into the woods.

He looked around, wondering what to do, and saw a woman who had come out of her door and was emptying some plastic into her recycling bin. She caught Robin's eye.

'I'm sorry,' Robin said, 'but I think someone's sheep must have gotten free.'

She looked him up and down. 'Not from round here, are you?'

'No, but . . .'

'Those sheep go where they please. They belong to the town.'

Robin took a look towards the woods again. 'Right.' Sheep wandering around freely? That was new to him. 'I'm looking for somewhere to stay. Is this the way to the town centre?'

'Follow the hill down. Pub called The Hamlet has the best rooms,' the woman said, like she'd said it a dozen times before to inexperienced tourists such as himself.

'Thank you,' Robin said, but the woman had already gone back into her house.

Robin did as he was told, and got to the bottom of the hill. At first, the town presented itself as a series of pubs. He came to two buildings, either side of the road. The Lucky Duck and The Grey Fox stood watching each other, acting as an unofficial gateway to the commercial part of the small town.

Past them was a main street filled with shops – a bakery, a charity shop, a Co-op, three cafés and many other small businesses. They all led up to a crossroads where a tall clock tower stood, white with red corners. The clock had stopped at 3.15, and Robin had to check his watch to see the real time.

It was just past 6 p.m., but Marsden was already deathly silent. There was no one on the streets and the shops had shut for the day. Robin walked up the street, expecting to see some sign of life somewhere. He passed the clock tower, seeing a crossroads but deciding to keep going straight, and kept going up the road, finally hearing a gentle thrum of noise coming from somewhere.

As he passed a Post Office and another charity shop, there was a break in the buildings, and he found what he was looking for. Set back slightly, he found the largest pub he had seen yet, although the outer decor matched every other pub he'd found in Marsden. A cream building with black siding and a sign with gold lettering. 'The Hamlet.' The sign jostling gently in the wind had a man in a puffy Shakespearean collar holding a skull. The windows and open door streamed light out of them and the sound of laughing and conversation washed out into the street.

Robin headed inside.

7

The Hamlet was thriving. He came through the door to find a quaint bar area, unmistakeably British with its rich mahogany furniture and country decor. Paintings of men on horses galloping after foxes hung on the walls. It seemed like all the people absent from the streets outside were in The Hamlet. It was packed with people sitting at the tables, and propped up against the bar. The whole place had a warm glow, friendly and inviting. There was a steady noise of chatter, punctuated every so often with a hearty laugh.

As Robin stood in the doorway, a few people looked up from their conversations. They smiled at him, and as he looked over to the bar, a man with a purple nose and rosy cheeks tipped his pint and smiled. Robin smiled back, a reflex he usually suppressed in London. But something about The Hamlet screamed safety, a real home away from home. The man took a deep sip from his pint and turned back.

Behind the bar, a young woman dressed in black, with her brown hair tied up in a bun, was smiling and laughing with a man at the end of the bar as she poured a glass of white wine. Robin stepped forward, leaning against the bar, next to the smiling man.

When the young woman had finished taking money for the wine, she came over. 'What'll it be?'

'A Coke, please. And I was hoping to get some food. Are there any more tables?'

'Downstairs, there's a few,' she said, 'I'll get your drink.'

While she was pouring out the Coke, the man beside Robin cleared his throat. Robin looked at him to see he was smiling again. 'My mother used to say, "Never trust a man who doesn't drink."' Closer, Robin could see that his purple nose was bulbous and attempting to eclipse his entire face. He had a grey pepper-pot beard and wore glasses on a chain. He looked kind, if troubled by years of alcohol abuse. 'Probably why she died of liver failure.' He laughed heartily and clapped Robin on the back.

Robin could only smile back, a little dazed by the off-colour joke and the physical contact. 'Sorry, it's been a long day.'

'You come far?' he said, taking another swig of beer.

'I . . .' Robin wondered if he really looked that out of place. And then remembered he was carrying a suitcase.

The man tapped his head with a finger. 'Everyone from Marsden. Up here. In the brainbox. I'm Jim Thawn – I run the bakery.' Robin shook his outstretched hand.

'Robin. Robin Ferringham.'

'What brings you to Marsden, Robin? I'm guessing it isn't the world-famous bakery, is it? Because I make a mean tiger bread.' His speech was not slurred, but it was a little too fluid. If his speech appeared in type as he said

41

it, it would be fuzzy around the edges. Robin suspected that the half-empty pint is his hand had not been his first, maybe not even his fifth.

Robin thought for a moment. He didn't want to talk about Matthew McConnell and the Standedge Five until he got the lay of the land. After all, the whole town had seemingly stayed silent about it. He had to find out why. So, he told the truth in a different way. 'Curiosity,' he decided on.

Jim looked at him for a moment, and then decided that was enough of an answer. 'Well, you picked a good place to be curious. Marsden's a beautiful place. Lots of history here.'

The barmaid came over with Robin's Coke and he gave her the money. As he placed the money in her hand, he noticed she was wearing two thick black sweatbands on her wrists – a bold and slightly odd fashion choice. When she came back with his change and a folded menu, he said, 'I'm also looking for a place to stay. Someone told me there'd be rooms here.'

'Yes, of course. How long are you thinking of staying?'

Robin thought. He didn't really know. Loamfield said that Matthew's day in court was Friday. But what if he met with Matthew and hit a dead-end? Matthew's information on Sam was the most important thing. If Matthew was somehow lying, would he be able to walk away?

'Don't worry,' the barmaid said, 'you can pay by the night. We don't have many tourists coming through here this time of year.'

Robin took a sip of his Coke. 'How much is it?'

'Forty-five per night.'

Robin spluttered. 'I'm sorry.'

'Forty-five pounds.'

'. . . Right. How much is breakfast then?'

'Breakfast is included.'

Robin looked from her to Jim. Jim was chuckling. 'Right?' he said, wondering why it was so cheap.

'Things aren't so expensive here, huh?' she said. 'You're a bona fide city boy, aren't ya?'

'You could say that,' Robin said uncomfortably.

The barmaid was called away by someone demanding another pint in shaky tones and Robin said goodbye to Jim, locating the narrow stairs that went to the basement. He made his way down, emerging into a snug small stone room with a roaring fireplace, tables around the edges and a plush red rug laid out on the floor. A Golden Retriever was lying in front of the fire on a leash which ran along the floor and disappeared under a table in the corner where a family – a father, a mother and two children – were poring over a large map. The basement was just as busy as the upper level, but at least no one was standing around. There was only one table free and Robin sat down at it, placing his backpack on the seat next to him and drawing up his suitcase so it stood alongside. Like upstairs, there was something incredibly homely about the place, and the tables of people creating a slow drum of conversation matched with the crackling of the fire made Robin feel suddenly very tired.

Robin realised that he hadn't really travelled anywhere further north than Milton Keynes in years. Seeing

Sam come and go at least twice a month made him feel that she did enough travelling for the both of them. And after she went missing, well, he barely had enough motivation to go to the corner shop, let alone a new city or town.

He closed his eyes, feeling oddly content. Like he could sleep. He snapped his eyes open and took a drink to try and counteract his drowsiness. He looked at the menu, catching the eye of the barmaid when she came down to collect empties. He ordered fish and chips and then tried to find something to keep himself awake.

He decided against getting the folder, full of the printouts he had collected on the Standedge Incident, out of his backpack. He didn't want anyone to spy what he was looking at. So instead he looked around the walls of the basement.

The walls were lined with pictures, but photographs rather than paintings like upstairs. Nearest him, in the corner, was an old framed map of the town and the surrounding countryside. He had seen it on the Web the night before and could trace the thin baby blue line of the Huddersfield Narrow through Marsden until it disappeared completely into the Standedge tunnel. The map covered the whole of the tunnel and he saw the tracks of the three tunnels running either side of it. The railway line that he had just been on, and the line adjacent to it, and the two disused railway tunnels to the left. The canal tunnel ran for a distance, and eventually came out in the neighbouring town of Diggle. Just viewing it on the map, Standedge seemed to stretch on forever.

Next to the map was a photo of a landscape Robin didn't recognise, but he guessed it was somewhere local. It was a rural landscape, a hill silhouetted by a cloudy sky. As he looked closer, he saw two white smudges at the top of the hill with black faces and legs. Two sheep. Was it possible that they were the same ones he met on his way here? Robin smiled at that.

There was an old detailed illustration of workmen working in Standedge, chipping away at rock, and loading boats with waste. There was a small plaque next to it, with some information:

Standedge Canal Tunnel: At 16,499 feet long and 636 feet deep at its lowest point, Standedge is the longest and deepest canal tunnel in the United Kingdom. It stands as an incredible feat of British engineering and construction.

Another illustration caught his eye. It looked more like a schematic, showing a drawn overhead view of the entire tunnel. In the almost exact centre of the tunnel was an S shape configuration. Something jogged in Robin's memory, something he had skimmed over but found slightly amusing. When the tunnel was built, it was started from both ends, but was woefully miscalculated. Thus when the two workforces got to the middle, the tunnel didn't meet. A slight deviation had to be made to get the tunnel to join up.

Robin could see why the tunnel was a tourist attraction – it was indeed an impressive thing, but the question for him wasn't why anyone would go through the tunnel, it was why Matthew and his friends were.

Glancing round, Robin saw the walls littered with more photos – all local and most pertaining to the tunnel. But there wasn't much he hadn't already seen, so most didn't hold his attention – that was until he looked above the fireplace, and saw there was a picture of a group of people sitting around a room that looked like the one he was in right now. He strained to look, but knew he would have to get up to see properly. Slowly, without drawing attention to himself, he slipped out of his seat and walked towards the fireplace, careful not to disturb the Golden Retriever.

The picture was of The Standedge Five. In this room – the basement of the Hamlet. Robin's eyes widened and he slowly looked around, matching details up.

They looked almost identical to how they looked in the picture he found online. Tim Claypath, Rachel Claypath, Edmund Sunderland, Robert Frost and Prudence Pack were sat around a table in front of the fire – it seemed they had arranged all the small tables to create a bigger one. The dog was sitting on Rachel Claypath's knee. Scattered across the table were poker chips and hands of cards. They were all looking at the camera and smiling – even Edmund's looked genuine this time. Matthew was nowhere to be seen.

Finding a framed photo of the five missing friends on the wall in a pub and taken in this very room, it made the disappearance seem realer. Five people. Vanished.

Robin looked at the faces of the five with sadness. Tim

and Prudence were waving at the camera. He realised they both had something on their wrist, some kind of black scrawl. A tattoo or some kind of writing. And by the looks of it, the marks were both the same. Robin got even closer but couldn't for the life of him make out what it said.

Slowly, he took his phone out and switched the camera on, holding it up to the picture. As soon as he pressed the button, he was blinded by a split-second of dazzling light. The flash. The room must have been dark enough to trigger it. He blinked away sunspots and realised the room had gone silent.

He looked around. Every single person in the room was looking at him. Everyone had looked up from their conversations and were staring – two people near the stairs who looked like they were on a date, two elderly men who seemed to be trying to out-drink each other, three women on a girls' night out, and even the family in the corner – all eyes trained on him.

Robin found himself looking down and met the eyes of the Golden Retriever who was also staring up at him. Robin suddenly felt very unsettled. He expected someone to break the silence, say something, but no one did. He turned back to the picture but that seemed worse – the eyes burning into his back.

He stepped away from the picture, picking his way around the dog, and got back to his table as quickly as he could. He kept his head down, and after a moment, he heard the sound of four conversations starting up again – overlapping each other into an inaudible mess of chatter. He dared to look up and found no one was staring at him anymore.

What the hell was that?

He looked at his phone to see the flash had consumed the picture. All he saw were ghosts of the Standedge Five fighting through the light.

'Fish and chips.'

Robin jumped out of his skin and looked up. The barmaid was towering over him, holding the food. He tried to smile, slipping the phone into his pocket.

Trying to suppress the urge to run.

8

Robin ate his food quietly, trying not to look around the room and attract the gaze of any of the other patrons again. As far as he could tell from his peripheral vision, no one even acknowledged that he was there, and if not for the incident with the photo, he would have wondered if he were invisible.

Slowly, the basement started to empty. The family with the dog were first to leave, and the others soon followed. When Robin finally managed the courage to look up, he was alone, with only the snaps of the healthy fire to keep him company.

He waited five minutes, and went back to the picture above the fireplace, taking a photo without the flash on this time. He was still transfixed by what was written on Tim and Prudence's wrists, but could not make it out.

He went back to his seat and looked at the picture on his phone, zooming into Tim's wrist. Definitely something there, but too pixelated to make out. 'Crap,' he muttered under his breath.

'Can I take your plate?'

Robin jumped. The barmaid was standing over him again. She had made her way down the rickety stairs without him hearing so much as a creak. Robin smiled despite his surprise. 'Yes, thank you.'

She didn't pick up his plate. Instead she sat opposite him. 'I'm Amber.'

'Amber. I'm Robin.'

'There's a room ready upstairs for you when you want it.' She pushed aside the empty plate and placed a large brass key on the table. It had a tag hanging off it with a large 4 written in felt-tip. Robin refrained from picking it up – it seemed Amber wasn't finished.

'You're a long way from home,' she said, but there was an air of friendliness about the remark.

'Yes.'

'Why are you here?'

Robin was quiet for a moment. 'It's a long story. I needed a change of scene, and I've never been here so . . .'

'If you don't mind,' Amber interrupted, 'that's not why you're here. No. You're here for them, aren't you?'

'Them?'

'Them.' She gestured towards the fireplace and the framed photo above it. 'The "Standedge Five" as they're called.'

'I don't know what . . .'

'Please,' Amber said, 'you've already got people talking about you. You're bad at this. And if you don't want to get run out of town, you have to get better.'

Robin opened his mouth then closed it. She was right after all.

Amber smiled, but it was friendly. 'I think the

50

'grown-ups' in town started labelling them the Stand-edge Five because they couldn't bear to call them by their names,' Amber continued. 'I guess it's easier for them that way.'

'Did you know them?' Robin said, dropping any pretence that remained.

'I was a year behind them in school. Knew them a bit. Well, I guess you could say that. I had a bit of a thing for Tim, truth be told. Just a silly little thing, but . . . We had one sort of . . . date, but . . .' She trailed off, fiddling with one of her sweatbands, absent-mindedly.

'What were they like?' Robin said, leaning forward. 'What were the Standedge Five like at school?'

'Well,' Amber said, 'it was the six of them at that point. Matthew McConnell too. They used to hang around together all the time, in and out of school. Thick as thieves. And the community liked them. A gang of kids who weren't going around kicking in shop windows or smoking pot – just hanging, being with each other. They used to come down here quite a lot, before I got my job here.' She got up, took the photo off the wall and sat back down, placing it in the centre of the table. She looked at it with something like longing. 'All us kids looked up to them. I think we desperately wanted to be one of them. But there were never tryouts, no auditions, no open spots. It was always the six of them, and the six of them it would always be. Until death they did part, I guess.'

Robin looked down at the photo. 'Do you know what brought them together?'

Amber looked up. 'I think it was the tunnel.'

Robin looked confused. 'What?'

'At Marsden Primary, there's a Geography field trip where classes go through the tunnel. It's quite famous. You have to understand, to a kid, Standedge tunnel is kinda scary. Bullies make little kids go and stand by the tunnel and look inside it for thirty seconds to prove they aren't cowards. There's a myth about a man living in there that parents tell their kids so they won't get too close – the Standedge Monster. You know, that kind of thing. So, to voluntarily go in there, at nine years old, with only a Geography teacher and some tour guides to protect you, that's a big deal.'

Robin nodded. He had never been claustrophobic. But even looking at pictures of the tunnel and knowing that it was a long journey through turned his stomach slightly.

'Well, they did it, and after that, they started hanging out. Inseparable. Like the tunnel changed them or something, brought them closer together. I dunno. And when they were old enough, they went again. Through. And then it became a sort of tradition, I think. I don't know the details, but it seemed all us other kids knew it. I think a lot of people felt left out.'

'Left out?'

'Of course. The chance of being in a gang with the Claypath twins – I mean who wouldn't be jealous, right? That's why Matthew, especially, worked to make sure he was important to them – I think he was afraid of getting left behind. He joined the Trust so he could take the group through Standedge without a tour guide.'

'So there were never any problems in the group?' Robin said.

'No. Well, the usual bickering and stuff but they always sorted it out.'

'There was nothing odd in the run-up to when they disappeared.'

'I don't know. As I said I was on the outside,' Amber said, and then thought for a moment. 'But it was obvious the group had fractured somewhat. They'd all spread across the country, going to uni. Tim and Edmund were in Edinburgh doing Physics and Rachel was there doing Psychology. Robert was in London doing Literature and Pru was doing Engineering in Manchester. It was only Matthew who stayed here.'

'Matthew was always a little . . . different . . . to the others. He didn't have any grand ambition – just seemed content with the day to day. More in step with folks round here. He joined the Canal Trust because he loved Standedge, not because he wanted to be rich or because he wanted to change the world. He just loved it.'

Robin stopped writing. 'Matthew was content with Marsden, while the others needed more?'

'I guess so,' Amber said, sighing. 'I wasn't one of them. But . . . after the five of them had gone off to university, things did start to change, I guess. When the group got back together in holidays, well . . . see for yourself.' She tapped the photo.

Not that he needed to see it. 'There's no Matthew.'

Amber smiled sadly. 'This picture was taken three

days before they went missing. Three days before Matthew piloted the boat through the tunnel, and the five of them disappeared. The only survivor in this photo is the bloody dog.' She thought for a moment, looking at the picture with wonder. 'It's all rather crazy, isn't it? Something like this happening in Marsden.'

'What do you think? About it all?'

'About the Incident? I don't know. It's so bizarre. Almost supernatural, you know. What do you think? As an outsider.'

'I think that there has to be a logical explanation.'

Amber looked at him, raising an eyebrow. 'Ah, you don't understand yet. You will.' Amber moved the photo aside and picked up the salt and pepper shakers. She placed one at the edge of the table, and then traced a line to the other side and placed the other. 'Standedge Canal Tunnel. For all intents and purposes, a straight line. Point A,' she touched the top of the salt, 'to Point B,' moving her hand to the pepper. 'The Standedge Five and Matthew and the dog enter Point A in their boat,' she moved a finger slowly along a straight line from the salt, 'there's nowhere to go except Point B. But somehow – the Standedge Five go somewhere else. Against everything, Matthew and the dog come out the other side without the others. You start asking around, and you'll hear a lot of theories. But I've never heard a single one that I believe. They are gone, but there's no way they can be.'

'But people don't just disappear,' Robin said. Even though a little voice inside him said, *But Sam did*.

54

'And yet, against all odds, the Standedge Five did,' Amber said. 'They aren't in any of the tunnels, they weren't in the water. The searches were thorough. Gone into thin air.'

Robin felt a shiver course through him. 'What are your thoughts about Matthew doing it?'

Amber shrugged. 'Whether he did or didn't, the major questions remain the same.'

Robin carried on. He didn't want to address the subject of *How?* yet – if only because the implications of the question scared the hell out of him. 'Do you think maybe Matthew was annoyed at being excluded?'

Amber thought for a moment, and then lightened, laughing. 'It's hard to think Matthew would be annoyed at the Five for anything. It was like the sun shone out of their arses for him. He worshipped them. He was like a . . . a rubber band. They could stretch him and twist him any way they wanted.'

'You make it sound manipulative.'

'No,' Amber said definitively. 'Matthew knew what was going on and was only too happy to let it happen. If that's manipulative, then he was welcoming it.'

'There was one thing though.' Amber looked around, even though she had to know they were alone. 'It's just a rumour, but word around town was that this year's Standedge trip was to be the last for them. This was something Matthew looked forward to every year, was probably mostly why he got that job at the Trust, and now there was a chance it was going to end. I dunno, people are saying that's why he did it. Hard to argue with 'em.'

Robin braced himself, and asked the question. 'Do you think Matthew did it?'

Amber looked from him to the photo, and then into the fire. The light danced in her eyes. 'What else is there?'

Robin changed tact. 'Before the Incident, would you have said Matthew was capable of something like that?'

Amber drew her gaze back to him. 'No,' she said definitively. 'He was always friendly, a bit too timid for his own good. Well, as I say, he let the others take the reins, he was someone who was happy just to be along for the ride. I wouldn't have thought he had a bad bone in his body. But, as my dad would say, takes all sorts to make a world, huh? I mean, take that whole thing that happened last year? That guy who locked that television presenter, the old *Resident Detective* guy, and all those people in that room, forced them to solve a murder or something. Stuff like this happens now, I suppose. Just like my dad said, all sorts.'

Robin nodded. 'Thank you, Amber.'

'No worries,' she said, 'if you ever need any more information, I'll do what I can. If I'm not at work here, you can usually find me at the church.'

Robin wondered why she was being so forthcoming. 'The church?'

Amber nodded. 'I help out there, run some of the groups, keep the place tidy – those kind of things.' She got up, and picked up his empty plate. 'You have everything you need for now?'

Robin was confused. 'Sorry. What do you mean by 'need'?'

'Your notes,' she said, pointing down to the open notebook. 'You're gonna write a book about the Standedge Five, right?'

Robin was a little taken aback.

And Amber laughed at his face. 'Sorry. You're Robin Ferringham.'

'Oh,' Robin said, never actually having been recognised before, 'have you read my book?'

Amber almost managed to look apologetic. 'Nope, I can use Google though. You told Jimbo your name, I needed it for the reservation. Don't see many Ferringhams knocking about, and renting rooms around here. So your second book, it's going to be about the Standedge Five?'

Robin talked before his thoughts caught up. 'Yes.'

'Well, tread lightly. Folks round here, they're trying to move on. Incident didn't happen that long ago, but to them, they've got the guy for it, it's resolved. There's a sort of vigil at the Church on Tuesday night if you want to see what I mean. Everyone wants to mourn the deaths of the Five and they want it to be over.' Amber went to the staircase, but before she began to ascend, she turned back. 'And if you see Roger Claypath . . .' she trailed off. She thought for a second, opened her mouth and then closed it again. Wordlessly she went up the stairs and left Robin alone.

Had she looked scared? Or was it Robin transplanting his feelings onto her? He didn't know.

He ran his finger over the notes he had made. The Standedge Five were starting to become more fleshed out in his mind, and so was his caller Matthew. Seemed like there were some complex feelings between Matthew and the rest of the group.

What had Amber called Matthew? He searched through his notes, almost unable to read his hurried handwriting. A rubber band, she had said, that was stretched and wound to fit the group.

Robin looked at the photo of the Five. What appeared to be a happy night in the basement of The Hamlet. Without Matthew. He wondered how the young man would feel if he saw this very photo?

How far could you stretch a rubber band until it snapped?

9

Robin put his suitcase and backpack in the room, and turned the small television on, but couldn't settle. He felt there was one last thing he needed to do before he went to sleep.

He had to see it for himself. He had to see Standedge. Even though he knew he couldn't go inside. He had to see it with his own eyes.

So he turned off the television, got his coat and went back out.

The evening had turned to a bitterly cold night. A wind was blowing through the empty streets with alarming speed. If Marsden seemed empty before, now it seemed like a ghost town. Robin retraced his steps up to the station, knowing from the maps that Standedge lay to the left instead of the right he had taken to get to the town.

He took the left and found himself almost instantly running parallel to the canal that had made its way under the bridge he had crossed earlier. He followed the canal, hearing the soft lap of water between the gusts of wind. He continued down a country path until he turned a corner, and paused as he took another bridge over the canal.

And there it was.

The entrance to the canal tunnel looked incredibly small – almost like a mouse hole in some old cartoon. But this was real – a little mouse hole in the side of the land-scape. It felt rather unassuming – the canal just ran up to it and disappeared inside. As though it swallowed the canal. Boats were moored by the tunnel entrance – blue and white narrowboats with plastic seating. Tour boats.

Next to the tunnel, stood a building that looked like a large holiday cottage. The Standedge Visitor Centre with an empty car park in front of it. The path from the bridge went down to the Centre and closer to the tunnel and Robin found his step hurrying.

He wanted to see closer.

The hole – gated up and chained, as though a prison for some horrific monster – grew larger with every step. Amber had said the children were afraid of it, and he could understand why. Staring into it, into the darkness inside, felt like staring into a void.

He came to the centre, but couldn't take his eyes from the tunnel. The wind was whipping through it, and somehow it was creating a whistling sound. Almost as if it were talking to him.

He thought of the game Amber talked about. Where you had to stand beside the tunnel and see how long you lasted. Would he have been able to do that as a child? Could he even do that now?

He chuckled to himself. No use getting spooked. It was just a tunnel after all. But he had to find out what Matthew's interest in it was. And why it brought the group close together. Did something happen on that trip?

Robin turned and started back toward The Hamlet. It was definitely creepy, and the ghost stories were warranted. But now Standedge was the location of a very real crime.

When he was crossing the bridge, he looked back at the tunnel. *People don't just disappear*, Robin thought again. And nodded to himself.

The tunnel whistled as if in agreement.

10

The girl watched Robin Ferringham cross the bridge and hurry back to The Hamlet. She hadn't exactly been hiding, having followed him across most of the town. She hid behind a tree when he turned back. It was a simple act of stealth – he wasn't exactly a secret agent or some such. But then neither was she. He didn't notice her at all. Simple.

She had to see if he was here for what she suspected. And lo and behold, he led her to Standedge. She didn't like being right all the time.

She got her phone out. Took a couple of snaps. She didn't really know what for. He was just standing there, like he was waiting for something to happen. She looked at them. If he was here for Standedge, what did that mean? She wasn't sure yet.

She watched him leave, spooked, and then she decided to keep the photos she took and slipped her headphones back on, making her way back to Marsden too.

Time to get back to work.

11

HMP New Hall was down an unassuming country road with trees along either side. Robin felt like he was coming into some country estate, more than a prison, but as he emerged out the end, he saw a large group of buildings surrounded by high imposing fences.

After breakfast, Robin had rented a car from a place in the centre of Marsden that seemed to double as an estate agent's. He wasn't entirely sure the woman there hadn't just rented him her own personal car. Whoever's car it was, it got him where he needed to go. New Hall was about half an hour from Marsden and on the journey he saw more fields than he'd seen in about a decade.

He followed the road up to the prison, watching as the large fence parted to let cars through. There was a small guard house positioned next to the road, with a rather bored looking officer inside. He gave his name and the guard let him through.

He found a space in a mostly-full car park at the front of the largest building, following signs that led to reception. As he got out of the car, he noticed that there was another fence surrounding the large building and stretching as far as he could see.

This was most definitely a prison. At least on the outside. When he entered the building, he found himself in a large hall that felt more like a museum. Marble floors and a glass ceiling dazzled him. Maybe that was the intention.

He was frisked and his backpack was put through an airport scanner, and subsequently rifled through before he could journey across the marble floor to a set of desks with officers enclosed behind glass.

'I'm here to visit a prisoner,' Robin said.

The officer on the other side of the glass looked at him with dull eyes. 'Name?'

'Mine or his?' Robin said.

The officer looked at him as if he were taking the piss.

Robin was given a set of forms, slid to him through an opening in the glass window, and told to fill them out. When Robin mentioned Matthew's name he had expected some sort of reaction, but the officer didn't even seem to recognize it.

Robin sat on a row of chairs by the wall, next to a young mother with a baby in her arms. By the time Robin had filled out the first form, an officer had come to escort her away – visiting the father no doubt. Visitors came and went as Robin ploughed on, the paperwork never ending. He had to detail criminal convictions, past addresses, any trips he'd made in the past five years – information that he thought couldn't possibly be relevant. By the time he was done, he felt like he'd written another book.

He went back to the officer and slid him back the stack

of papers. The officer took them and placed them behind him on a pile. 'They'll take a day to process.'

'What?' Robin said, 'No, I don't have a day. I have to see him now.'

The officer almost smiled at his misfortune. 'If you'd done it online in advance, it would've been quicker.'

Robin opened his mouth and closed it. He expected saying that he hadn't intended to be visiting anyone in New Hall a mere thirty-six hours ago, wouldn't exactly reflect the best on him.

He was about to turn away when a voice boomed from close behind him. 'Now now, Miles, I'm sure we can make an exception.'

The officer, Miles, suddenly came alive. His eyes widened and he sat up straight so violently it looked as if he'd been shot by a taser. 'Sir.'

Robin looked over his shoulder to see a tall, tidy man in a crisp suit standing a little too close to him. His eyes were sharp, and his prickled smile traced by a thin black moustache.

'I'm sure Mr Ferringham can go and visit who he likes, and we can rush the paperwork through while he's still in the building. Yes?'

The officer named Miles was as still as a mannequin, looking as if he was trying not to shake. 'Of course, sir.' Without taking his eyes from the crisply-dressed man, he reached behind himself and found the paperwork. He instantly started clacking at his computer keyboard, obviously happy to tear his eyes from the newcomer.

Robin turned to the man. 'Thank you.'

The man had his arms behind his back in a pose that showed off his broad chest. He wore a dazzling red tie, with a sparkling tie clip. Robin noticed this most, as it was at his eye level in relation to the man. 'Think nothing of it.' He unfurled one of his long arms and offered a hand with equally long fingers. 'Roger Claypath.'

Robin's heart skipped a beat, although somewhere he had known that the man in front of him could not have been anyone else. His face looked familiar – he had the same bulky jaw as his son, and he shared his daughter's nose. Even without having met the Claypath twins, there was no doubt they could have come from anyone else, like they were artists' impressions of the man in front of him.

Robin shook his hand. 'I'm Robin . . .' Was it an accident that Claypath was here?

'Ah, no need to introduce yourself,' Claypath said, still managing to boom even though he'd lowered his voice, 'you are Robin Ferringham. My wife's book club read your book a few months back.'

'Ah,' Robin said, uncomfortably. Even in such a vast airy room, he felt vulnerable. 'Did they enjoy it?'

'Haven't the foggiest. I leave her to that kind of stuff.' Claypath laughed. His eyes twitched – flitting up and down Robin in a motion that was almost imperceptible. 'I'm more into the macho stuff, you see – the Chris Ryans, the Tom Clancys. Something to get your pulse racing. But then, these days, the job does that for me.'

'Yes.'

'Aren't you going to say you're sorry?' Claypath said, bluntly, and not at all friendly. His demeanour changed in an instant.

'What?' Robin felt very small.

'My children disappear, killed by a perverse maniac who once was a friend, you stand before me trying to see this monster, and you don't at least tell me that you are sorry for my loss?'

Robin opened his mouth to say sorry like a quivering subject, but instead he straightened up and said, 'In my experience, a sorry from a stranger is probably the most insulting thing to hear after losing a loved one.'

Claypath considered this for a long moment, and the ghost of a sad smile played on his lips. 'What it is, hmm?'

'Pardon?'

Then Claypath did smile a joyless smile. 'What it is to find someone who understands.' Claypath leaned in close and whispered, 'You know, sometimes when some idiot comes up to me and says sorry, I just want to wring their bloody necks, choke them until I feel the life ebbing from them, just so they can feel what I feel.' He considered what he said, and leaned back again. His smile was genuine this time. He turned and beckoned to Robin to follow him. 'You can see Matthew McConnell on two conditions – the first being that there will be guards directly outside the door. This boy is dangerous, and he is manipulative. There will also be guards watching the room on the closed-circuit cameras. Anything happens, you must alert the guards, I cannot stress that enough.' He led Robin to the waiting area, and a guard appeared from down a long and comparatively dark corridor as if on cue. 'Stanton.'

The guard jumped slightly and looked at Claypath. 'Sir.'

'This is Mr Robin Ferringham. He has come to see Matthew McConnell.'

If there was any surprise at that, Stanton hid it perfectly. 'Yes, sir.' He turned to Robin. 'Will you come with me, please?'

Robin went to follow Stanton. And then turned back. 'Wait, you said there were two conditions.'

'Yes,' Claypath said, 'the second is you must come to the vigil being held at Marsden Church on Tuesday afternoon. You can see first-hand the sorrow that Matthew McConnell has caused. And then,' Claypath's face changed, like a cloud had come over him, his eyes sparking with a vindictive fire. 'You can tell me exactly why you're here.'

Robin quickly nodded and wilted under the man's gaze.

Roger Claypath was good cop until he was bad cop.

And now Robin was on his agenda.

12

The guard named Stanton led Robin through limitless corridors that all looked alike. He couldn't help feel it was to keep him off balance. Finally Stanton stopped in front of a large window that looked into a dark room with only a table and two skeletal chairs either side of it.

Stanton frisked him again, and seemingly satisfied, let him into the room via a heavy steel door. Stanton told him to sit, so he did, while the guard disappeared through a door on the opposite side of the room.

Robin looked around – no other windows, no connection with the outside world – and placed his notebook and pen on the table. He'd had to leave his backpack back with the officers in the lobby – even though there was nothing else in it. He looked at his watch. And tried to remember whether Stanton had locked the door behind him. Was he stuck in here?

Seconds piled up into minutes and Robin watched as the big hand on his watch whipped around from half past to the hour. The room was so silent he tried to strain his hearing to listen beyond it. But he couldn't.

Eventually, the door swung open and Stanton pushed a small figure – dressed in a grey T-shirt and trousers, his hands cuffed in front of him – into the room. Stanton almost threw the young man down into the chair opposite Robin.

'I'll be right outside the door,' Stanton said.

Robin nodded, as Stanton took one more look at the scene, assessing it and deeming it adequate, before he disappeared through the door.

Robin turned back to the young man in the chair. He looked different to how he appeared in the photographs – smaller, somehow even less realistic. His hair was tousled and he seemed generally dirty – his face slightly smudgy. He also looked a lot thinner.

His eyes, framed by lack of sleep, found their way up to Robin, with almost no drive, no motivation. 'You're really him?' he said.

'Hello, Matthew,' Robin said.

13

'I want to make one thing perfectly clear,' Robin said, before Matthew could say anything else. 'I'm intrigued. I'm intrigued by the Standedge Incident. I'm intrigued by what happened. And I'm intrigued by you. But I don't want you to think that I won't drop this and go back to London if I find out that you are lying about Sam.'

'I'm not lying,' Matthew said defensively, although still in his small voice.

'How do you know her?' Robin pressed.

'I don't.'

'Then why did she call you?'

'I don't know. It was a random call. I thought it was someone taking the piss. I thought she was drunk.'

'How'd she get your number?'

'I don't know.'

'Where was she calling from?'

'It was an unknown number.'

'And she said something about trusting me?'

'In a roundabout way. She wasn't making much sense.'

'What did she say?'

'She said your name. She said you were the greatest man she'd ever known. And that you were someone to rely on. She said if you asked for help, Robin Ferringham would help,' Matthew said plainly. He stated it so unenthusiastically it was hard to not see it as fact.

Robin's tone softened, although not consciously. 'I don't understand why she would call you and not me.'

Matthew sniffed. 'Neither do I.'

'And she didn't mention anything else?'

Matthew faltered. 'No.'

Robin didn't believe him. No one would. 'You're lying. What else did she say?'

'She muttered some incoherent stuff about . . . a black hound . . . and a horse's head.'

'What?'

'I didn't understand it. That's where I got the idea she was drunk, or on drugs, or something. It didn't make any sense, who would understand that?'

A black hound. And a horse's head. He definitely didn't understand it. 'When was this?'

Matthew brought up both his cuffed arms to wipe his nose. 'It was the middle of the night. Like 3 a.m.'

Robin interrupted. His patience was thin. 'I mean when? What year? What month?'

Matthew's breath hitched creating something between a sigh and a yelp. 'I don't . . . It was October. Nearly Halloween. Not last year. And it was before the others went to university. But I didn't tell them about it. Because they'd gone quiet. And then I just forgot it. So . . . it must have been . . . 20 . . . yes, 2015.'

Robin stopped. His signing pen dropped out of his hand and clattered onto the table. His vision became hazy. His mouth quivered as he formed the next sentence. 'Are you sure?'

Matthew regarded him, as though he were a time bomb. 'Are you okay?'

'Are you sure?' he said, through clenched teeth.

'I . . . I think,' Matthew searched himself. 'Yes. Yes. I'm sure.'

Robin sniffed, blinked away his tears. 'I think you were the last person to speak to Sam before she disappeared.'

14

Robin retrieved his pen. His voice was sure again. 'Why didn't you tell anyone?'

And Matthew was defensive again. As though they had settled back into their roles, and found comfort in them. 'I didn't know she was missing. I didn't know until you told me. I just thought she was some drunk.'

'She wasn't a drunk. She was my wife.'

'I didn't ask her to call me,' Matthew said.

Robin slammed his fist down on the metal desk. He knew Matthew was right. But he still couldn't bring himself to think that he wasn't the one she called. There had to be a reason. 'And that is all? That's it?'

Matthew's expression seemed to hold nothing but sorrow and understanding. 'Yes.'

But Robin felt like walking out, leaving, not giving this man a moment more of his time. 'You're lying. There's more.'

Robin couldn't place the look on Matthew's face until he heard his voice. 'I am lying.' It was disgust. He was disgusted. With himself. 'I can't tell you everything. And I'm sorry about that. But I need you to help me.'

So there it was. The incentive. The one bargaining chip Matthew held.

'You'll tell me now.'

'I can't do that. I need to know you'll help me.'

'I will help you if you tell me.'

'I'm sorry,' Matthew said, as tears rolled down his face. He seemed to be thinking, his face screwing up into a concentrated frown. 'But I have to get out of here. I didn't do it, Mr Ferringham. I loved them. I could never do it. If you at least try to help, even if it doesn't work, I'll tell you everything else I know. I promise. I trust you – I'm asking you to please trust me.'

'It's hard to trust someone who's been arrested for the murder of five people.'

Matthew shook with tears. 'I know.'

Robin stopped as Matthew composed himself. He wanted to believe the young man. He seemed genuine – he seemed in pain at the loss of his friends. But what if it was all an act? What if the real person he was mourning was the innocent Matthew that died in the tunnel?

It was hard for Robin to think with the mess of humanity in front of him, but he had to remember that currently the evidence pointed towards Matthew as the killer.

And yet, even then he might be a killer withholding information about Sam.

He had to know what Matthew knew. Maybe it was something that could help him find her, find out what happened three years ago. 'I need you to give me your word. Right now. I help you. You tell me everything.'

'I promise,' Matthew said. 'Really. Honestly. I promise.'

Robin looked at him. 'Okay. Okay. I'll help you.'

Matthew looked at him through his tears and Robin saw hope dawn on his face. 'Thank you.'

Robin smiled slightly, but he could only think of what Matthew was withholding from him. Robin wanted to help Matthew, was as intrigued by the Standedge Incident as anyone could be, but the driving force was Sam. It always was.

And if Sam sent Matthew to his doorstep, then who was he to turn him away?

Robin picked up his pen, and opened his notebook. 'I know a little. But I guess we should start with what happened on 26 June this year.'

Matthew sniffed away the tears, wiped his face with his cuffed hands. 'Okay yeah. Of course.'

'I know you worked for the Trust so you could go through the tunnel unsupervised. But where did the boat come from?'

Matthew straightened somewhat. He cleared his throat. 'It belonged to Edmund's uncle. It was moored down the canal a ways. I was so excited I went a few hours early, just to get it ready for the guys, like do all my preliminary checks and stuff. When I was finished, I just waited for the rest of them on the boat. There was a TV, so I switched it on, and ended up watching some daytime rubbish. That talk show thing that used to have that famous guy, Sheppard, on, but they replaced him after . . . What's it called?

'Something like *Resident* . . .'

15

26 June 2018
11 a.m.

'. . . *Detective*. I'm Thomas Mane and Nothing Gets Past Me! Let's start the show.'

Matt smiled. What a load of rubbish.

Everything seemed in order. The engine seemed fine, and the small living quarters were as quaint and inviting as any boat he'd been on before. Matt loved narrow-boats, would like to buy one some day. But they were expensive. And although he had the money from his parents' estate, he couldn't help but feel there were more pressing things a twenty-one year old should spend his money on.

He sat down at the dining table and watched as the presenter ushered on his first act – a couple fighting about some affair or whatever. He yawned – hadn't been able to sleep the night before for excitement. He rested his head on the table and before he knew it, he was asleep.

'Matt.'

Matt's eyes snapped open. He was no longer alone. But he didn't jump.

Pru and Robert were sat on the bed. Pru was reaching over and prodding him. 'Matt, hey. You're not drunk, are you?'

'Can you get done for drink driving if you're driving a canal boat?' Robert mused to no one in particular. 'I mean, you're not gonna get pulled over.'

'Ever the thinker,' Edmund said. Matt looked around and saw that Edmund was in the kitchen area, unpacking two plastic bags of cans and putting them in the fridge. Edmund put a can in front of Matt.

'He is right,' Matt said, smiling. 'I am driving.'

Edmund laughed. 'One'll be fine, surely. You're going to have to be a little tipsy, at least, to cope with us lot.'

Matt took the can, shrugged, and popped it open.

'Attaboy.'

Matt just stared at Edmund and then Pru and then Robert silently. Finally they noticed. 'What?' they seemed to all say in unison.

'You're just . . .' Matt seemed to struggle for the words, and settled on, 'You're just all here.'

They all laughed, the booming sound seeming to echo throughout the cabin. It sounded good.

'Of course,' Robert said, 'it's 26 June. Where else would we be?'

Matt looked around at them – it seemed so right. 'I haven't seen you all since Christmas.'

'Yeah,' Edmund said, 'sorry about that.'

'We'll . . .' Pru trailed off, and very quickly looked from him to Edmund and back. 'We'll make it up to you.'

Matt didn't know what to say, was processing the

look, when he decided to change the subject. 'Where's Tim and Rachel?'

'They've just gone to get our final passenger,' Pru said, nicking Matt's can and opening it herself, 'we thought our final voyage should have a special guest.'

'Who?' Matt said.

'Well, DCI Claypath, of course,' Edmund said. 'He particularly wants to try the weed I brought from uni.'

Pru threw a pillow at Edmund. 'Don't listen to him.'

Matt was just about to ask – 'Who then?' – when there was a loud barking coming from outside the boat. Two dogs were making a play for loudest and most unruly and the barks segued into growls. Muffled voices started growing louder – two people arguing.

Everyone got up and filed out of the cabin in turn to see what all the fuss was about. Matt emerged to see Tim, carrying two crates of beer, arguing with a middle-aged woman. Rachel was trying to keep two dogs apart – one familiar, and dwarfed by the other, less familiar.

The dogs were dancing around each other in a circle. Amy, the Bedlington, wasn't letting the hulk of a black Newfoundland out of her sight. 'Amy,' Rachel was snapping, 'Amygdala, down!' Rachel had named the dog herself, when she had got interested in psychology. Amygdala – the part of the brain that processed emotion, fear.

Amy didn't have a lead, had never needed one as long as Matt had known her. She loved all other dogs, although clearly not now. The Newfoundland snarled and lunged at Amy, Amy jumped out of the way and continued to circle.

'This dog should have a lead, little terror.' The woman was lecturing Tim, but Tim was having none of it.

'How about your dog should have a lead? It's practically a horse,' Tim shouted. 'Or maybe a donkey.'

Matt, Pru, Edmund and Robert just stared at the entire scene, not entirely knowing what they had just walked out into. None of the participants seemed to notice their audience.

'Your dog is terrorising mine.'

'Your dog could eat mine three times over. Which looks like its primary strategy.'

'Rodney doesn't like Bedlingtons. Never has.' The old woman almost looked like she was revelling in the ruckus.

'Great, so it's racist too. I might have to tell my father about this mutt.'

'Father? What do you . . .' The woman stopped, looking at Tim.

Matt didn't see this stopping anytime soon, and he had a quick idea about how to finish it. He ducked inside, swiping his Canals and Rivers Trust raincoat and slinging it on. He went back outside, and cleared his throat loudly.

The scene at the side of the canal froze. It almost seemed like even the dogs looked round at who had made a sound. Of course that was silly, but they at least seemed to quieten down. The humans finally acknowledged the boat and the occupants of it. Rachel looked at

Matt and smiled. Tim looked a little confused. And the woman turned her thunder on him.

Matt gave it a beautiful second before he spoke up. 'Sir, I have done all the preliminary checks I need to do. So when you wish, we are ready to set off. Do you need help with those crates, Mr Claypath?'

Matt had said the magic word. Claypath. Tim smiled as he understood. The woman's face quickly changed, from the initial thunder, to a stormy, to a weak rainfall. 'Hmm,' she said. The dogs were still quietly going at it, but she grabbed the Newfoundland, almost mounting it, and pushed it on. She gave a snide look at Tim as she passed and the Newfoundland followed its master by growling at him. Amy looked after them, still yapping away.

'Amy,' Matt said, and her little head whipped around. In a second, she had jumped onto the boat and leaped up into Matt's outstretched arms.

'Not sure who was happier to see you,' Robert muttered.

Tim and Rachel beamed at him. 'Smooth work, Mc-Connell. Very nice and stylish. Using your station to great effect.' He jumped on to the boat and gave Rachel a hand across the gap. The boat bobbed slightly, settling as it got used to its new passengers. 'This is a nice boat. Props go to Edmund's uncle, huh?'

Matt didn't want to tell Tim why exactly saying his name worked so well. That woman with the dog was Liz Crusher, and her fear of the Claypath name was for a different reason entirely. Even if it was woefully unfounded. He shook away the thought and forgot Crusher.

81

Tim went inside the boat and deposited his crate of beer. There was hardly any need for it, with all Edmund had brought. But too much was always better than too little, Matthew guessed.

The others followed Tim in, including Amy, and as Matt turned, Rachel pounced on him and seized him in such a big hug he had to struggle for air.

'Hi, Rachel,' he said – all he could think to say.

Rachel let go of him and held him by the arms, almost surveying him. 'Has it been dreadful staying here? We talk about you all the time, you know.'

'I didn't die,' Matt said. 'I'm still here. And I like being here. I like Marsden. Always have.' Marsden was his home. And he loved it as much as he loved the group. It was like their unspoken eighth member (if Amygdala was considered the seventh). That was why he was puzzled that the others found it so easy to leave to go to university – to go to big cities and forget where they came from. Matt could never do that.

'How's your aunt?' Rachel said. 'Still giving you a tough time?' Rachel was staring at him strangely, with a lost look, as though if she looked away for one moment, she would lose him forever.

'You know how it is.' He wanted to ask her what was wrong, but couldn't bring himself to do it. So he just nodded and said, 'How's Edinburgh?'

'You know how it is,' Rachel said, parroting him, 'classes, books – books, classes. Parties, then more books and classes.'

Matt smiled, and opened his mouth to say something,

anything, else, but Pru interrupted by sticking her head out of the hatch. 'Bloody hell, Rachel, leave the poor guy alone,' Pru laughed, handing Matt his open can. Matt and Rachel shrugged to each other and followed Pru back through the hatch.

She sat down next to Edmund at the table. Tim was waving about a handful of beers. 'Why did we bring so many again?'

'Classic young person overcompensation,' Rachel said, taking one and opening it. She made a face. 'Too warm. Chill them.'

'Can't,' Edmund said, 'the fridge is full with mine.'

Tim gawked. 'Well, I'll lower myself to your level and have some of your pig swill.'

'No,' said Edmund.

'Please.'

'No.'

'Please.'

Edmund sighed, 'Fine,' but not before Tim had already swung open the fridge and helped himself to one.

Behind them, Pru and Robert had resumed a heated conversation. 'It doesn't recognise it,' Pru was saying, 'it's like my phone is embarrassed to acknowledge yours' existence.'

'You have to put me in your contacts,' Robert said defensively.

'I have you in my contacts. Of course I have you in my contacts. But you still come up as Unknown.'

'Well, that's hardly my fault.' Robert caught Matt's eye, although everyone was looking at the two bickering now, and flashed a friendly smile. 'Matt, when I call you, my number comes up right.'

Matt shook his head and laughed, 'Sorry, U.N. Owen. You're an enigma for me too.'

'Just get a new phone,' Tim said.

'This is perfectly adequate.' Robert reached into his pocket and brought out a mobile phone that looked like it was circa 1999 to a collective groan from the others.

'How can you have that out in public without being embarrassed?' Edmund said.

The conversation continued but Matt didn't hear the rest. He was too busy watching his friends in front of him, once more sliding back into their usual roles like they were born to play them. For him the group was more than family, it was fate. And they all worked together in harmony.

Robert was the lovable butt of everyone's jokes. He was timid and quiet, but the most diplomatic of the group. At an early age Robert found out that he had been named after a famous poet, and had a deep crisis of the identity of the self. It resonated to this day, as he weighed up outcomes before acting, as though to live up to his namesake.

Pru was vicious – a girl who talked first and thought later. This had gotten her into a lot of trouble at school, but her good grades and inquisitive mind often saved her. Her love of mechanics really kicked in when she borrowed a school laptop from the library and brought it back in pieces. The librarian made her put it back together, which Pru did right in front of her.

Edmund was classically handsome and fiercely intelligent. In any other group, he would have risen to the top. But instead he was relegated to be the right-hand man to Tim – anyone else might have been miffed by that. But not Edmund. He was always one to go with the flow, content to be needed when he was needed. He was Tim's friend from kindergarten and possessed many of the same traits, but he was never quite as good. But Edmund didn't possess Tim's intensity, which made him more approachable.

They were all in orbit around the twins, having a regard for Tim and Rachel that, although unspoken, was never really hidden. Tim and Rachel were untouchable – people tread lightly around them. The Claypaths were the most important family in Marsden, with Roger Claypath casting a formidable shadow in the police force and Ava Claypath casting an equal one in the social scene. This was a rather silly thought, as Matt had met both of the Claypath parents and they were the friendliest people in whose company he had ever been. Tim and Rachel shared that friendliness, although sometimes Tim clearly revelled in his power. And power he most definitely had.

Rachel shared the Claypath intelligence, although she was much quieter than her twin brother. She seemed to understand people at a fundamental level, and whenever Matt talked to her, he had the uncomfortable feeling that she was reading his mind. Luckily, she countered this with a fierce sense of humour and a warmth which radiated the fact that even if she did read your mind, it wouldn't be the worst thing.

That left Matt, who didn't feel like he added much, but the others seemed to accept him. Except recently, the group had started pulling apart. They had been radio silent for months – their WhatsApp group totally silent. It was only exacerbated by Tim suggesting this should be the last trip through Standedge – the annual tradition was to come to an end. The group was falling apart.

Or was it Matt who was falling away? Didn't someone in the town say they saw the other five at The Hamlet – without him?

That was why today was so important. He knew that this journey was going to reignite their friendship. It was going to pave the way for many more trips to come.

Matt checked his watch. They had all afternoon to go through the tunnel – no other boats were scheduled for passage today. Matt had the key to the gates, now he was part of the Trust. They had time, so he sat down with the others and listened to them as they talked and laughed. He sipped at his beer and just enjoyed feeling safe in the familiar company.

He didn't know how long he sat there, happy, but the others had got onto their third or fourth cans of beer, when the discussion turned to Standedge.

'How many times have you been through the tunnel now, Matt?' Pru asked, having to slightly lean around Rachel in the narrow space to see him.

Matt shook himself. 'Sorry?'

'The tunnel. How many times have you been through?'

Matt thought. He had asked himself the same question and was slightly annoyed with himself that he hadn't counted. But like all good ideas, it had come just a little too late. 'Not sure. Maybe fifty times?' he guessed.

'Fifty times,' Tim marvelled, 'and you're not sick to death of it yet? I like it once a year but more than that and I think I'd get bored.'

'No,' Matt said and genuinely meant it. 'It's still awesome. Every time I go in, I feel that same way we felt back in Year 7. Every time, it feels like a marvel and it is. Every time, I feel lucky to do something amazing.'

He looked around the group and didn't see quite the same enthusiasm. Edmund smiled at him but there was an element of sadness to it. 'Yeah,' he said slowly, 'but you are really just going through a tunnel, very slowly, on a boat.'

Matt's smile dropped. He looked around and saw that the spell had been broken for every other member of the group. No one could meet Matt's eyes. Suddenly the cabin seemed too small, as if cramming them all together only exacerbated their indifference. He stood up and grabbed a can of his own, angry, but trying not to show it. 'It's what brought us all together.'

Tim put a hand on his shoulder. 'It wasn't really. Remember we were all on that boat, but we didn't know each other really, not at the time.'

'No one else remembers how it felt? Like life was so much more than we thought? Like human beings were capable of so much more than we thought? It was like riding a bike without stabilisers the first time. It was . . .'

'Matt,' Robert interrupted, 'I appreciate the irony of what I'm about to say, seeing as I'm studying literary

87

fiction but you don't have to drown everything in mysticism to make it seem more than it really was. We thought the tunnel was cool and then we became friends and we decided to make an annual pact. That's it. The tunnel is a tunnel. It's not alive, it's not a portal, it's not something that can provide a springboard for cosmic ideology. There was a hill. Humans decided they needed to go through the hill. So they did. It's very cool, but it's just a tunnel.'

Matt looked around to see the others wordlessly nod in agreement. He'd never felt so segmented, so cut off from the rest of them. 'If you all thought that, why did you all come back here?'

They all remained quiet and looked to Tim, as if they were waiting for their leader to speak. Reluctantly, he did, putting a hand on Matt's shoulder. 'We didn't come back here for the tunnel.'

Suddenly, Matt felt upset, incredibly so. He flung his hands up in the air, spilling about a quarter of his beer, and shrugged off Tim. 'Then I don't know what you did come back here for, because it certainly wasn't me.' He pushed past Tim, and went to the door, expecting someone to stop him, say, 'No, it was you, silly. We came back for you!', but no one did. He turned to look at them all again sadly.

'We should get going,' he muttered. And went outside.

The motor started up quickly, spluttering slightly as if shrugging off a few months of slumber. Matt cast off on his own, knowing what he was doing, even though it was better done with two people. No one came out to help him. He felt like he was on the boat alone.

As the boat started to move up the canal, Matt steering into the centre, he finally started to hear the others talking in the cabin. They had been mysteriously silent in the period between Matt leaving and now, and he wondered what had been happening in there. Silent drinking, no doubt. Matt left the hatch closed. He couldn't hear what they were talking about, didn't want to know if it was about him or not. He didn't know which would be worse.

Matt accelerated, shifting his weight on the steering stick, preparing to steer into a slight curve. It was supposed to be relaxing, canal boating, and in a way, it did calm him down – to have something else to think about.

He went on for ten minutes, listening to the muffled conversation and the water parting as the boat cut through it. It seemed the atmosphere inside had changed as he heard laughing – including Edmund's drunken laugh – and lighter voices. He wanted to open the hatch and forget everything and join in. He wanted to enjoy the last boat ride they had together.

Just as he was about to open the hatch, Rachel's head popped out and she tentatively smiled at him. She had in her hands three cans of beer (not Edmund's cheap stuff but her own slightly better quality stuff). She stepped through the hatch and Amy scampered out too, woofing delightedly and sticking her tongue out to lap at the fresh air.

'Thought you could use these,' she said, indicating the beers and put two of them down by Matt's feet. She held the last one out to him and he took it and smiled.

'Thanks,' he said, cracking it open and taking a swig. He glanced around the banks of the canal to see if anyone was watching. He might lose his job if anyone saw him, but for some reason, it didn't seem incredibly important anymore. If everyone was going to leave Standedge behind, maybe he should too.

'No,' Rachel said, as if reading his mind, 'you're thinking too much. I can see it in your face.'

'What?' Matt said, wondering if he had been talking out loud.

'You screw your face up when you're thinking,' Rachel said and then laughed, 'Yeah, just like that.'

'Am I that easy to read?' Matt said.

Amy yapped, as if in confirmation. She started making laps of the small outside area, and poked her head under the railing to watch the world go by slowly. A cyclist was passing them on the bank and Amy barked happily at him.

'Well, kind of, yeah.' Rachel leaned against the railing. 'But I didn't mean it as a bad thing.' She tilted her can at Matt. 'You know we all love you, right?'

'Yes,' Matt said quickly, and hated himself for it. He didn't know anything of the sort, and why should he bother to make Rachel, or any of the others, feel better about it? He should be more assertive, stick up for himself a bit more. 'Maybe.'

'Well, we do.' Rachel leaned over and opened the hatch. 'Guys,' she called, 'do we love Matt?'

Whatever conversation Tim, Edmund, Pru and Robert were having died down, and quickly there was a resounding 'Yes!' before it started up again. Rachel left the hatch propped open, and righted herself. 'See.'

'Thanks,' Matt said.

'Anytime.' Rachel touched him on the arm, and he couldn't help but look down at her hand, welcoming her touch.

'What's that?' he said.

'Hmm?'

'On your wrist.' He had thought he'd seen it before, something out of the corner of his eye. But now he was sure – there was something there at the top of her wrist, written in black just under her palm.

'Oh this.' Rachel withdrew her hand, and looked at the writing as though she were seeing it for the first time. 'It's nothing really.' She held her wrist out for Matt to see. On Rachel's left wrist in small letters, almost incomprehensible, was a six-letter word, all in capitals in strong black ink.

ASCEND

'Ascend?' Matt said. He ran his finger over the letters, and felt her shiver at the touch. He looked up and their eyes met for a glorious second that he could live in forever. She smiled. And he did too.

Amy barked at a runner going by, and the moment was broken.

Rachel withdrew her wrist as quickly as she had offered it. She clutched it with her hand as though it hurt.

'What does it mean?' Matt said, wanting that moment back.

Rachel just looked at him sadly. 'I told you, it's

nothing.' And without another word, she went inside the cabin.

Matt just watched her, trying to ignore the fact Amy was staring at him. 'Don't look at me like that. I'm going to tell her.' Amy barked, as if to say *Yeah, right*.

He took a swig of beer and then another and before he knew it, he'd finished the can.

He focused on the journey, watching the world go by at a snail's pace. The canal was quiet, as if everyone had made way for the famous Standedge group. He passed a couple of boats moored to the side of the canal but there was no sign of life in either of them. Amy settled down at his feet, stretching across the deck. A serene calm came over him and for half an hour he just enjoyed the ride.

As the sound from inside the cabin grew rowdier – no doubt thanks to the insane amount of beer – he saw a sign for Standedge and saw the outskirts of Marsden and knew they were getting close.

He poked his head in the cabin. 'We're nearly there.' They were now sitting in a circle, as best as they could in the small space. It looked like they were playing some form of spin the bottle with a can, providing even less legitimacy by Amy bouncing in and out the circle patting the can.

Matt realised that he had done it again – segmented himself off from the rest of them. They hadn't done anything. It had all been him.

Tim jumped up from the circle, using Rachel and Edmund's shoulders as support. 'Come on then, I'd like to see it coming up. For last time's sake.'

There he was again, insisting it was the 'last time'. Matt went back to the deck, clearing the way for Tim to join him. He slipped a little and Matt grabbed him for support. 'Just a little drunk is all.' He looked around. 'Standedge, eh?'

'Yeah,' Matt said.

Tim tipped the rest of his can into his mouth, upending his head. Matt caught sight of it before he even knew what he was looking at. 'What is . . .' But he stopped himself. On Tim's left wrist, just like Rachel's, a small word. Six letters. Ascend.

They were getting closer to Standedge, but Matt couldn't look away from Tim's wrist.

'Why do you have that tattoo?' Matt said. 'And why does Rachel have the exact same one?'

'What?' Tim said, in the exact same tone Rachel had. 'This thing?' He showed him the tattoo.

'What does it mean, Tim?'

'Ascend? I think the dictionary definition is . . .'

'Cut the shit, Tim, what does it mean?'

Tim took a step backwards, an impressive feat in such a small space. 'Matt, mate, calm down, it's just . . .'

Matt didn't wait to hear the end of the sentence, and he didn't even care to see that Tim swung for the steering lever when Matt launched himself inside the cabin. Inside, the others were sat in the circle again. This time they seemed to just be watching Amy chasing her tail in the centre. Matt didn't think about what he was doing, operating on some kind of instinct that he knew what to do. He ignored the greetings the others gave him, and he just grabbed Pru's left arm, as she was nearest to him.

'Hey.'

He pulled Pru's sleeve down. He didn't want it to be there so much that, for a moment, it almost wasn't. But a micro-second later, when reality set in, there it was, exactly the same as Tim and Rachel. On Pru's wrist – 'Ascend'.

'What the hell is going on here?' Matt barked, rather like Amy. The dog jumped and looked around at him as though he were a canine. The others looked equally shocked.

'Matt,' Rachel said.

Suddenly the boat came to a stop. The others probably didn't notice, but Matt had been on boats for a long time. He felt the small shift in direction stop and the motor stop. It seemed like Tim had at least worked that out.

'Someone tell me what this means,' Matt said before Pru wrenched her arm away from him.

'What are you doing, Matt?' Pru said, not knowing he had seen two other tattoos exactly the same. The realisation seemed to dawn on her as she looked at her own wrist. The fact they didn't care enough to even know what he was talking about was somehow even worse than the act itself.

'Edmund, Robert, show me your left wrists,' Matt said.

'Don't be crazy, mate,' Edmund said.

But Matt's look obviously convinced them to do what he said, because they looked at each other and both held up their wrists. The word on each wrist was too small to read from any distance but he knew what it was. On Edmund's and Robert's.

All of them.

'Why? What is . . .' Matt said, whirling around, not knowing where to look. 'Have you all joined some crazy cult or something?'

'Don't be stupid,' Edmund said, grabbing Matt. Matt tried to force himself away. But Edmund wrapped his arms around him.

'Tim,' Rachel called.

'Are you okay?' Edmund said in Matt's ear.

'I'm fine,' Matt spat and Edmund let go of him.

Matt just stood there, in the middle of them all. He didn't know what to think. Thoughts came fast and short. He couldn't clutch onto any of them long enough to decipher them. What was happening? Why—

Tim had entered the cabin and suddenly a calm came over the space. Even Matt felt it. The others seemed to freeze, waiting for their leader. Matt looked at him and saw him jump down into the cabin, calm as always. 'What's going on?'

'Ascend,' Matt said, trying to temper his speech. 'What does that mean?'

'It's just a word,' Tim said, like that was that.

Matt tore his eyes from Tim, to look around before returning. They had all adjusted their bodies to gravitate towards Tim. It was like seeing some weird congregation worship a priest. 'Just a word . . . tattooed on all of your wrists.'

'We just . . . wanted something to remind us of each other,' Tim said.

'Everyone except me, huh?' Matt spat.

Tim sighed. 'Matt, your lack of self-worth isn't endearing. In fact, it's starting to piss us all off.'

'I have done everything for this group.' Matt was fighting back tears. 'And you all repay me by ignoring me, sneaking around behind my back, talking about me, freezing me out . . .'

'Matt . . .' Rachel started, stepping towards him.

Matt pushed her away, harder than he meant to. Rachel was forced onto the couch, any harder and she would have gone into the wall. 'You've all been meeting without me. Haven't you?'

Matt looked from one shocked face to another, and he stopped at Rachel. The one he trusted most. 'Yes,' she said, almost in a whisper, 'but I can explain, Matt.'

'You all lied to me. Saying you were staying at uni? Why?'

'Matt . . .' He didn't even know who it was. Didn't care.

'Why would you come back to Marsden and not tell me?' He was crying now. 'Someone, please just tell me.'

'Matt,' Tim said, stepping forward and putting his hand on Matt's shoulder, 'I promise you, everything will be explained. We just need to do one thing first. We need you to take this boat through our tunnel, *our* tunnel – you, me, Rachel, Ed, Robert, Pru – *our* tunnel. And when we come out the other side, everything will be better. What did you say once? Going through Stand-edge is like leaving the world and coming back to it? Let's do that. And let's enjoy it. And afterwards, you can ask anything you want. Promise.'

Matt looked at him through tears. He didn't know what to think. But he knew one thing. 'I don't know who you people are anymore.' And he pushed past Tim to the hatch, looking back long enough to see their reactions – Pru, Edmund, Robert and Tim (even, Amy) were staring dumbfounded, Rachel was crying. He didn't care – they were meant to be his best friends.

He went outside, slamming the hatch behind him. He started up the motor again, almost on auto-pilot looking down on himself. He picked up one of the cans of beer on the deck and wiped it across his forehead before opening it. The air was cold and he looked up to see the sunny day had turned sour, with dark clouds threatening rain, as if the weather was being dictated by him.

Matt leaned against the steering column, watching the mouth of the tunnel grow ever closer. He drained a can from full in less than a minute. He didn't care anymore – he didn't care if he lost his job. There was only one real reason he had gotten it in the first place – for this exact scenario. And it was ruined. All of it was. His friends were ruined.

Tim popped out and said they all had to get the annual photo by the tunnel. It was obvious to Matt now that he didn't care. He didn't care about the tunnel, he was just trying to save face – damage control. Everyone filed onto the side to take the picture but Matt stayed in the background. And then when they were done, they just went straight back to how they were before. Tradition done – for the last time. Good riddance. So long, Matt. He started the boat up again, noticing Tim had made sure to shut the hatch when he'd got on the boat.

Standedge got ready to swallow them, as the tip of the boat entered the tunnel. Every second more of the boat disappeared into darkness and, for once, Matt didn't blame himself. Whatever had happened between him and the group wasn't his fault, it was theirs. They met in secret, they got matching tattoos, they spent a Christmas without him. They chose to do that.

Half of the boat was in the tunnel now, more every second. And Matt looked around at the world one last time, as he always did. But he didn't feel excited or awed. He just felt empty. He felt like he had invested so much of himself in a group of people who treated him like a joke. He felt like the life he had been leading had been the wrong one, a planet orbiting a fake sun made out of cardboard and LED lights. He felt that who he was as a person was wrong. And, as the tunnel swallowed him, he started to feel an emotion he had never felt towards the group before.

Anger.

16

Robin looked at Matthew. The young man had stopped talking. He was staring down at his hands, as though wondering what they'd done. They were shaking. 'What happened next?'

He jumped, as though coming back to the present, tucking his hands under the table. 'That's it. That's the last thing I remember. The anger. And then – nothing. Then I woke up, lying in the hospital with a doctor standing over me and my hands cuffed to the side of the bed.'

Robin rubbed his eyes. Matthew's story was relentless – he told it with the pace and emotion of a painful experience – like he was reliving every second. It hadn't given Robin much time to think.

'So you remember going into the tunnel, and nothing else?'

Matthew thought for a moment. 'Yeah. I don't remember anything afterwards. No getting hit on the head, nothing with the others, nothing at all. The doctor said it's probably short-term amnesia brought on by the concussion.'

'Hmm,' Robin said. He couldn't help thinking how

convenient that was. But he also thought Matthew had seemed truthful – he had willingly told Robin the story, even the parts that made him look bad. It was hard to think he could be lying, seeing as he made himself look pretty guilty.

'They're gone and those were the last things I ever said to them.' Matthew was still wading in the past. Robin looked at him, and wondered how Matthew would go about killing and disposing of his friends? As usual, he came up with nothing.

As soon as questions started with 'How . . .?' this whole case slammed into a brick wall.

Because, well. How?

Robin took out his phone, swiped to the picture of the Standedge Five in the basement of The Hamlet. He slid it across to Matthew, pointing at the smudge on Tim's wrist. 'This was the tattoo you saw?'

Matthew only had to glance at it. 'Yes. That's it. Ascend.' And then he looked at the picture, really looked at it. 'What is this? I don't remember this.'

Robin realised his mistake too late.

Matthew's eyes sparkled, with equal amounts of regret and redemption. 'This proves it. This proves they were meeting. I was right. Where did you get this?'

'It's hanging in the basement of The Hamlet.'

'When was this . . .'

Robin sighed and ran his hands through his hair. He decided to tell the truth. 'It was taken three days before the Incident.'

Matthew looked up from the photo and surprised

Robin – by laughing. Uncontrollably. 'Three days. Three. Days.' He gave out a fresh cackle. 'I was right. I was damn right.'

Robin just watched as Matthew rapidly went through the stages of grief.

'Why the hell would they do that? Three days before . . . I was right there. Right there.'

Robin changed the subject. 'So you'd go through the tunnel a lot – like a ritual? Like the tunnel was important to the group? Did something happen that first time you went through the tunnel when you were young?'

The question helped Matthew calm down. He sniffed. 'Nothing tangible, physical. I think as kids, we spent so long being afraid of that place – afraid of what was lurking inside Standedge. Then that day, we found out that we were afraid of nothing. And even more than that, it was actually kinda cool. You understand?'

Robin mulled it over for a second and then nodded. He'd had things like that when he was a child too. He had been afraid of dogs until his grandma got an old sheep dog. Now he was a dog person. It was a coming-of-age moment – when you realised your worst fears were utterly unjustified. Of course that led into the discovery that there were far more tangible fears in the world, but that was by-the-by. 'So the trip was what brought you all together?'

'Yes,' Matthew said, 'before that I hadn't really said two words to the others – not any of them. But the trip changed that – I think we all felt exactly the same. We came out the other side a little different – a little older.

And we felt we had some kind of bond because of it.'

'What about the other kids? The ones that were in the class but didn't become part of the "group"?'

'Some of them didn't get it. Some of them hated it. Two of them even had to get off.'

'I'm sorry, get off? How would someone "get off"?'

Matthew looked at him as though it were obvious, but seeing Robin's confused expression, dropped his. 'Sorry, I forget people don't know, but you wouldn't if you hadn't gone through at least once. When you go on a trip through the tunnel – if you're going on one of the tour boats anyway – there are four pilots that go through with you. Two are drivers – one at the front and one at the back – one is the tour guide, and the last takes a van through the abandoned rail tunnel next to the canal tunnel. There are half a dozen cut-throughs between the canal and the rail tunnel where the guy can appear and ask if anyone wants to get off. Say someone's suddenly claustrophobic – panicking, screaming, I had someone projectile vomiting once – the driver can take them back in the van far quicker than the boat can. And that way, everyone else can carry on.'

Robin wrote down 'Abandoned Rail Tunnel' – this wasn't a mystery of one tunnel, it was a mystery of two. If someone could've gotten into the abandoned tunnel, they would have had access to both. He paused, then wrote down 'Other workers??' too.

'Let's get back to the group,' Robin said, 'you seemed to all be quite loved in Marsden. Why was that?'

Matthew shrugged. 'I think the "grown-ups" liked to

see young people not acting like hooligans. We were a "gang", I guess, in the true sense of the word, but we didn't go around making trouble for anyone. We kept ourselves to ourselves mostly, and when we didn't, we liked to help out around Marsden. Marsden is my home – I love it – so I like to help out any way I can. We used to do charity events, help out at the old folk's home when they needed it, stuff like that . . .'

'You were proud of the group?'

Matthew frowned. 'Of course. What kind of question is that? They were my best friends and we were good together. At least . . . Nearly ten years of friendship and then . . .'

'You said it was Tim's idea that this year be the final trip? Do you know why?'

'It was Tim's idea,' Matthew said, 'but everyone agreed. Just like Standedge helped us to grow up, I think he thought it was holding us back. He thought we could be friends without the rigid structure.' Matthew stopped.

'Go on.'

'I think Tim – and the others kinda – wanted to leave Marsden behind. I guess the Claypaths were done living in their dad's shadow. And Edmund, Pru and Robert . . . well, maybe they thought they were destined for something bigger. They were prepared to turn their backs on where they came from. And turn their backs on . . .' Matthew couldn't finish the sentence.

'Turn their backs on you?' Robin said.

Matthew nodded, sniffling. 'I never thought I was

bigger than Marsden. I never wanted to be. I love it, it's my home, and it has done just as much for me as I have done for it. I knew I was never as clever, or as creative, or as handy as my friends – but I never wanted to be. I wanted – want – a quiet life. And Marsden is perfect for that.'

Robin didn't even want to think, let alone say, that that future was gone for Matthew McConnell. Even if he were totally exonerated, Marsden – and the people in it – would likely never forget his part in what happened in Standedge. Matthew's love for Marsden was as genuine as Marsden's hate for him. But looking at Matthew, he realised that he hadn't had to say it. Matthew already knew. And that made Robin feel a pang of the young man's pain.

Robin pressed on, 'When did your friends start to exhibit some of these feelings?'

Matthew didn't need to think. 'When school started pushing us to apply for universities that was when it came to the forefront, I guess. But even before then, I suppose. They were always more than the town, more than me. Tim and Edmund were razor sharp so fell into Physics and other Sciences, Rachel understood people so was a natural psychologist, Pru wanted to know how things worked and Robert could write a mean story. If they'd stayed in Marsden, they would have been bored. I guess that's what it really comes down to. Boredom.'

Robin knew what he meant. He had often wondered if Sam was bored with their life. She was so much more – so much more than him. 'It's only natural you felt angry.' And Matthew saw his understanding and warmed slightly. 'When the group started to pull away, you must have felt incredibly upset.'

Matthew surprised him by giving a joyless laugh. 'That's the thing. Looking back now, I see I was kidding myself. But I had never really known that they were going to leave me until that day. The Incident. But then, I saw it – life without them. I guess that's what I'm living now.'

'You said someone told you that the group was meeting without you? Do you remember who told you?'

Matthew went to dry his eyes again. Robin handed him a tissue. 'It was a guy named Benny Masterson. He works in Marsden Butchers. We used to be friends at school . . . before . . . Before them.' He gestured to the photo.

Robin nodded, writing down the name. Maybe Mr Masterson would be able to shed some light on the group without Matthew.

'I gave them everything,' Matthew said, and pushed the photo away.

Robin ignored that. 'Do you have any clue why they chose the word "Ascend" to tattoo on their wrists?'

Matthew shook his head. 'You don't think I've been wondering about that ever since? No, I have no idea.'

Robin suppressed another sigh. Matthew was there – on the face of it, he was the only person who could unlock what happened in that tunnel. But he didn't know much. And Robin didn't think he was lying, didn't even think he was holding back.

Robin needed to think. And he was glad when Matthew said softly, 'Do you mind if we finish for today, Mr Ferringham?'

He had a thousand more questions, but they were not for today. There was just one he needed to ask. 'Do you know anyone who would want to harm your friends?'

Matthew started crying again.

'Matthew.'

Matthew looked at him through his tears. 'I don't know. I don't know.'

Robin straightened up. 'Do you know anyone who would want to hurt you?'

Matthew stopped crying instantly. He looked into Robin's eyes, making it clear that he had never been asked that question before. He had never had to think of an answer. And he knew he wasn't going to get one anytime soon. 'What do you think happened, Matthew? To your friends? What happened in Standedge tunnel?'

Matthew seemed to think for a long time. When he finally spoke, he spoke the truth, hard and fast and breathless – 'I honestly have no idea.'

Robin watched him, almost as breathless as Matthew. He caught his breath, and nodded slowly, closing his notebook and putting it back in his backpack. He got up.

'Mr Ferringham . . .'

'I think you'd better call me Robin.' Robin smiled with no joy.

'Okay. Robin. What do you think happened to my friends?'

Robin didn't say anything. He looked at the young man in front of him, scared, alone – staring down the barrel of multiple life sentences in prison.

He mulled the question over in his mind. He had been running from it ever since Matthew had called him, ever since he had learned of the Incident. What did he think happened? Six went in. Only one came out. Now you see them – now you don't. He had no idea where they went either.

But he was going to find out.

17

There was something niggling at him as Stanton led him back through the rabbit warren – something on the edge of his mind that he couldn't quite get a handle on. Something important.

Stanton deposited him back in the entrance hall without a word, and he nodded his thanks.

'Mr Ferringham,' boomed a somewhat familiar voice.

He looked up to see a small, thin, mousey man in a terracotta coloured suit coming towards him with his hand outstretched. Robin took it without thinking.

'I'm Terrance Loamfield, Matthew's defence. We spoke on the phone.'

'Yes. Yes. Of course.'

'You warmed him up for me?'

'What?'

'You saw Matthew just now, yes?' Loamfield was squirrelly. He looked like a man who would run away if you so much as glanced at him aggressively – not a solid candidate for a defence lawyer. 'Never seen a boy so deluded in my life.'

'If you think he did it, why are you representing him?' Robin said.

Loamfield's face stretched into something horrible and he laughed. 'You kidding? Case like this is going to be big. Doesn't matter what side of the battlefield you're on, you still make the history books.'

'Nice,' Robin said, wondering why he'd even bothered asking.

'I assumed that's why you were here too,' Loamfield said, and Robin's stomach turned just at the insinuation.

'That's my business,' Robin said.

'Hey.' Loamfield held up his hands, including the one carrying a black briefcase, 'I don't get paid to ask questions.'

Actually, you do, Robin thought, but said instead, 'You were appointed as Matthew's representative?'

'Yes,' Loamfield said, 'Matthew didn't have an attorney. And he didn't find one himself. So, they appointed me.'

Robin watched him. A man in his natural habit. 'They? Who are they?'

Loamfield smiled. 'I'm afraid I have an appointment to keep.' Loamfield gave Robin a wide berth as though he might catch some humanity.

Robin quickly turned. 'Mr Loamfield.' He looked back. 'You said Matthew had no chance in hell of getting bail on Friday. What would change that?'

Loamfield chuckled. 'By Friday? You're an optimist. Optimism doesn't get you far in this part of the world.'

Robin shrugged. He'd had more than enough of this man. He just wanted an answer to his question.

And he finally got it. 'Do something the police

haven't,' Loamfield said. 'Find someone else who could have done it.'

Loamfield grinned and turned away, nodding to Stanton, who was still hovering about. Robin turned the other way, a bad taste in his mouth.

As he made his way back to the main entrance, he found his eyes drifting over to the waiting area. There were a few people waiting – an old couple looking out of place, a father with a teenage boy and a young woman. Their eyes met.

The young woman, barely more than a girl, wearing a hoodie with her hands tucked inside, was watching him. She had headphones on and was regarding him with a strange intensity. He pulled his eyes away, shook off her gaze and continued out of the building.

He didn't see her follow him to the entrance, and watch as he got into the rental car and pulled away.

He didn't see as she pulled out her phone and took a picture of the number plate.

18

Robin's niggling feeling followed him all the way back to The Hamlet and when he got back to his room, he found himself looking through his folder of articles. Something Matthew had said had struck something in his memory, something he had read or found or . . . something.

The papers spilled off the desk and onto the floor and Robin cursed under his breath. He knew he wasn't a detective. He wasn't used to this kind of stuff. But he had to do this. If he wanted to find out what Matthew knew about Sam.

And wasn't he invested enough now? Couldn't he admit it? He needed to know – what had happened to the Standedge Five? And how was this connected to Sam? Because he really couldn't imagine any scene where Matthew killed his friends, and even if he had, what had happened then?

But he had to prove Matthew wasn't responsible somehow. And he couldn't do that without first understanding what had actually happened.

Robin scooped up the papers in a clump and threw them on the bed. What he was looking for wasn't there.

He got out his notebook and looked at the notes he had taken during the visit.

He had written 'ASCEND' in bold capitals – gone over it multiple times so it bled through to the next page. It must have looked similar inked on to the five wrists of the Standedge Five. The more he looked at the letters, the less he saw.

He got his laptop out and connected to the wi-fi. He found himself scrolling through the same online articles, the same pages, examining the same pictures. He didn't even know what he was particularly looking for. Ending his journey, he drifted to the personal Facebook pages of the Five, not entirely knowing why. He scrolled through the comments of people mourning the lost – hundreds and hundreds of them. Nothing jumped out at him. He randomly went to Rachel Claypath's 'About' page and scrolled down. A normal young woman.

And then . . .

He found himself getting closer to the screen.

He opened a new tab and went to Robert Frost's 'About' page. And then Prudence Pack's. And then Edmund Sunderland's. And finally Tim Claypath's. His niggling felt satisfied. He'd seen it without even knowing he'd seen it.

He popped them all out into different windows and lined them all up.

At the bottom of all five 'About' sections, alone, isolated, was the word -

ASCEND.

19

'Well, I always liked Matt. We used to hang out back in primary school. We were best friends – until you know, they came into the picture.' Benny Masterson was moving some very unprepared parts of a dead pig around the closed butchers' shop and it was very distracting. Robin was standing as far away as possible.

It was the next morning – Tuesday – and Robin had been waiting for the butchers' to open, when Benny let him in early. The young man seemed almost impossibly friendly, clashing with his gruesome surroundings.

'I saw them a few times. Around the town. Without Matt. So I told him. Didn't know he was going to "go postal", did I?'

Robin opened his mouth and some kind of smell entered. He masked a choke and then pressed on with his question. 'This was recently that you saw them?'

'Yeah,' Benny said, 'I saw them just before the Incident, in the basement of The Hamlet. That was their usual place. Didn't bother me – kept them out of the way. But yeah, they were there. When I told Matt about it, he went quiet but I could tell he was fuming. That's why I didn't tell him about the other times.'

'The other times?'

Robin had to wait a moment as Benny ducked in the back, and brought out a pile of what looked like lambs' livers. Sure enough, he placed them in the counter display by the very same label. 'Yeah, I saw them a few other times too. They were at the Claypaths' at Christmas, even though Matt had told me over a pint they were all staying at their unis. I went over to give the Chief their Christmas order – turkey the size of Spaceship Earth and all the trimmings. Had to strap it onto my bike just so it wouldn't bounce off if I hit a kerb. Anyways, the Chief opened the door and I could hear them all having a grand old time in the front room. Knew Matt wasn't there cos I'd seen him on the way shovelling snow off Frank Jaegar's driveway. You know Frank Jaegar? Owns The Grey Fox. Nice guy.

'Anyways, same thing happened when I went to deliver at New Year's. They were having duck. Who has duck for New Year's? Not me, at least – not on my wages.' He gave out a great guffaw.

Robin wanted to stay on track. He looked at his watch and saw that the Standedge Visitor Centre would be opening soon. 'You don't seem to like the Standedge Five very much.'

Benny smiled as he struggled with a string of sausages. 'What gave it away? (Don't write that down in your little book mind. I'll deny it.) Truth is, none of us other kids liked them very much at all. The grown-ups treated them like the sun shone out of their collective arses and we could never really understand exactly why. Probably something to do with the Claypath twins. Maybe they were just all happy the twins calmed down.' Benny came to the end of the link of sausages and thus to his sentence.

'Calmed down? What do you mean?'

Benny smiled. 'Back in primary, those two were utter psychopaths. Tim used to bite people and Rachel used to accuse people of touching her – you know, on the . . . But put both of them together and they were evil geniuses. They used to trap animals, you know. They started off with rats and what have you. Used to corner them and play with 'em – like cats play with food. Then they progressed somewhat – rumour has it they got a cat themselves once.'

'What do you mean by "got"?'

Benny picked up a batch of steaks and started un-wrapping them, placing them inside the counter. 'What don't I mean would be more apt. It was never proved but kids round the playground said Tim took it out in the woods and skinned it alive. Just a rumour, maybe a tall tale. But still, makes you shiver – makes you think.'

'He skinned a cat?'

'Allegedly. There weren't no proof, but you know kids – there doesn't need to be. Anytime a cat went missing, we always thought it was the twins. Hell, even to this day, I'd think that one was him if he weren't dead.' Benny waved a raw steak in the general direction of a wooden noticeboard. There was a poster of a black and white cat named Mittons with the headline 'MISSING'.

115

Benny looked at it for a soul-searching moment. 'You think they actually wanted to call it that or they just misspelled Mittens?' He thought for a moment and then shrugged the thought away.

Robin didn't follow the diversion. 'But the group calmed the Claypath twins down?'

'Yeah. Well, that or the rumours died down anyway. To some they just became more boring after – kids like to gossip, I guess. But I think all the adults of Marsden were happy to see them settling into something. The adults heard the whispers of the stuff that they were doing and they were obviously a little unsettled.'

'The adults heard about the cat?'

'Yeah. No surprise. You can't take a dodgy poo in Marsden without it being written up in the *Chronicle*.' He paused, his hand outstretched to reposition a steak as though he had disgusted even himself. Then the moment passed and he continued. 'People round here gossip faster than usual.'

'Is there anyone in the community who doesn't like the Claypaths?' Robin said.

Benny scratched his chin, leaving a small amount of animal blood mixed in with his stubble. 'Liz Crusher maybe.'

Liz Crusher. The name rang a bell and it took Robin a second to remember where he'd heard it. The woman who had had an argument with Tim Claypath on the side of the Huddersfield Narrow the day of the Incident, according to Matthew's story. Robin wrote her name down. 'Why Liz Crusher?'

'Well, that's the easiest question you've asked me yet,' Benny said smiling. 'It was her cat.'

Robin raised an eyebrow. 'The cat that Tim Claypath skinned?'

'Allegedly,' Benny added.

Robin nodded and closed his book. Benny had finished loading the counter and had come out around into the shop. 'Thank you, Benny. You've been a great help.'

'Anytime,' said Benny. 'Just, you know, make sure to cite me. Spot in the acknowledgements wouldn't go amiss either.' He went to clap Robin on the back but mercifully thought better of it, given he was still wearing the gloves covered in blood.

'Acknowledge—?' Then it dawned on Robin what Benny was talking about and what Amber had said two nights ago.

'I told you, gossip.' Benny beamed and Robin took his leave.

Benny shut the door behind him and Robin looked back as the young man turned the 'Closed' sign to 'Open'. Their eyes met through the glass, and they nodded to each other.

For them both, the day had just begun.

20

'Standedge is closed for the season. I'm afraid there are no tours going through the tunnel now until after the winter. Good day.' The small, frumpy woman in the blue polo shirt emblazoned with the Canals and Rivers Trust insignia went to close the door, but Robin shot out a hand and stopped it.

He was standing outside the Visitor Centre with the tunnel, chained and gated, looming off to his left. The canal was deathly silent – no traffic, not even ducks. The Visitor Centre was similarly devoid of life standing empty and dark. Robin wouldn't have known anyone was in there, if he hadn't seen the woman arrive.

She clearly wished he hadn't.

'Can I just ask a few questions at least?' Robin said through the open crack in the door.

The woman sighed. 'I need to clean the cobwebs out of this place, and then go to my other two jobs, so you'll have to be quick.'

'That's fine,' Robin said, 'of course.'

The woman opened the door to let Robin in, and quickly shut it behind him, as though there were a thousand other people demanding entry. Then she went round a corner and disappeared.

Robin looked around. He was in a small reception area with a wooden counter and a stand full of leaflets and brochures. There was a chalkboard with a faded menu written on it (a few months ago, it seemed a cheese ploughman's was on offer, among other things) behind the counter. To the right of him, there was a cut-through to another room. It seemed the Visitor Centre doubled as a café.

Lining the walls were pictures of Standedge all throughout the years – modern ones, drawings of schematics, old photos of men in moustaches with pickaxes clunking away at rock. There was also a pinboard with pictures of all the Trust staff, although all Robin could discern before the woman came back was that Matthew was not there.

'Taken down,' the woman said, when she saw what Robin was looking at. She had dragged out a mop and bucket full of soapy water. She started sloshing the mop in the water.

'You've heard the gossip too?' Robin said.

The woman tutted as the water sloshed over onto the floor, annoyed, even though Robin was sure that was going to be her endgame anyway. 'Don't need to hear anything. I can read your type like a book. Know what you city people would come to a place like this for.'

'And what am I here for?'

The woman looked up, rested the mop against a wall and folded her arms. 'Blood.'

Robin got out his notebook, not even trying to hide it. In ways he guessed the woman was right – as long as she was talking metaphorically. 'Well, so long as the pleasantries are out of the way, I had a few questions if you don't mind.'

'Not before mine,' the woman said. 'Who are you?'

'My name is Robin Ferringham. I'm a . . .'

'No, I know *who* you are,' the woman said. Gossip had attached itself to his name. Was it really making the rounds of Marsden already? Where did the chain begin – and did Roger Claypath have something to do with it? 'What I'm asking is who you *think* you are? Waltzing around town with your little notebook like you're Hercules frickin' Poirot.'

He opened his mouth to correct her on the name, but shut it again – she didn't seem like someone who would appreciate it.

'You should be ashamed of yourself. This was exactly what everyone didn't want – what we were trying to avoid. The Chief said it best – Murder Tourists. That's what you people are. Want me to take your photo by where McConnell killed them all? Be nice for your wall, wouldn't it?'

'Wait,' Robin said. There was a lot to unpack and the woman wasn't about to give him time. He put his notebook back into his pocket, partly for the act of it and partly because he couldn't write fast enough anyway. 'Sorry, I didn't catch your name.'

The woman almost looked like she wasn't going to tell it. But eventually she conceded. 'Martha. Martha Hobson.'

'Martha, what did you mean by "trying to avoid"?'

Martha turned her nose up, but talked nonetheless. 'We didn't want your kind coming here. All looking for the Standedge Five. Playing armchair detective. Pretty much exactly what you're doing is what we didn't want.'

'How did you try to stop this though?'

'It was Chief Claypath mostly. Held a town meeting a week or so after the Incident. Pretty much everyone was there – to show solidarity to the Claypaths, as well as the other families –' she said *other* like they were lesser, '– we all agreed unanimously that Marsden should be protected. We know that the guilty party is already found. No need to make a big fuss – no need for this to be a big thing. Because we knew it would be if the ghouls had their way.

'I mean, we'd seen it in action. How many godawful people go to get a snap by the room where that television detective was held now, eh, ever since that awful thing happened up there last year? Our world is getting over-run by bad guys, and the idiots who romanticise their every move. Murder Tourists.

'Good was the Standedge Five. Those kids were wholly good. And now they're gone. Because of a boy I used to eat my packed lunch with. (Even went through Standedge with him on a couple of occasions.) And we don't want him to be glorified. We want to remember the Standedge Five without having to remember him too. That's what Claypath proposed and that's what we all agreed to.

'We kept our heads down about it and kept quiet.

And when Matthew McConnell is behind bars for good, that's when we can grieve more openly.'

'You're putting a lot of stock in the fact that Matthew is guilty,' Robin said.

'That's because he is, sweetheart. He's a crafty bastard, but guilty as sin.'

'Can I ask what makes you so certain?'

'Well, the police say he is, even after their investigation. There are no other suspects. And there's no way it could have been anyone else.'

Robin thought as Martha went back to squeezing the mop and then finally splatting it onto the stone floor. 'Can you talk me through the logistics of going through the tunnel? Explain the ways, as someone who works here, that it couldn't have been anyone else?'

'Ooh fancy,' Martha said, 'sounds like a GCSE question, dunnit?'

'Please.'

'Okay, but not because I want to help you. I'm only telling you because it supports my argument,' she said, gliding the mop across the floor and sloshing Robin's shoes in a way that was almost certainly deliberate. 'The five and *him* went through on a private boat. *He* had the keys to the gate across the front of the canal tunnel. *He* opened the tunnel before he went to get the boat at the mooring site about a mile out of Marsden. *He* piloted the boat through the tunnel. There was no third party, no bogeyman – *Him*. *He* was the only one who could've done it.'

'What about the abandoned tunnel? The one you take the van through?'

She looked almost impressed. 'You've done your homework, well done. That tunnel was locked up tight. We had trouble with kids getting in the tunnel a few years back – the whole thing is fenced off either side but they used to burrow under. So we poured concrete along the fence boundary. Those gates are unlocked with a keycard – a keycard that was locked up in here on that day. No one else could have done it.'

'Did Matthew have a key to the Visitor Centre?'

'You're thinking he took the keycard and replaced it somehow. Benefits of it being a computer system on the gate – you can see when the gate was unlocked. It wasn't – at all – that day. And anyhow *he* took the tunnel gate key the day before. Visitor Centre was locked.'

'So Matthew couldn't have used the abandoned tunnel to move the bodies of his friends?'

'He could have accessed the tunnel through the multiple cut-throughs in the canal tunnel but he couldn't have got out.'

'What about the other side of the canal tunnel? The train tunnel?' He was saying and hearing 'tunnel' so much, the word was starting to lose all meaning.

'It's not quite as easy to get to the live train tunnel. There are still cut-throughs but we don't really use them, so they're far more dangerous. And even if you did get in there – well, they're called "live" for a reason.'

Robin grew silent, and watched Martha go up and down the floor. She paused and nodded to Robin to move and he stepped back, up the step into the doorway to the table area. 'You've said that no one else could have done it, but by your description, it doesn't seem like Matthew could have done it either. What do you think happened?'

Martha stopped, leaning on the mop. 'I thought he drowned them. Then the divers came back and they weren't in the water. Then I thought he'd hidden them in the abandoned tunnel. And that search was a bust too. Then I just sort of stopped wondering.'

'How can you do that?' Robin said, stepping forward and nearly sliding on the wet floor. He steadied himself on the doorframe. 'How can you be content with not knowing something which happened mere metres away?'

Martha scoffed. 'You sound like one of them Ghosts of Marsden lot. Always wanting to find a way for it to be over. That's how you start getting theories in your head like aliens and ghosts and monsters. Dangerous talk.'

'What could have possibly happened? Think.' He was getting angry, his voice ballooning in the quiet.

'I dunno,' Martha said, clearly thinking hard but coming up short. 'He could have cloned the keycard, tied up the steering, hacked into the computer system and carried the bodies out the abandoned tunnel, rejoining the boat at a later cut-through.'

'Also hiding the bodies somewhere the police search would never find?' Robin said. 'No. Be better, Martha.'

Martha looked around, as though she'd find an answer on a wall. 'Maybe he hid the bodies in the boat somewhere, and moved them again later.'

'Again somewhere the police search didn't find? Not

to mention the fact he was unconscious in the hospital, no doubt with a guard on the door. Nope.'

'I don't . . . maybe . . . scuba equipment?'

'Scuba equipment? What about scuba equipment? No.'

'I don't know, okay. Sometimes, in certain situations, being rational is difficult. But the police have McConnell. McConnell did it.'

Robin gritted his teeth, his temper flaring,'I came to this town to see if there was any way that Matthew McConnell could not have done what he has been accused of, but what I've found is no logical theory to say that he did. This boy is about to go up against a court who are going to decide if he can come home or not, and the most damning thing I've found so far is his own goddamn testimony.'

Martha looked at him with a mix of contempt and poorly constructed anger. 'Okay, city boy, since you're all about the theories, what do you think happened?'

And that was when he realised he hadn't been angry at Martha. He had been angry at himself.

Because he honestly had no idea.

21

Martha slammed the door behind him, and bolted it. He wasn't getting inside Standedge any time soon, not in any official capacity anyhow.

He should have been ashamed at how irate he had gotten, but (it was the strangest thing) he wasn't. He was relieved. He hadn't got so upset at anything in a long time, not since Sam and the screaming at the police officers to take him seriously. He had thought the fire was gone.

But this case. This case that Sam led him to. This tunnel.

Robin looked at it, thinking of how Amber described the games they used to play. He stepped forward, and suddenly a gust of wind flew out of the tunnel and whipped into his face, as though it had been waiting for him. He made his way down the canal side as far as he could, until he was almost sticking his head through the bars.

Stare into the black. See how long you last.

'One,' Robin muttered under his breath.

There was nothing. Beyond the bars was an abyss. It wasn't like he saw the beginnings of the tunnel and it faded away. As soon as the tunnel mouth started, the world was gone.

'Two.'

It was as if he could step inside and be erased. Fall into eternity.

'Three.'

But as he looked more, shapes started to manifest. They had no real form, no real tangibility. It was like looking into an ever-changing lava lamp. Looking into thought.

'Four.'

He was seeing what the mind saw when presented with absolutely nothing.

'Five.'

And then there was something else. Something to grasp onto. Something that felt fathomable. An oblong shape coming through the dark.

'Six.'

The more he looked, the more he saw, and he didn't know if he was regarding it or it was regarding him. Something long and gaunt.

'Seven.'

And hairy.

Robin snapped his eyes away, stepping back from the tunnel and turning away. His breath came in thick gasps and he suppressed a yelp. He held his head in his hands and told himself to pull himself together. It was what the game did. That's why the children played it. With the absence of stimuli, the mind invents.

But for a moment there, he too was a child standing in front of a hell hole, goaded on by the bullies. Staring into the tunnel.

And it scared the hell out of him.

22

Robin barrelled through the front door of The Hamlet. He'd been mindlessly walking around for hours, trying to get the image of what he'd seen – what he'd thought he'd seen – in the tunnel out of his head. He'd lost time, time that he didn't have, and now the afternoon was in full force. He didn't know why he'd come back here – he guessed he just needed to see somewhere familiar, somewhere the closest to home that he currently had.

The pub was quiet. There was one man who looked scruffy and drunk sat in the window seat, but he was the only patron and then he remembered why.

It was Tuesday afternoon. The vigil at the church.

As if on cue, Amber came out of a door behind the bar, said goodbye to the barman, and made her way towards the door. She looked up to see Robin. 'Robin, are you coming to the vigil?'

He was apprehensive about it. After all, Claypath was gunning for him. But it could be useful. So he said, 'Yes.'

'I'll show you where the church is.' Amber smiled.

Outside, Amber led Robin into the heart of the town, and turned left at the clocktower.

'How's the investigation going?' Amber said.

Robin didn't even really know how to answer that. 'It's hitting a few speedbumps.'

Amber laughed. 'Don't want to say I told you so, but . . .'

'Yeah, you were right. People around here, they just seem content with what's happened. The Five – they're just . . . gone and people are carrying on like nothing happened. How is that possible? How can you live next to a mystery like this and not wonder what happened to them? I mean, how does something like that happen?'

Amber turned a corner onto a village green. And past that, a church. There was a stream of people going inside. Everywhere else was quiet. But the church, even standing across the green like he was, seemed to pulse with activity, as if everyone in town was there.

Amber stopped and turned to Robin. 'I think you'll find your answer here. You'll see why people need to accept they're gone, need to draw a line under what happened.'

Robin watched as more people filed into the church. They were all dressed in muted colours as though this were a funeral instead of a vigil. He guessed in some ways it was.

Robin nodded. 'Okay.'

And Amber nodded too, leading him across the green and into the church.

23

The church was busy with many of the pews already full with people. Robin and Amber slid into a pew at the back. Robin looked around to see a sea of faces he hadn't seen around Marsden before, but eventually he saw people he recognised. There was Benny Masterson, and Martha Hobson, and a couple of people he knew by sight from the pub. Most people were keeping their heads down. If they talked, they talked in hushed tones, careful not to be too loud.

Suddenly, Robin felt eyes on him, shivering, and he turned his head to see a young woman in the corner of the room. A young woman he recognised from somewhere. She was looking directly at him. She stood out, as she wasn't all in black. She had the same purple hoodie on and had her hands in her pockets, just like at . . . the prison. As Robin met her gaze, she didn't look away. Finally Robin did. But he could still sense her watching.

'I'd like to thank you all for coming,' a voice said, and Robin looked to the front of the church to see a man in black with a vicar's collar. Behind him, several people had appeared, sitting on the stage area.

'Are they the parents?' Robin whispered to Amber.

There were only five people on the stage but there were eight seats. 'That's Mrs Pack,' Amber said, gesturing to the woman at the far end. She looked incredibly old and exhausted. She was dressed in a ragged-looking jumper and jeans – not something he would have expected of an event such as this.

Next to her were three empty seats, until there was a couple. They looked slightly more together, dressed in formal wear, although they matched Mrs Pack's tiredness. 'Mr and Mrs Frost and next to them Mrs Claypath and then our Chief of Police Roger Claypath.' The Claypaths looked the most together of them. Mrs Claypath was dressed in an expensive-looking black dress, while Roger Claypath had his uniform on. He looked as intimidating as he had the previous day at the prison.

'Where are the others?' Robin said, 'The Sunderlands and Mr Pack?'

But Amber didn't have time to answer.

'We will begin with a reading,' the vicar said. And started to read from a Bible.

After a passage and a prayer, the vicar invited the families up to say a few words. Mrs Frost was the first to stand up, but as soon as she got to the podium at the front of the stage, she erupted into tears. Mr Frost hurried up to her. 'Let me, Sandra.'

Mrs Frost nodded.

'Our Robert,' Mr Frost said, his arm around his crying wife, 'he was always gifted with knowing what to say. And I don't know where he got that from, because it certainly wasn't from me. He was a fantastic writer, uh, he wrote stories and scripts and songs. But mostly he wrote poems. Which as I'm sure you understand was ironic. Because we named him after a poet.' Mr Frost smiled and sniffed, 'I was going to read something out that he'd written, but looking through the many poems he wrote, I realised that he never wrote anything sad. He focused on the good in the world and that's what we should do. We should all remember the good of them. The Standedge Five were the best of us, and I am proud to call Robert Frost my son. Thank you.' Mr Frost stepped away from the podium and led his wife back to their seats.

Next Mrs Pack stood up, but she was crying so much that her entire speech was lost. Everyone just watched as she stumbled and sobbed through whatever she was saying. No one stopped her, she just continued until she was done, and when she was, she just stood there, swaying slightly, looking out to the crowd.

Roger Claypath got up and took Mrs Pack back to her seat. Then he went back to the podium. 'I have no doubt that all of you understand the pain we are all going through, and if you didn't understand I'm sure you do now.' And then Claypath somehow stared directly at Robin. How had he known exactly where he was? His gaze was fierce, and piercing. The message was clear.

Leave us alone.

'I understand now,' Robin muttered under his breath, maybe to Amber, maybe just to himself, 'they move on because they have to.'

And Robin found tears coming to his eyes. And

suddenly the room felt like it was closing in on him. He had to get out of the church. He didn't care what anyone else would think. He just had to leave.

So he did, pushing past some people he didn't know, and opening the door as softly as he could.

Outside he burst into tears. He didn't really know why. And then he thought – they're moving on even though their children were lost. They were managing it, even though it was difficult.

Did he have to move on?

Was the only reason he was still fighting for her because it was less painful than being faced with the prospect of finally letting go?

24

With the whole town in the church, Robin's walk back to The Hamlet was uneventful and lonely. He went through the doors to find the pub was very much as he left it. The same barman was behind the bar, and the same man was sitting at the window table, finishing an obviously fresh pint.

Robin ordered a Coke and then whispered to the barman, 'Who is that man by the window?' If the whole town was at the vigil for the Standedge Five, then this man was the odd one out. Why was he not with everyone else?

Robin wasn't prepared for the answer though. The barman looked to the man then back at Robin, 'That's Ethan Pack, Pru Pack's father.'

Robin's eyes widened and he turned to look at the man. He was wrapped up in a raincoat, even though it wasn't raining outside and it was plenty warm in The Hamlet. He had a thick beard, and hair that was jutting out at odd angles. There was a newspaper on the table next to him, but he seemed to have no interest in it, just content with drinking. The sight of him just made Robin feel sad.

'What's he drinking?' Robin said.

Thirty seconds later, Robin placed a fresh Marsden Ale in front of Ethan Pack. Ethan Pack looked up. His eyes showed no life. 'I saw you were running a little low.'

'Thank you, stranger,' he mumbled.

'Robin Ferringham. Can I sit?' And he sat when Pack waved his approval.

'Robin, huh?' He drained his pint – over half – and started on the fresh one. 'You passing through?'

'You could say that,' Robin said, and Ethan shrugged. Subtlety wasn't going to be necessary for this conversation. Ethan was drunk. 'I couldn't help noticing that you weren't at the church? The vigil for the Standedge Five?'

'What's that to anyone?' Pack said.

'Because . . . of your daughter. She was one of them, right? One of the Five?'

Ethan looked at him, and Robin thought that maybe he had overstepped his bounds. But Ethan just took another drink. 'Don't mean I have to band together with all those arseholes and sing Kum By Ya, does it? I'm fine exactly where I am.'

'I'm sorry about what happened to you.'

'Yeah, well . . .' Ethan said breathlessly.

'I lost someone too,' Robin said, 'A while ago. You never stop wondering.'

Ethan looked at him, really looked at him for the first time. 'No, you never do. And I can't stop. All the time, round and round in my head. She's nothing now – just a . . . a question mark.'

'What was she like? Your daughter?'

'The usual young woman. Ran rings around me and May, May was my . . . Pru's mum. Pru had big plans. She was a hell of an engineer. She had just got an internship designing things for spas. New kinds of hot tubs, swimming pools, saunas. It wasn't what she really wanted to do, but it was a step in the right direction. She really wanted to work on space shuttles. Move to Florida and go to work at the Kennedy Space Center. Imagine that.' He tipped the beer to Robin and took a sip. It left a foam moustache on his upper lip and he didn't seem to have any interest in rubbing it off.

'She must have been very special.'

'She was. Not like me. I work at the City Council – I mean, I used to. Not anymore. Not these days.'

'I . . . you don't have to explain . . .'

'I know what they think . . . what they talk about behind my back. But it doesn't matter anymore. The day Pru disappeared, it was like part of me disappeared too. You know?' Pack absent-mindedly picked up his newspaper and put it on the seat beside him. 'That's when it all fell apart. I'm going to put it back together. But . . . Just some day, right?' He gave a laugh that had no joy in it at all. 'I was out there for days at a time, out there looking for my little girl. But she wasn't there. There's only one person that knows where she is. And he's sitting there in his box not talking.

'People see prisons as a bad place. A punishment. I see it as protection. There's a dozen or more people in this town who'd like to beat it out of him. Beat out . . . where

136

he . . . where he put them . . .' Pack's speech cracked up but he still didn't cry. He just took another drink. 'Pru never did anything to anyone. Never even hurt a fly. And she trusted every one of her friends. She would die for them all. And this is what he did to her.'

Robin couldn't help it slipping out. 'There doesn't actually seem to be any concrete proof that Matthew . . .'

Pack slammed his fists down on the table and there was finally something in his eyes. He looked like a man ready to kill. And Robin knew he'd made a mistake. 'Proof is superficial. I know what happened. I can feel it. This memory loss thing he's pulling is bullshit. He knew what he was doing from the instant he got in there to the second he got out. Thank God for people like Roger Claypath who are prepared to do the things that have to be done.'

Robin was confused. 'What do you mean?'

Pack stopped himself. 'I just mean that kid has to be held accountable. Everyone here loved them. My Pru. Tim, Rachel, Edmund, even that awkward Robert kid – they were good people. They made Marsden a better place. They reminded us of being kids ourselves. Running around, getting into trouble, having adventures. They were the good of the world, and that . . . viper . . . had to turn them into the bad.'

'Did you ever meet Matthew personally?' Robin said.

Pack recoiled, even at the name. 'Yeah. So what? That was before. He just seemed like a normal kid. A bit quiet, a bit clingy – now I know why. He was a little psychopath, just waiting to happen. You know, even when he was fine, I always thought something was wrong about him. Looking at him, it was always like looking at a puzzle. What was he thinking about? What was behind his eyes? Everyone knew he was the outlier of that group, even us parents. Every other one was someone, every other person added something, but he . . . he was just a blank slate. I guess he finally found out who he was. A psychopathic mass murderer.'

Robin just listened. Pack was almost shouting now, and he was glad the pub was empty. Pack lowered his voice – leaned over the table and whispered, 'They all know it. We all know it. But the messed-up thing is, I don't really care how many years he gets, or how many more hearts he breaks, I just want to know where my little girl is.' He slammed his hand down again, but this time spread his palm out on the table. 'It's sick, in its own way. You get that, right?'

'Yeah,' Robin said, 'of course.'

And as fast as lightning, Pack grabbed Robin's wrist and gripped hard. 'Could you kill someone? Could you kill the person who took your loved one away?' Pack's face stretched into a grin. 'Sometimes I think I could.'

Pack's grip was ferocious, unyielding. Robin watched as his hand started to go white, his wrist throbbing under the drunk man's locked hand.

'Ethan,' the barman shouted as he came over.

At the sound, Pack's grip loosened – Robin's hand immediately erupting into pins and needles. But he didn't let go, not completely. 'My daughter . . .' Pack snarled.

'You've had enough, Ethan,' the barman said. 'You're done for tonight.'

'This bastard . . .'

And as quick as Pack had attacked him, the barman was pulling at Pack's arm. His hand suddenly pulled away, so Robin could get out of his grip. He clutched his throbbing wrist. 'Get out of here,' the barman said, still wrestling with Pack's arm, 'Now.'

Robin took one more look, but it seemed like the man was holding his own. He didn't want to know what Pack would do when he got out of the man's embrace. He was deranged. And as he watched, Pack shrugged the man off.

Robin didn't wait any longer. He launched himself out of The Hamlet and into the brisk afternoon. The sun blinded him momentarily, but he shook his head and found himself heading down the street.

He heard a clatter behind him and an enraged scream. Ethan Pack leaving The Hamlet. And then loud booming steps coming closer. He didn't look around – couldn't bring himself to. What was happening? Had the world suddenly gone mad?

No. Just one man.

Robin didn't want to know what would happen if Pack caught up. But Pack had the advantage. He knew the town, and if he was intent on pursuing Robin, it was only a matter of time before he caught up.

Robin flew down the street, knowing Pack wasn't far behind. He had to find somewhere to . . .

There. Between one of the charity shops and a café

was an incredibly narrow alleyway. He didn't even think. He just ducked down it.

It was dark and cluttered, barely wide enough for him to walk down. His footfalls seemed to echo, bouncing off the walls. About halfway down the alley were a collection of bins and two doors either side, leading into both businesses. He heard Pack somewhere behind him and ducked behind the bins.

His heart quickened as the footfalls behind him stopped. He looked down the alley through a minute gap between two bins. Pack was standing at the entrance to the alley, illuminated by the daylight. He almost looked biblical. He turned away.

And at that moment, Robin accidentally nudged one of the bins with his shoulder, and it came crashing down – a horribly final sound of mistake. He was still concealed, but Pack's attention was back. Pack stepped into the alley.

Robin's heart missed a beat.

And then a hand reached out and grabbed his.

He jumped out of his skin, looking round to see a young girl peering down at him. She looked familiar. Hoodie. Black hair tied in a bun. Headphones. 'You . . .'

'Run,' she said and pulled Robin up.

Robin was up before he could think. And the girl started pelting down the alley away from Pack. Robin followed her. Right to the end of the alley.

The girl emerged into a street he hadn't been on before, and Robin was about to as well, when a noise behind stopped him.

Crying.

He looked back. Ethan Pack had collapsed by the bins, lying and writhing on the ground. He was wailing, screaming, crying – like a newborn baby. He didn't look hurt, he just looked . . . pathetic. In a way Robin could wholly understand. Pack's sobs came thick and fast, bounding off the walls, consuming the alley in sadness.

Robin took an instinctual step towards Pack, instantly forgetting his fear of him. He wanted to help, tell him that it was going to be okay.

A hand clasped his shoulder, and he didn't have to look to know it was the strange girl.

'We have to help him,' Robin said.

'We can't,' the girl whispered, 'at least not yet.'

And Robin knew the girl was right. Comforting Ethan Pack wasn't going to help anything – not really. He would still wake up tomorrow without a wife, without a job, without his daughter. He would still go to The Hamlet and drink himself into a violent rage.

Helping Ethan Pack would be finding out what really happened.

Robin looked at the girl and she nodded as though agreeing.

'Come on,' she said, 'I have somewhere we can go.' And with that, she turned away and started walking up the street.

And, with one final look at the sorry form of Pack convulsing on the ground, Robin followed.

25

The girl led him through the town, pausing by the clock tower to take a side road, and get back onto the main street he was familiar with. She kept two or three steps in front of him, maintaining an unyielding pace. When he tried to catch up, she sped up too. They met no one else as they strode through the town – a bizarre convoy where Robin was to be the follower. They got to the duo of pubs at the bottom of the hill leading to the station before Robin recovered from the situation with Ethan Pack and managed to speak up.

'Who are you?' he called to her, as she started up the hill, him following. 'Why were you watching me at the prison? Or at the vigil just now.'

She didn't look back but she did speak. 'I've been watching you ever since you got here.'

'Wait, what?'

'Don't take it personally. I had to know why you were here. And now I do.' She stopped by the path about half-way up the hill. The one that led to the woods, where he had seen the sheep disappear just after he'd got to Marsden. 'It's because you're an idiot.'

'Now, hang on . . .' But she had set off again – not

up towards the station, but down the path towards the woods. Robin looked around, considering just abandoning her, but she had helped him out of a jam, and she seemed to want his attention. He jogged down the path, catching up. 'Where are we going?'

But she didn't respond. She kept leading him towards the woods, across a vast field. The woods were further away than they looked – an outcrop of trees. She disappeared into them. And so did Robin.

What followed was a trek through swathes of trees that could have taken five minutes and could have taken half an hour. He wasn't sure – everything looked so similar that time seemed to run in a loop. The crunching of their feet in the autumn leaves was rhythmic. The only thing that kept him on a straight path was the girl in front of him ducking between the thin trunks, with a conviction that showed she knew where she was going.

Finally she paused and then disappeared over the crest of a hill. Robin got to the drop and saw that the woods carried on as far as he could see. He saw the girl at the bottom of the hill, pausing by a large bush. He went down to join her, all the while realising that the bush was actually some kind of wooden structure, covered in leaves.

The girl disappeared around the corner of this thing that took the form of a shack. Robin went round the corner too to see an opening, with the leaves creating an awning of sorts. He guessed the girl was inside.

'Where are we?' he called, trying to suppress the feeling he was about to get murdered.

There was something jutting off the opening and Robin saw it was a tattered screen door which was woven into the landscape by plants and vines. It was like he was standing on the doorstep of a ruined house, shrouded in leaves. Robin poked his head inside to find an outdoor porch area that was overgrown with all manner of weeds and plants. The screen door had been left open for all manner of undergrowth and wildlife to come in. There was what looked like a pig trough buried in some nettles, but that wasn't what grabbed his attention.

Robin stepped backwards in surprise.

He was directly in front of it. The leaves and bush parted as if to show the majesty of it. Pristine, grand, almost sparkling.

A red door.

26

The door stood ajar. Beyond it, darkness. He found himself reaching for it. The girl had gone through here, this was where she had led him. If this was where he thought it was, maybe it was exactly where he needed to be.

Maybe.

He ran his hands over the door, then pushed on it. The room beyond was pitch black, as though the door opened into nothingness. He scrabbled in his pockets for his phone, pulled it out and switched on the torch function. Why hadn't the girl turned on the lights?

A beam of light illuminated a dusty table and cabinets, with dirty plates on both. Robin swung the torch around to see an oven and fridge. This was a kitchen. The cooker had pots and pans littered over the stove, and there seemed to be a thick layer of dust over it. Dust particles danced around in the torchlight. Everywhere seemed to be incredibly dirty, as if no one had been there in a decade. In fact, the only thing that seemed to be clean was the fridge-freezer. It was gleaming white, and practically shone in the light.

He stepped into the kitchen and was conscious that as soon as he let the door go, it was going to swing shut. He did it and was plunged into utter darkness, apart from the torchlight. There was silence. No, there was a small sound, a rhythmic clicking. It was inconsistent – sometimes it was slow, sometimes it was fast, sometimes it was barely there at all.

The kitchen opened into another room and he made his way around the table to see where it led. He slipped on something on the floor, and pointed his torch down to see it was an old copy of the Marsden *Chronicle*. He bent to pick it up, saw that it was extremely soggy and decided against it.

He rounded the table and pointed his torch into a long hallway. It seemed to go on forever, past the torch's reach at least, but the light did hit on a slightly ajar door to the side. From the crack of the open door, although incredibly faint, it looked like there was a small strip of blue light.

Finally – some sign of life. Some sign that the girl was here at least.

He willed his legs to carry him into the hall, and closer to that blue light. The click-clacking sound grew louder as he inched down the hall, but as he came to the door, it stopped.

He could feel the electricity in the air.

The light seemed manufactured, artificial.

The sound started up again.

He reached out to the door and with one great push, flung it open. The blue light flooded the hall and he reached up an arm to shield his eyes.

He blinked away sunspots and lowered his arm as his

eyes refocused. The electricity in the air was no mistake – the room was filled with electrical equipment. Computer towers lined the walls and the floor was a mess of interlocking cables, weaving in and out of each other. The server towers were practically pulsing with life.

In the centre of the room was a metal shelving unit, loaded up with all kinds of scrapped electronics – old printers, microwaves, telephones, fax machines, all piled up and in various states of disrepair – blocking whatever was behind the shelves, where the clicking sound and the light was coming from.

He picked his way through the cables and as he reoriented, the scene behind the shelves revealed itself. First, he saw a mess of monitors – there had to be five or six all stacked up on top of each other, all old and chunky, but all up and running. They were all displaying the same thing, a ream of text, growing bigger and bigger by the second. He realised what the click-clacking sound was before he saw the girl sat at the keyboard, in a large desk chair. She was typing.

She spun around towards him.

'Welcome to The Red Door . . . Robin.'

She beamed.

27

'Can I interest you in a chocolate beverage?' the girl said, as she took a swig from a milk carton.

'This is The Red Door? The website?' Robin said.

'Yes. Hence the red door. It doesn't look like much, but it's my home. And my secret base.' She looked around, almost lovingly.

'You have a habit of bringing strangers to your secret base?'

'You're hardly a stranger, Robin,' the girl said, smiling like she was pleased with herself.

'So you've been following me?'

'Yes,' she said, bluntly. 'I had to know why you were here. At first, I thought you might be a Doory, but . . .'

'I'm sorry – a Doory?'

'A fan of the site. Had a couple of spikes in popularity the last few months. The report on the North Fern Phantom. My expose on The Faceless Ones. The only public interview with Kace Carver. Site's been lighting up like a Christmas tree. But nothing seems quite as big as . . . Standedge.'

'Who are you?'

'You're not a Doory though. You were at the prison

visiting Matthew McConnell. You were at the tunnel. You went to the Visitor Centre this morning, no doubt trying to get inside. That and you're a journalist – or at least were. More into long form writing these days, huh?'

'You seem to know who I am, so tell me who you are,' Robin said, forcefully.

She raised her eyebrows, took her headphones from around her neck and put them on the desk beside her keyboard. She hesitated a little. 'Sally. Sally Morgan.'

'Sally?' There was something in her voice, or maybe it was the hesitation. Something made him think that she wasn't telling the truth. But for now, Sally would do. 'You live out here alone, Sally?'

'Yeah. Problem with that?'

'This just doesn't seem like a place typically for a young girl to live.'

Sally raised her eyebrows and frowned, as though that was answer enough.

'So,' Robin started looking around, 'you work the website all by yourself?'

'Yep,' Sally said chirpily, 'it's been me and only me ever since I started this thing up. Thought it would be more secure for me to just do all the work myself. I do the coding, the maintenance, the programming, the investigating and the writing.' She swung around in her chair to tap a few times on the keyboard. The home page of The Red Door came up. He saw that the latest article was a new one about Standedge and Marsden that he hadn't read. 'Impressive, right?'

'But what else do you do?'

'What?'

'The Red Door had no advertisements on it. So what do you do . . . to make money?'

She sighed, and adopted a tone like she was talking to a two year old. 'You see those server towers?' She gestured and he looked to the large black plastic structures with blinking lights lining the walls, 'I rent out a large amount of my processing power remotely to people who mine crypto-currency.' She saw his face. 'Don't bother saying you don't understand, because I'm not going to explain.

'What is your interest in the Standedge Incident? And don't lie.'

He realised he wasn't in control of the conversation. And for some reason, he trusted this person in front of him. She was part of the reason he was even in Marsden. Her articles about Standedge had piqued his interest. 'Matthew McConnell called me.'

Sally laughed. 'Now that . . . that was not what I was expecting.' She pulled up another desk chair so Robin could sit down, which he did. Over the next half an hour, he told her the entire story – the truth. He told her about Sam, and about Matthew, and about everything that had happened since he'd arrived. And when he was done, she just regarded him. 'When I said "don't lie", I didn't mean for you to tell me the whole damn thing.'

'Sorry, just . . .'

'So you think you help Matthew and he tells you about your wife.'

'What choice do I have?' Robin said.

Sally shrugged like a petulant child. 'You have . . .' She was interrupted by a loud 'baa'. Robin jumped – the sound was so out of place. Sally just sighed and got up. 'I'll be back in a minute. Teddie wants feeding.'

'What?' Robin said. 'Those sheep are yours?'

Sally shook her head. 'No. But I still feed them.'

She passed Robin and he looked around as she expertly picked her way around the shelves. He listened as her footsteps grew quieter, and when they had disappeared, he looked around at the desk. It was cluttered with weathered knick-knacks – an executive toy missing a ball, a half-solved Rubik's cube, a book of word searches open, with the cover weighted by a stapler. He looked at the book to see Sally had not found any of the words listed but had instead highlighted her own. Past the book was the clattery old keyboard, and Sally's headphones, and past them was a toolkit, and what appeared to be a stack of computer hard drives taken apart. There was nothing on the desk that was personal – nothing to tell him who Sally Morgan was. Or anyone else for that matter.

He slid closer to the mess of monitors and looked at the nearest one – the front page of The Red Door. He read the title of the article that, from the date, had seemed to be posted the day Robin had got to Marsden. He started to read:

Ghosts of Marsden Unite to
Question Standedge Incident
by The Red Door 23/10/2018 13.45

On 26 June 2018, five students, well-loved among the Marsden community, disappeared inside Standedge canal tunnel, leaving their friend and local tour guide Matthew McConnell unconscious on the deck of their canal boat, along with their Bedlington Terrier.

Consensus among police and the community is that McConnell viciously attacked his peers inside the tunnel and used the disued tunnel connected to the canal tunnel to dispose of the bodies and re-enter the boat resuming the journey before the boat re-emerged at the other end of the tunnel.

This writer has noticed the public opinion of McConnell turn incredibly sour as of late, with the latest gossip being that his court date might even be fast-tracked (I guess we'll see soon enough at the hearing). McConnell's guilt largely rests on the fact that the crime cannot be explained any other way, and although there are factors going against the 'McConnell Theory' (such as the CCTV evidence at both sides of the disused tunnels, that The Red Door covered in last week's QUICKFIRE NEWS) police seem confident that they have the right party in custody.

However, there have been reports of a splinter group emerging who believe in McConnell's innocence. They call themselves the Ghosts of Marsden, and seem to believe that the chosen students were spirited away by some more rather otherworldly means. The Red Door uncovered the secret location of the Ghosts of Marsden's meetings – the Community Centre in Diggle on Tuesday nights (they implore you to bring baked goods) – and went to talk to them.

Every meeting the 'Ghosts' attempt to come up with a simpler theory for what happened to the greater half of the Standedge Five. The Red Door sat in on a meeting and heard tales of aliens, spectres, poltergeists and (in a rather illustrious tale) space dogs, being the reason the five students became figurative ghosts themselves.

One attendee, who wished to remain nameless, said that the tall tales were no more than 'therapeutic' – 'It is important to remember that McConnell is being punished when there is no concrete evidence against him. We, as a group, firmly believe in the idea of "innocent until proven guilty". We tell of fantasy theories that are actually more probable than the McConnell yarn the police have cooked up.' The attendee added, 'Although there is significant evidence that space dogs did it.'

The group as a whole are working on a substantial theory that would have the students teleport from inside the tunnel to a neighbouring county. They even claim to have amassed a bevy of evidence, including bizarre energy fluctuations on the date and time in question and a sighting of figures who fitted the description of the Claypath twins emerging from a hedge in Sussex.

Of course, the group has gained some traction with the 'Standedge Monster' theory. Locals will be aware of the legend of a homeless man living in the abandoned train tunnel alongside Standedge. There are numerous, rather shaky, accounts of people seeing a ghostly face staring at them throughout their journey, popping up at each of the cut-throughs. Of course, this is totally unsubstantiated, and no police or members of the Canals and Rivers Trust have ever actually laid eyes on this spectral hobo.

Overall, The Red Door saw the Ghosts of Marsden to be a mostly harmless group about hope – a hopeful future where maybe the five students are still alive. In every story, they seem to be living happily somewhere, albeit with the aliens, the spectres and the poltergeists. Even the Standedge Monster theory has them being whisked away by a man to a better, more exciting life. Although The Red Door wishes to keep many of the groups' identities secret, two noted attendees were Mary and James Sunderland – the parents of the missing Edmund Sunderland.

The Red Door attempted to talk to them, but they declined to comment.

'It appears our situations have aligned,' Sally said loudly, obviously trying to get Robin to jump out of his skin. He didn't oblige. She stood next to him, with a tuft of long grass in her hand. 'I need someone to boost popularity of the site. If I could put your name in these articles, there'd no doubt be a renewed interest.'

Robin shook his head. 'No one knows who I am, *Without Her* wasn't exactly a commercial barn-burner.'

Sally scoffed. 'Do you want my help or not?' She reached under the desk, pulled out a small ziplock bag, and sealed the tuft of grass inside. Robin wanted to ask why she was doing that but she continued, 'You need me because I know the lay of the land here. I know not to piss off Martha Hobson. I know Benny Masterson runs his mouth and would talk to anyone given half the chance. I know Stanton works for Claypath, and Loamfield . . . well . . . he's a snake. And I know Amber . . .'

'What about Amber?' Robin said.

Sally sighed. 'Well, let's just say that maybe you should watch yourself around her.'

'Why?'

'She tell you her surname? Amber Crusher.'

Crusher. Like Liz Crusher – the surname of the woman whose cat Tim Claypath allegedly skinned. But Amber said she had a crush on Tim Claypath – even though she had to have been around when the rumours started. Was she not telling him something? 'What?'

'Keep on track, Robin.'

He switched gears. 'This Incident. Standedge. Why are you so interested? Did you know them? The Standedge Five. You're going to have to give me something more to go on than just your name.'

Sally shook her head, placed the bag of grass in a drawer, and sat in the empty chair. 'My father died. Back in London. Six months and some change ago. Drank himself to death. I didn't even know he was doing it. High functioning. That, and we didn't really spend any time together, despite living in the same house. He blamed himself for . . . something that happened. To me.

'I realised I had nothing keeping me in London. So I came here. Wanted to start up a website so I did. Used the inheritance to buy the place, a couple of server towers, this stuff . . . And then one day, 26 June, Standedge happens. Six people go into a tunnel and one comes out. Right on my new doorstep. Right where I start a website about these kinds of things.'

Robin nodded. 'Coincidence.'

Sally smiled but shook her head. 'Or maybe it's a sign that I'm exactly where I need to be.'

'No,' Robin laughed, 'it's a coincidence.'

'Whatever – it doesn't stop the itching, the feeling to need to know what happened. The whole town seems to be under some kind of spell, like no one really wants to talk about the Five. Roger Claypath held this meeting and after that, everyone shut up about Standedge. Even the people that worked there stopped mentioning it. No one'll dare bring them up, even the local papers. That's how The Red Door is the only place reporting on it.'

'How did Roger Claypath silence an entire town?'

'You don't understand yet,' Sally said. 'Things work differently round here. Community is still a part of the vocabulary. That's why you need me.'

'Okay,' I said, 'so what are you suggesting?'

'I'm suggesting we pool our resources, you help me and I help you. We use The Red Door to get out information about Standedge. You find something and I can upload it for the world to see. If you find anything that might suggest McConnell didn't do it, we might be able to get through to the folk round here. And maybe even get McConnell home by the end of the week. And then we can see if he really does have more information about your wife.'

Robin opened his mouth to say that he definitely did, but then realised Sally had voiced something he hadn't dared admit to himself. What if Matthew was lying? What if there was nothing else? What if Matthew needed him far more than he needed Matthew?

'Come on, we're going to be late.' Sally got up, picked up a heavy-looking backpack from under the desk and slung it over her shoulder. 'News doesn't happen when you're sitting on your arse.'

'What are we going to be late for?'

'That article,' Sally said, pointing to what Robin had just read, 'is out of date. James Sunderland wants to talk, says he has something. We're going to the Ghosts of Marsden.'

Robin looked at the article and then back to her. 'Did you just leave this here because you knew I would read it?'

Sally smiled. 'I couldn't be bothered explaining. Come on, Diggle's about an hour's walk from here.'

Robin got up, and, slightly miffed, followed Sally.

28

Diggle was a small hamlet town, managing to be even smaller than Marsden. Sally followed the canal and Robin followed her. She knew where she was going. They passed the opening to Standedge and walked down a country path until they rejoined the canal.

The other side of Standedge was much the same as the Marsden side, albeit even quieter. The opening was chained up and gated, and there was no Visitor Centre, or boats moored outside. It looked even eerier than Marsden's as there were no signs of life.

Sally didn't stop or even look at Standedge. She just led him into Diggle, up a sparse street, and into a boxy building which looked like a cross between a doctor's surgery and a school, both options abandoned. A slightly crooked sign labelled it as the Community Centre. Sally didn't pause, just pushed open the door and went inside. She didn't hold it open for Robin, and in the incredibly short time he had known her, he wouldn't have expected her too.

Robin looked around, knowing he was going to follow but feeling strangely apprehensive about it. He reached out for the door and then stopped.

A figure, an older woman, had just rounded the street and was coming towards him, being pulled by a black Newfoundland. He instantly knew that this had to be Liz Crusher. He took one more look at the door, and stepped away. Liz Crusher had crossed the road and Robin did too.

'Excuse me.'

The woman looked up. She was short and stout and wore a scowl that looked all but permanent. She was quite a sight next to her dog. If people looked like their pets, she was a perfect example. The dog was so enormous, it was unclear just who owned who.

As she came up to Robin, the dog finally looked up at the reason it had stopped. It growled at Robin, until the woman bonked it on the snout. 'Rodney, please.'

'Are you Liz Crusher?'

The old woman looked at him, with no recognition in her eyes. 'What's it to you?'

'I'm Robin Ferring—'

'I know who you are, boy.' They both looked at him, unimpressed. Robin started to think that this had been a bad idea. Maybe he should have heeded Sally's warning, and played it a little smarter. 'You want to talk about them.'

It wasn't a question. Robin was a little taken aback. 'Excuse me?'

'The Standedge Five. That's what you're here for, ain't it? Christ almighty, the Chief was right about all this. You people smell blood and you come running wanting to point your cameras, and make your videos, and write your books.' There was a snort and Robin couldn't tell if it came from her or the dog.

'Did your daughter tell you about me?'

Crusher's eyes narrowed. 'It's none of your business, but me and my daughter don't talk. Everyone knows who you are. And everyone's gonna shut their mouth from now on.' The way she said that made them sound tied into something more than a community.

'I didn't see you at the vigil,' Robin said.

Crusher squawked a laugh. 'That'll be because I wasn't there.'

'Some people are saying you had some troubles with Tim Claypath?'

'I obviously didn't make myself clear,' Crusher said, 'I'm not talking to you.'

'Please, just . . .' Robin trailed off, not knowing what to say. Something nudged at his leg, and Robin looked down to see the dog wiping his nose on his leg. Robin smiled and patted the Newfoundland on the head. 'How old is he?'

'What?'

'Your dog? How old is he?'

'Seven,' Crusher said apprehensively. 'Name's Rodney.'

'I heard that you and Rodney here had a run-in with the kids on the day they went missing.' Robin crouched down and Rodney rested his paws on Robin's leg. Crusher looked at them, looking as though she was thinking hard. And then softening slightly. *Thank God for the dog*, Robin thought. 'Did you see anything on that day? Anything strange?' Robin said. 'Anything that could maybe explain why what happened happened and maybe how. You were there – right by the boat that carried them through the tunnel.'

Crusher said nothing.

'Of course I'll give you full credit if I find anything. You and Rodney here could be responsible for a break-through. And there'll be monetary compensation of course.'

'Yes,' Crusher said slowly, 'I was there.'

'There was nothing out of the ordinary?'

'No, there wasn't. It was a canal boat, with a bunch of stupid kids on it. That was all.' Crusher smiled as if she knew something he didn't. 'And what makes you think I would tell you even if I did see something.'

Robin persisted, changing the question. There was something that didn't add up. 'Why did you not recognise Tim Claypath that day?'

'What?' Crusher's vindictive tone was back.

'Matthew said that you didn't know who Tim Claypath was, until he said it.'

Crusher breathed out of her nostrils so they grew to twice their normal size, and said through gritted teeth, 'You talked to him? You talked to that psycho? Are you friends with him? Have you come to rescue him?'

'I've come to find the truth,' Robin said, surprised at his conviction.

'Well, you can go home, because the truth has already been found.'

'I don't know about that.'

Crusher sized him up. 'What else do you think you know?'

'I know that there was a rumour going around that Tim Claypath killed your cat? Back when he was in school.'

Crusher didn't look surprised, in fact she gave him absolutely nothing. 'Well, ain't you a nosy bastard.'

'What happened?'

'I don't want to talk about Mr Sammy. In fact, I don't want to talk to you about anything. Good day.' She went to go, but Robin blocked her. 'You're going to want to get out of my way. Now.' He couldn't help feel a little intimidated. The woman stared at him with a ferocity he had never seen matched. 'I am well-respected in this county and I will not be terrorised.'

'I'm not terrorising you, I'm just asking a question.' Robin stood up.

'Mr Sammy never hurt a soul. And then they find him out there in the woods without – They wouldn't let me see him. Because of what he did.'

'Claypath?'

'Yes,' Crusher said, sadly. Rodney seemed to notice her tone and looked up at her, rubbing his head against her leg.

'Was there any evidence that it was Tim? Any proof at all?'

'Whispers. Among the kids. Too many of them came out and said it for it to be not true. Both of them – the Claypaths, they were monsters when they were children. I would have tried to press charges, but I wouldn't want to go against that family.'

Robin said, 'How did you not know Tim Claypath?'

'After what happened to Mr Sammy, I kept myself to myself. My doctor said I had some kind of anxiety – he put me on some pills. I hardly left the house, and then I just didn't at all. For three years I kept myself to myself, shut the curtains until my husband got me Rodney. He was just a little puppy when he gave him to me. Now look at him. He saved me, reminded me what was important. And the first walk I took him on . . . I ran into him.'

'Tim?' Robin said.

Crusher nodded. 'And his dumb friends. Set me back about two years – well, I thought it did at the time. But then, maybe what happened helped that.'

'You're talking about the Incident?' Robin said, not expecting an answer.

And he was surprised when Crusher nodded. 'Imagine being afraid of clowns, then have all clowns disappear inside a tunnel. Does wonders for your anxiety. The doctor tried to convince me I was afraid of bad people. Turns out, I was just afraid of Tim Claypath.'

'You're the only person I've talked to that seems to hate the Standedge Five. Everyone else seems to think they were God's gift.'

'Well,' Crusher said, 'let's just say I keep my opinions to myself.' Robin didn't buy that seeing as how easily she had offered her opinions. He expected the reality was more that Liz Crusher didn't really have anyone to tell those opinions to. She didn't seem like the easiest person to talk to, her abrasive manner leaving a lot to be desired.

'You still think McConnell's crazy though?'

Crusher's mouth twitched up. 'Of course he is. Maybe I'm not openly grieving about what happened, but what that psycho did – you've got to have more than one screw loose to do something like that.'

'You saw Matthew McConnell that day too. How did he seem?'

'I didn't know who he was. He had his uniform on so I assumed he was just a guy who was taking the others through the tunnel. He seemed fine, normal. Whatever a man who's just about to murder five of his friends looks like, he didn't look like it.'

Robin nodded.

Rodney looked up at him, and pushed past him. Robin stepped aside. Crusher nodded and started moving, then stopped abruptly. 'I'd appreciate it if you kept what I said to yourself.' She almost looked friendly.

'Of course,' Robin said, smiling his confirmation.

Crusher's friendliness vanished in an instant. 'Because if you write any of what I said in your book, I'll bloody sue. Say you took advantage of my worldliness.'

Robin dropped his smile and nodded.

He watched as Crusher walked away. And then just as she was moving out of earshot, he thought of another thing to ask her. 'Mrs Crusher?' he called, half-thinking she wouldn't look back, and pleasantly surprised when she did.

'What?' she grunted.

'If you don't mind me asking, why do you not talk to your daughter anymore?' Robin knew he was stepping

164

out of bounds. But if he didn't try, then he wouldn't get anywhere.

Crusher mulled over the question, as though wondering whether to throw him a bone. And just when he was about to give up, she obviously decided to allow him something. 'I found out that my daughter was canoodling with him, with Tim Claypath. So I forebade her to see him. She said that if I enforced it, she'd never talk to me again. Let's just say, we both kept our promises.' She turned and walked away.

Robin looked after her. Amber had gone out with Tim Claypath – it sounded a lot more serious than Amber had made it out to be. She had downplayed it. Had Amber been lying to him? And more than that, he had another thought – intrusive and a little out of turn. If Amber held a candle for Tim Claypath, well – no.

Was she involved somehow?

29

Walking into Diggle Community Centre was like going back in time. The lobby reminded Robin of his old primary school in London. It was small and cramped – an empty reception area was cordoned off at the start of the room and beyond that was a small waiting area with a couple of budget grey sofas. The overall impression of the area was one of clutter – the walls were lined with overlapping flyers and pamphlets and posters stuck on with Blu Tack: flyers about the classes and happenings in the Community Centre, pamphlets open in all their glory about drink and drug awareness, and posters about shows happening at the Community Centre. Apparently, Diggle was about to be shaken by an amateur production of *Glengarry Glenross* by Diggle and Marsden Theatrical Society.

Sally was nowhere to be seen and with no idea where in the building the Ghosts of Marsden was, Robin started his search. For the next ten minutes, he completely covered every corridor of the Community Centre looking into all the rooms. Most of them were empty, with only a few having a semblance of life. He walked in on a pasta making class in the kitchens and an AA meeting on the second floor.

Finally he found the last room with anyone in it. He looked through the small window to see an empty round of chairs, and a table at the back with assorted cakes on it, and a man with his back turned.

Robin opened the door as quietly as he could and entered the room. It was a pale classroom-type set-up and there was no indication of what he had just walked in on. The man seemed to be doing something at the table at the back, and didn't show that he had heard Robin. Sally was leaning against the window, looking out. She didn't hear him either.

'Hi,' Robin said, and they both turned.

'Where the hell did you go?' Sally said.

Edmund Sunderland was the spitting image of his father. James Sunderland was taller, slightly more rugged and weathered but he was definitely his son's father. He was middle-aged with a grey streak through his unkempt hair. That coupled with the dark bags under his eyes and his thin frame made him look a lot older than he actually was. It didn't help that he wore small circular glasses that looked incredibly old-fashioned. Robin's mind, rather cruelly, went to a walking corpse. 'Hello, friend.'

Robin tried to smile. 'Hello. I was expecting more people to be here.' He gestured at the empty circle of chairs – a sure sign of absentees.

James looked at the circle with a mix of sadness and tiring anger. 'No. They're all gone, I'm afraid. Have been for a while now.'

Robin looked to Sally to see she had turned back to the window. 'Do you mean we're late or . . .?'

'No.' James reached behind him and picked up a biscuit. He got it halfway to his mouth before he decided against it, and put it down again. 'Unless you mean late by about two months. The Ghosts of Marsden are dead.' He laughed, flatly. 'There's nothing left here for anyone. Just silly old me.' He reached up and took off his glasses, wiping them on a handkerchief. Robin saw his eyes were tearing up. 'I'm sorry,' Sunderland said, replacing his glasses. 'Sally has told me why you are here. I just want to say thank you for trying to find out what happened to my son. I don't suppose anyone else in this godforsaken place has offered you such a courtesy.'

Robin shook his head, but said, 'Where is everyone else?'

James sat down. 'Quit. They don't believe in the cause anymore. Or they've had their fun speculating. That's what most of them were here for, I expect. Frivolous talk – busy-bodies getting their rocks off. But there's only so much talk you can do about ghosts and witches and spells and aliens until you have to step back and take stock, I suppose. I'm the only one left who thinks McConnell's innocent. Even my wife has gone and I can't even blame her. I don't blame any of them, not really. What is that saying? "There are many truths of which the full meaning cannot be realised until personal experience has brought it home." Who said that? John Stuart Mill, I think. That's why I think she left. She left the group. And she left me. And she left Marsden. After that, everyone else was gone soon after. If my wife was gone, why shouldn't they be gone too.'

Sally stepped away from the window. 'I have a feeling Robin's about to get his notebook out, so I'm going to get a drink.' She left without another word.

Robin sat down and did indeed get his notebook out. 'That must have been hard – after everything that happened.'

James smiled sadly. 'You can only play make believe so long until you have to accept the reality, I suppose.'

'You accept that it was make believe?'

'Of course,' James said, like it was the most obvious thing in the world. 'You don't really think I believe in all that stuff, do you? It was about hope. Hope in the human race, if you want to get all grand about it. Hope that one boy couldn't be so evil. That was what it was for me anyway.'

'What was your son like?'

James sniffed. 'Edmund was a good lad. Not perfect, but wholly good. When he was having trouble at school, and could have gone down a different darker path, he found them. They all found each other. Tim, Rachel, Robert, Pru, Matt – and my son. And when they did, everything just clicked for them. They were like pieces of a jigsaw – and when they all got together, you could finally tell what the picture on the box was. Any of them would have happily died for any other – maybe Matt most of all.'

'What do you mean by that?' Robin said.

'Everyone knew that Matt was the odd one out. Everyone except the group itself. They didn't treat him any different from any other member. In fact, sometimes I think Edmund liked Matt most of all. But Matt was different to the others. It's going to sound terrible, but he was simpler, had a less complex view of the world. He didn't have such lofty ambitions – didn't seem to have any interest in going to university, or broadening his horizons – he just wanted to stay in Marsden and become a tour guide for that damn tunnel. So he did. And none of the group thought any less of him for it. They all loved each other – sometimes in weird ways. It wasn't like they loved each other as friends, but it wasn't like lovers either. It was like they were all tied together by something deeper – true love.

'That's why there's no way McConnell did it. No way in hell.'

'You truly believe that?' Robin said, already knowing the answer.

'Yes, sir,' James said. 'And what's more it's blatantly obvious to me, and it should be to everyone. Matthew McConnell is not a killer. And I don't like Roger Claypath going around convincing everyone he is.'

James Sunderland, a father just like Claypath – but he wasn't letting his emotions get the best of him. Claypath and Ethan Pack were taking the easiest path by blaming Matthew, and now Robin almost understood it. James was feeling more pain than those two could ever take on, all because he believed in Matthew. He had lost everything for that.

Robin braced himself for the next question. He thought he was going to get one hell of an answer. 'What

170

do you think happened to them? Your son and the rest of the Standedge Five?'

'I can't say for sure,' James said, as if stating fact. 'It's hard to believe I'll ever meet anyone who could. But I know one thing. It has to do with the hole.'

Robin thought he'd misheard for a second. 'The hole? What is "the hole"?'

The door opened behind him and he didn't have to look around to know that Sally had returned. He heard her opening a plastic bottle with the familiar fizz of a carbonated drink. 'We all caught up? I hope so because I'm all boned up over here waiting.'

'James,' Robin said, trying to get him back on track. 'What are you talking about?'

Sally sat down next to Robin with a clatter, the chair scraping backwards slightly. 'Ditto.'

James's eyes flitted around the room, as if making sure they were alone. Robin could have told him there was barely anybody else in the building, let alone the room. 'I'm in construction – work for a building company in Huddersfield called Laker's. A couple of years back, we were hired by the Canals and Rivers Trust to perform some maintenance on the disused tunnels that run parallel to Standedge. I'm going to assume you know what they use them for – the vans that follow the tours.'

Robin nodded and so did Sally.

'The tunnel with the live train lines is fine. But. Well, the two other tunnels are notoriously unstable. When they built the canal tunnel, they started from either end. One team started in Marsden and one team started in

Diggle. They came together slowly, but they misjudged it. When they got to the middle, they had to create an S-type shape to join it up. There have been loads of patch jobs throughout the years to the canal tunnel – that's why if you go through you can see that some parts have brick walls, some parts are stone, and some parts are just rock.

'The railway tunnel has fared a little better, but still had plenty of repairs done to it. And a couple of years ago, my team was hired to do some. An employee's lights had gone out when driving through the tunnel and his van had slammed into a lode bearing column. Part of the outer wall of the tunnel was damaged and we had to go in, assess the damage and see if it was safe.'

'And was it?' Sally said, sharing a look with Robin.

James shook his head and laughed. 'No. No. Not by a long shot. The guy who did it was lucky that the whole damn tunnel didn't come down on his head. We instantly told them that they had to shut down, until we could stabilise the structure. The disused railway tunnels and Standedge are intrinsically linked. A house of cards. One weak link and everything could come tumbling down.'

'I don't suppose the Trust took kindly to the fact that they had to close up shop,' Robin said.

'Of course not,' James agreed. He shuffled his chair closer to Robin and Sally. Robin remarked that he had come a bit more alive since starting his story. His voice had become stronger. 'We spent two weeks reinforcing the tunnel, with the Trust leaning on us the entire way. If I'd had it my way, it would have taken four weeks. I wanted to do an entire sweep of the tunnels – both of them, hell, all of them – make sure that no other areas had been compromised. Like I said, house of cards. But the Trust wanted the job done so they could re-open – it was peak business time for them; July, I think. And we didn't have time for the overall survey. The higher-ups said no. So it went unchecked.

'Not that that was what the public heard. Laker's said it was all fine and dandy – we did a great patch job and the place was as safe as a padded cell. That was when the rumours started.'

'Rumours?' Sally said.

'Among the grunts at the firm, including me. There were whispers that the collapse had opened up a – a hole of some kind in the side of the railway tunnel. Tiny but there. No one actually went to find it, no one offered up any proof that it actually existed. But one man – I don't remember his name – went to ask the boss about it. Next time we saw him, he was carrying his belongings out of the office in a big plastic bag. He didn't come back.' James scratched his nose and looked at them. 'That helped to get people to shut up about it. And I forgot about it – even when . . . it happened . . . if you can believe it. It was so far from my mind. That job's long gone, and my memory ain't what it used to be. Still, I should have remembered. I should have . . .'

'What jogged your memory?' Robin asked.

James ran his tongue over his top row of teeth. 'I want to trust you. Both of you.'

Robin looked at Sally and then back. 'We just want

to help. We want to do what the police aren't doing. We want to find out what really happened to your son and his friends. We want to ask the question everyone in this place seems to be avoiding.'

'And that is?' James said.

'How?' Robin said simply.

James looked at him closely and then gave a small, almost imperceptible nod. 'Okay.' And then he did the same to Sally. 'Okay.' He reached in to his back pocket and brought out a folded and crumpled yellow piece of paper. 'A couple of days ago, someone knocked at my door. I don't really answer it anymore. I know it's not going to be anything important, and I don't want to talk to some arsehole about how I need new double glazing. You could say, losing a son puts everything into perspective. Still, I wish I answered the door then.

'I forgot anyone had ever knocked, just went on watching television until I fell asleep on the sofa. I woke up in the early hours and went up to bed. Wasn't until the next morning when I came down the stairs that I found this,' he held up the folded note, 'on the damn doormat.'

He held it out to Sally and she took it, and unfolded it.

'It took me a moment to realise what it meant. And then it all came flooding back.'

'Who do you think left this?' Sally said, staring at it. From the way she was holding it Robin couldn't see what was on the paper.

James shook his head. 'I have no idea. Wish I did.'

Sally held the piece of paper out to Robin and he took

it. It was sheet of weathered yellow lined paper, seemingly ripped out of a pad. On it, in hard pencil, someone had drawn four thick parallel lines down the page. They were each spaced out equally, with no deviation. At the top of the page, where the lines ended, there was written an M. At the bottom a D. Two thirds of the way down the page, just next to the fourth line, there was an X that looked like it had been gone over in pencil about five times.

'What is this?' Robin ran his finger over it and felt the bump that happened when you ran something over too much.

'Isn't it obvious?' James said. 'Four lines, four tunnels. M – Marsden. D – Diggle.'

'X marks the spot,' muttered Sally, nodding.

Robin looked at them both, finally getting it. He looked at it again.

'It's a map.'

30

Robin was out the door and into the late afternoon air. He heard Sally behind him but he didn't stop. He was halfway down the street before she caught up, grabbing his arm.

'Robin, wait, let's just think about this a bit first.'

He realised he was still clutching the piece of paper, squeezing it so hard it had ripped a little. Sally was looking at him, wide-eyed. He almost shrugged her off and kept going, but she looked genuinely concerned. 'What?'

'We need a game plan here. We're going to lose the light in two hours. Do you think now is really the time to go on a treasure hunt?' Sally said, as he looked behind him. James Sunderland was standing in the entrance to the Community Centre watching them. 'We need to re-group. Really think about this.'

'Think about this?' Robin said, holding up the paper. 'I think it's pretty bloody obvious, don't you? It shows where the hole is. This is it – what we need to get the police to see reason – if the hole really exists then this is it. A real tangible way that this could have happened.'

'In the morning at first light, we will . . .'

'No – we go now,' Robin said.

Sally stepped back, some kind of disgust on her face. 'No, we don't.'

Robin shrugged. 'Fine, then see you around, Sally.' He started walking again, even if it was just for effect. He knew the conversation was nowhere near over.

'Robin.'

He wheeled around. 'We're not a team, okay. We're not a detective duo or something. I was doing fine before you came along.'

Sally scoffed. 'You were halfway towards getting yourself run out of town. And let's not forget this was my lead. I brought you here. That paper is mine.'

'This isn't about whose lead it is, Sally. There is a young man sitting in prison right now, and maybe he shouldn't be in there. And maybe we can do something about it. And maybe, just maybe, we can do something about it right now. Not at first light, *now*.'

Sally slowly walked towards him, until they were close, almost intimately so. 'Why are you doing this, Robin? What's your prime motivation? Is it Matthew McConnell's well being? Or is it just about the information in his head?'

Robin held her gaze for as long as possible, before looking away.

'I thought so,' Sally said, 'maybe you should save the lectures about a moral compass for when you get one.'

Robin sighed, and tried to formulate a sentence. It was a while before he did, and even then it was only two words. 'I'm going.'

Sally nodded. 'If it comes to finding one – if it comes to finding out what happened to the Standedge Five, and what happened to Samantha Ferringham – I don't really know you, Robin. You seem like a good enough man – meat and potatoes. You say what you see, think the world is black and white just enough to think you're on the right side. Your paths are aligned at the moment, but you have to start considering the very real possibility that at some point they are going to diverge. And then you're going to have to start asking yourself some very hard questions.'

Robin knew she was right, but wasn't going to let her know it. He felt like a petulant child who only wanted to add to the petulance. 'Are you coming or not?'

'I'm coming,' Sally said. 'You need me. Because you're going the wrong way.'

Robin looked at her as she turned and started walking the other way. He found himself following once again. Sally was speaking the truth and hadn't he wondered himself, in the back of his mind, what would happen if he had to choose? In that moment though, he saw Sam at the end of a long road.

And following this scrap of paper would lead him closer. To her.

And that was what mattered. That was *all* that mattered.

31

Sally led him back to the Diggle entrance of Standedge tunnel. She followed the canal a little the other way until they came to a bridge. She looked back as she started to cross.

'I've never gone to the abandoned tunnels, so I'm just guessing here, but I assume it's this way.'

Robin nodded as they crossed the bridge, and watched Sally as she hopped over a fence into a probably private field. Robin didn't even think – just climbed over the fence too (a little less easily than Sally).

There were three horses in the field, hanging around further down the fence and they looked around to regard the intruders. Robin stopped to watch them, and started getting left behind. He caught up to Sally halfway across the field.

'How old are you?' he said, slightly awkwardly.

Sally looked around, mirroring his awkwardness. 'You wanna check my ID or something?'

'No,' Robin said quickly, 'just . . . what you said back there made a lot of sense. That's all.'

'I'm twenty,' Sally said.

'Your dad teach you to be so wise?'

Sally laughed. 'No. No, he did not.' They got to the end of the field, and Sally hopped over the fence onto a gravel path, and watched Robin as he precariously picked his way over, seemingly to enjoy the spectacle. She waited until his feet were back on the ground and set off up the gravel path, crunching with every step. Robin walked too.

'Your mother then?'

'Mother?' she said it like it was a foreign word. 'No . . . I don't have one of those.'

'Everyone has a mother.'

She stopped, looked at him thoughtfully.

'What?

She shrugged and carried on. 'You just reminded me of someone for a second.' Before Robin could respond, they rounded a corner, and Sally gave a small whoop of joy. 'Well, that was easy.'

They were confronted by two reasonably-sized train tunnels, completely fenced off and padlocked tight. Inside the tunnels was darkness. They were completely abandoned and small sounds echoed throughout. The whole place felt wrong – structures made for life devoid of it. Robin stepped forward, looking at the fence across one of the tunnels and specifically, the bottom of it. He saw that there was indeed a layer of concrete that spanned the width of the tunnel – both of them – just like Martha Hobson at the Visitor Centre had said, making it impossible to dig under the fence.

Sally tapped him on the arm and pointed up. He looked to where she was pointing. 'There's the camera.' There was a small nondescript box in the brickwork between the two tunnel openings, with a red light blinking on it. Robin suddenly had the feeling of being watched.

'There really is no way you could get through here,' Robin said.

And Sally nodded. 'This isn't what we're here for though. I guess we'll try and get round the side.' With that she crossed in front of the tunnels, looking at the hedges that lined the entrance. With a shrug, she reached out her hands and started to hack through. She disappeared.

Robin looked back at the two mouse holes, lined up, into the same nothingness he saw inside of Standedge. Train tracks worn into the dirt disappeared into the dark. He thought of the rugged face he'd seen the previous night. He imagined it – must have. But as he looked, the likelihood of that was in flux. He shivered involuntarily and hacked his own way through the bushes.

He emerged into a clearing of trees and bushes, all bare of leaves. The cold weather had already cleared them, and after a second, he understood why. A thick and cold wind smacked him in the face, almost blowing him over. He shielded his eyes, and, when it was over, he blinked away the cold.

'Jesus,' Sally said, clutching her coat and wrapping it around herself. She reached out in front of her to rest her hand against something, and through the skeletons of bushes, Robin saw the side of the railway tunnel. It was uneven and just gave the impression of a rocky hill. The surface was jagged but complete – there were no gaps,

181

just a hill. Solid. No hint of a way through. 'Well, let's see if our mystery mapmaker has good intel.'

They started to walk – slowly and steadily, charting a course as close to the edge as they could. There was an incredible amount of undergrowth to contend with, and if it had been the height of summer when the leaves were lush, it would have been impossible to traverse. Over the next twenty minutes, they searched in silence – following the hill.

'Can I ask you a question?' Sally said, as she snapped through a bare bush.

'You want to know how old I am?' Robin said, smiling.

Sally looked at him before continuing. 'Well, I do, now. But no, not that.'

Robin reached out and traced the side of the hill with his fingers. The light was failing – Sally had been right about that. The sun was visible through the tree trunks Soon they'd have to work by torchlight. 'Shoot.'

'Why do you trust McConnell? How do you know he's not lying about this phone call with your wife.'

'I know,' Robin said, looking the hill wall up and down.

'Yes, but how?'

Robin sighed. 'There was something that he couldn't possibly know. Something that Sam must have told him.'

'What was it?'

'He said 'Clatteridges. 7.30 p.m. 18 August 1996. It was something I never wrote about in the book. Something hardly anyone knows.'

'What happened?'

Robin considered it, and then said, 'It doesn't matter anymore.'

'Okay then,' Sally said, but not as flippantly as the words suggested. She sounded content to let it go, and Robin was thankful to her for that.

They continued quietly. Robin watched the hill, seeing nothing of note. Just a steep hillside. As impenetrable as it was unremarkable.

They carried on for another twenty minutes or so, as the sun dipped and then started to disappear. Robin got his phone out, casting its torchlight through the undergrowth.

'McConnell give you anything to go on,' Sally said, getting her own phone out doing the same, 'except Clatteridges?'

Robin smiled to himself. It was kinda dumb. 'Nothing concrete, except . . .' He shifted his weight, so he could get into his backpack. He reached in and pulled out the notebook. With one hand, he awkwardly shuffled the notebook to the page and tapped Sally on the shoulder. She shone the torch at him and took the open notebook. She stopped to look at it, and Robin took over in front.

Robin watched her, before going back to the search. 'He said that Sam said something about a black hound and a horse head.'

'A horse head?' Sally said, behind him.

'That mean something to you?' Robin said, raising his

torch to look up the hillside, and then down. The hill became bare, divulging into a rock face. The undergrowth was incredibly thick here, and . . .

His torchlight hit on something.

'No,' Sally said, but Robin didn't hear. He was too busy ripping through the bare thin branches, trying to see what was on the rock face, right at the base. It was a stack of wet cardboard, stuck to the rock face. He battled with the plant life and reached for it. He pulled it away, and shone the torch into the gap.

'Sally.'

He looked back.

'Sally.'

She was still looking at the notebook, and she muttered something. Something that Robin would probably have recognised as 'A horse head . . .' if he was listening.

'Sally,' he shouted, and she looked up.

Robin smiled, as he pulled away the cardboard and shone the torch at what he'd found behind it.

A small crack in the rock that had loosened everything under it, creating a small hole. Just big enough to squeeze through.

32

Robin went first – he cleared more of the undergrowth so he could lie on his stomach and shuffle himself forward. Sally trained her torch on the hole as Robin pulled himself forward. He slid his own phone into the hole so the torch illuminated ahead of him. He took one look at Sally who smiled her good luck and he stuck his head inside.

The hole was slightly bigger than it first appeared but not by much. He looked above him and his head grazed against a jagged rock. He resolved to keep his head down, shuffling his arms forward and pulling himself further into the hole.

'Are you okay?' Sally said, as Robin felt his feet graze the sides of the tunnel.

He didn't respond – he felt like even the slightest noise could cause a shift in the rock and send the whole thing tumbling down around him. He inched forward again, wondering how far it would be until he hit the tunnel.

As he moved, he wondered if this was really it. Was this really what they had been looking for? Is this how the Standedge Five had been taken out of the tunnel? The hole was only big enough for one person – it would have been difficult, almost impossible, to push a body through the hole. It would just get stuck.

What did any of this mean? This was the first tangible step in the right direction – the first thing that made sense in the quest for finding out what truly happened, but it only brought up a dozen more questions.

Robin caught up with his phone – the torch beam shining directly up and not helping him see ahead at all. He instinctually started to reach for it, shifting his right arm – dragging it against the side of the hole. He snagged it against a loose rock and something fell onto his back.

He stopped stock still. There was a shift above him – fine rubble fell on his face as he held his breath. There was a sound of tumbling rock, and for a second he thought that this was it. He was about to be crushed.

But then the sound stopped. And he stayed still a minute more, breathing out slowly. He was okay.

He retracted his arm and started shuffling forward again, nudging the phone ahead with his nose. It was inherently ridiculous, and he wondered what he looked like crawling through this hole like some kind of animal.

He nudged the phone forward and suddenly the light shot up, extending beyond the ceiling of the hole. At first he thought it had just widened but he craned his head up as far as he could to see and started to hear the wind. Suddenly, as he levered himself forward into the opening, a gust hit his face. It wasn't an opening, it was the tunnel.

An inch more forward and his arms were free. The ground was wet and slippery but he could reach out his hands and grasp a ridge of rock in the ground. He pulled himself out of the hole awkwardly, trying to make sure not to touch the sides with his feet. But soon enough, they were free, and in the tunnel.

He pushed himself up onto his knees and reached out and grabbed his phone. He shone it around the open space. The tunnel was big, with a high curved ceiling that was mostly smooth. There were a few weathered patches where bricks had come loose, and exposed uneven rock. It didn't look unstable, but wasn't in the best condition. He could see how a body could cause some kind of collapse.

He shone the torch along the floor to see wooden planks slotted into the old train tracks creating a path of sorts and making the floor more level – undoubtedly to help when the tunnel was used as a road to take a van through, following the boats inside Standedge. The rest of the floor was shingled, but the loose gravel rocks were sparse having been shifted around for what must have been decades.

Robin pointed the torch each way. Left was where they had walked outside and he could see a small pinprick of dull light in the centre of the tunnel that had to be the Diggle entrance. Right – there was nothing but darkness.

Robin wrenched himself to his feet, feeling more exhausted than he'd felt in years. His arms and legs throbbed with pain. His shins stung, and pointing the phone down, he saw that his trousers had ripped at the knee and his skin was red raw. For some reason, he touched a knee – obviously a mistake. A shot of pain ran through his body into his brain.

He clenched his teeth, trying to get through the pain by focusing on what he could hear. A steady dripping sound echoed up and down the tunnel probably only from one source but sounding like the drips that surrounded him. There was the wind of course, providing a steady blunt whistling backdrop, and strange sounds he didn't think he could even describe. They sounded like throwing a bowling ball at a padded wall – sort of hollow thuds with no real weight behind them. Those sounds seemed to be inconsistent but constant – almost like the tunnel was living and breathing around him.

He shivered.

He had never believed in ghosts or anything like that, but if there was anywhere they existed, it was here.

He heard Sally's quiet voice through the hole. 'I'm coming in.'

Robin knew he should wait – should be there to help Sally if she needed it. But it was almost like he was mesmerised by the dark. He stepped into the centre of the tunnel, turning right and shining the torch into nothing but more of the same.

And he started to walk.

33

The tunnel had him now. He started to realise why Matthew had been so entranced by somewhere like this. It was like the outside world didn't exist. The only thing he could count on was the ground in front of his feet – the ground that came alive in the circle of torchlight. Nothing that was behind him mattered. Just that ever-moving circle – always staying one step ahead of him.

The sounds were still there. The hollow clunks, the dripping. Sally was behind him somewhere – he had heard her get through the hole, and into the tunnel proper. But she wasn't with him. And neither was her own hovering light. Maybe she had gone the other way.

He walked on the tracks – the wooden planks had ended and he was stepping over the sleepers now. He stopped every so often to point the torch around himself, but all he saw was the same – the walls of a railway tunnel. It was sleeping, having been forced into slumber.

Robin smiled at that, and stepped halfway over the railway line, tripping. He dropped his phone and it went flying ahead of him, the light whipping around, until it slammed into the ground. He cursed under his breath and scrabbled around in the dark in front of him, his hands finally finding the phone. But not before he discovered something slimy and slippery. He picked up the phone and shone the light down on what he had found.

It was a damp and soggy piece of plastic bag. An orange bag for a loaf of bread.

What the hell was that doing in a place like this?

Robin looked around him. And he saw something to his left. It looked like a brick doorway without a door. This must be a pathway to Standedge.

He got up and walked to the doorway exiting the railway tunnel and coming out onto a landing of sorts, with a railing off into nothingness. And then another tunnel.

He leaned on the railing and shone the light onto a set of three stone steps that descended into water. The canal. This was the canal.

He poked his head over the railing as far as he could reasonably manage and looked left and right. The waterway carried on as far as he could see both ways. This was just what he had expected when he had heard of the cut-throughs where panicked people could be rescued from the claustrophobic confines of Standedge.

And Robin could kind of understand why someone would panic. In comparison to the large and empty railway tunnel, the canal tunnel was tiny. There was no space beside the canal at all, and it looked barely high enough to be able to fit a boat through. It had to be a surreal experience, being so hemmed in to your surroundings. Robin couldn't see why anyone would willingly want to travel through it.

He turned away from the canal and went back into the

railway tunnel, the torch bouncing light off the far wall. Something flashed.

Robin thought he had imagined it at first, but on another pass, he saw it. There was something almost reflective in the wall. He went over to it, and saw that there was a piece of blue tarpaulin slick with water. He reached out to touch it, expecting to press his hand against it. But his hand kept going, pushing it. The tarpaulin was covering something.

He wrenched the tarp aside.

Two sheets of metal were resting in a gap in the wall. They looked like they were painted some kind of red, but they had been dulled as though they had rusted. The two pieces came together as though they were doors. Robin almost had the urge to reach out and knock, but instead he ran his finger over the metal. There was something odd about the left sheet of metal and he had to reposition his torch to see what had caught his eye. But finally he saw.

The entire left sheet of metal had small holes all over its surface. And there seemed to be another sheet behind it that closed the holes. He reached out and pulled the sheet of metal back. It swung open. There was a slider on the other side – he pushed it and the slats opened so he could see through the holes.

He didn't know what it was, but it was hardly important. Instead he shone the torch beyond the door.

And stared into the small, narrow recess in the wall of the tunnel. It was covered in blankets – the walls of the recess, the floor. They were all incredibly dirty and damp, and there was a bunch of them at the far end with two pillows. A makeshift bed. To the side of the 'bed' was a crop of cardboard – three pieces positioned like a house of cards. It looked like someone was trying to make a sort of table structure. Under it were empty boxes of food – cereals, ready meals, packets of crisps, all so waterlogged they had all sort of fused together to create a mush of rubbish.

Robin looked around at the shelter in disgust. Something glinted on the ground and he picked it up, almost not even thinking.

It was a cat collar. The disc said 'MITTONS'. And as he regarded it, his torch bobbed over to something else. A small mound of something, a dull red. He didn't know what he was looking at, until he retched. He doubled over and retched a few more times but nothing came out. When he had recovered, he looked again at the thing in the corner. It was a dead cat carcass – half consumed and the rest of the flesh festering and mouldy. He turned away – a disgusting smell filling his nostrils as though it was waiting to shock him. His eyes stung and he blinked away the sensation of the smell attacking him. He wiped his eyes and looked down, his gaze falling on something else.

There was a piece of clothing on the floor, lying on the blankets. It looked cleaner than the rest of the shelter – and therefore newer. It was a purple hoodie – looked like a girl's. He picked it up, turned it over in his hands. His eyes widened as he saw writing emblazoned on the back.

UNIVERSITY OF EDINBURGH.

He instantly understood who's this hoodie was – it was Rachel Claypath's. It had to be. But what did this mean?

He heard footsteps behind him. Someone coming up the tunnel to meet him.

Sally.

He turned. 'I've found something.' No one was there. He shone the torch down the tunnel. No one.

He looked the other way.

And saw only the rock flying towards his face. His forehead erupted in pain, and his legs slipped out from under him.

He was unconscious before he hit the ground.

34

'Do you see them too?'

The voice drifted to him, and he tried to grab the words as they flew in front of his face.

He wafted in and out of the world, or maybe it wafted in and out of him.

'Or are you one of them?'

He opened his eyes, as best he could. His left eye didn't seem to want to open – it was stuck shut by something sticky – something leaking from his forehead. It was hot. His head felt like it was about to rip open, his pulse hammered at his temples.

'He lies.'

Robin's fingers sang with pins and needles. His hands were tied behind him with something. He was resting against the back of the shelter which was illuminated by some kind of battery-powered light in the centre of the place.

There was a man standing at the door.

He swam in and out of Robin's vision. Like he was on a partially tuned old television set.

The man was scruffy. A dirty white T-shirt and soiled grey trackpants. Long hair matted with sweat and rainwater, sticking up. A tangled, unruly beard. He was standing there. Looking at him with impossibly wide eyes.

'Who . . .' Robin spluttered – his mouth as dry as sandpaper.

'I saw them. The other day. This isn't what you think.' His voice was high-pitched. It almost sounded like a child's. 'I know what people say about me. Me.'

His forehead pulsed and unconsciousness became the easy option. But he battled against it. 'Who are . . .'

The man stepped forward, twisted his head around. 'He lies. I saw him do it. I saw him.'

'Who are you?' Robin said.

And the force it took for him to utter those three words was just too much. And the pulsing and the pain and the stench was just too much.

He watched the man stare at him and disappear into darkness.

And then it was all gone again.

35

'Robin. Oh God, Robin.'

He opened his good eye. The world seemed a little more real this time. He was still in the shelter, the light was gone – and so was the man. The pain in his forehead had dulled. Sally was standing over him.

'Where is he?' Robin said, trying to get up. His hands were untied – had they ever actually been bound? He used the rock face to inch himself up and staggered forward. He started to dip down but Sally caught him. 'Where the hell is he?'

'Who?' Sally said. 'God, Robin, your head. I think it needs stitches.'

'Did you see him?'

'No,' Sally said.

Robin shrugged her off and barrelled through the two metal sheets into the tunnel. Darkness flooded him. 'Robin.' Sally came up behind him, tried to grab him by the arm, but Robin evaded her – he almost slipped on a rock but managed to keep upright. He got to the train track – the sleepers – and knew that following them would take him back to the hole.

The man was going there. He was going there to get away. He just knew.

He started staggering at a fair pace, ignoring the throbbing above his left eye.

Sally was behind him. 'That place . . . was he living there . . . was that . . . the Standedge Monster?'

Robin didn't answer. He just quickened his pace.

His vision came in swathes. Time didn't really make sense anymore. All he could rely on was the pulsing pain in his forehead. He kept on up the tunnel seeing nothing that suggested a man had gone through there recently.

'Robin, stop.'

'No.'

'Robin, who was he?'

Robin didn't stop. Didn't look back. 'A man. In a white top. Grey trackpants. Beard. Long hair. Living in the tunnel. Doesn't matter who he is. All that matters is that he's out there.'

'Someone else can do this, Robin. It doesn't have to be you.'

The blood from his head had trickled down and into his mouth. He spat out a mouthful of it. He looked up to see a small glimmer of moonlight on the wall of the tunnel.

The hole. It had to be. It had grown slightly since he had last been through it. Either Sally or the man must have caused some more of the rock face to fall away. It looked even more precarious now.

Robin didn't even think – he launched himself at

the hole, retracting his arms to his side and wriggling through it. The rock above him shifted, but he didn't even hear it. He just kept going.

Soon enough, even more moonlight flooded his vision, and he was pulling himself out of the hole back into the clearing that he had created. It was empty – there was no one there. He got to his knees and looked all around – it was like the man was a ghost, and had just disappeared.

Who knows how long he had been out? The man could be miles away by now.

But that didn't matter. Not to him. He had to get up. He had to keep going. Because this is what he'd been searching for.

This was to get him closer to her.

He wrenched himself upright. With nothing to hold onto, he staggered and almost fell. But he was okay.

He almost smiled then, but caught himself. Instead he took in a deep breath of fresh air – his first in God knew how long. It felt good.

But then – a feeling. The sharp cool air was rushing to his head and his vision was going blurry.

He was going to—

He fell.

36

Ringing.

Not in his head. No – actual ringing.

He opened his eyes – both of them. He was lying on the bed in his room in The Hamlet. He sat up and traced a finger over his forehead. It was clean, but the cut above his left eye stung to the touch. He winced.

He swung his legs over the side of the bed. He felt like he'd slept for days, and looking at the clock he saw it was 10 a.m. He wondered what day that referred to.

He got up, looking around for his phone. He found it on the desk, plugged in, charging. It stopped ringing before he was able to reach for it.

Next to the phone, there was a packet of cookies. And a neon yellow Post-it note:

Gone back to The Door. Called the police about Man.
Going to write article. (Don't worry, I've got this.)
SALLY

Sally. Had Sally got him back here all on her own? And what did she mean 'I've got this'? How could she possibly 'have it'? They had nothing. The monster had gone.

Matthew was going to go in front of a judge. And their arrangement would be void. Would Matthew still tell him what he knew about Samantha, from behind a set of bars?

No. The answer was no.

The phone rang again, and Robin unplugged it, holding it to his ear. He suddenly felt incredibly hungry and ripped into the packet of cookies, stuffing a whole one in his mouth, not caring about the person at the other end of the line.

'You beautiful bastard,' a familiar voice said. Loamfield. He sounded happy. 'You know, I must admit I didn't think you had it in you. The trial of the century just became the trial of the millennium. And I'm at the forefront. I just want to personally thank you for letting me be a part of this. I'm going to be a superstar. I just can't believe it. I can hike up all my fees now. I can . . .' He continued jabbering on. Robin had no idea what he was talking about. He just finished his cookie and swallowed.

'What are you saying?'

This stopped Loamfield. 'Don't act like that – no need to be all humble around me, you glorious son of a bitch.'

'Loamfield, I have no idea what you are talking about.'

It seemed Loamfield believed him, because he grew quiet, and then just said, 'Turn on the TV. Right now. BBC News.'

Robin sighed and fumbled around the room, finally finding the TV remote. He clicked it and the small box suddenly spluttered into life. He went to BBC News and saw a banner saying 'Breaking News'. The image was of a building that looked very familiar – it was New Hall. A semi-circle of people were gathered around the front steps, seemingly waiting for something. They all had microphones, or cameras, or boom mics and there was a steady thrum of chatter. Until suddenly everyone collectively silenced.

'This was you, right?' Loamfield was saying on the phone but Robin put it on the bed, staring intently at the television.

Roger Claypath walked into shot in his shiny suit. He mounted the steps, standing directly in front of the main entrance that Robin had used himself. He held no sheet of paper, no cue cards. He didn't look happy, and as he looked at the camera, Robin couldn't help but feel he was looking directly at him. 'Thank you all for coming. This is a public statement about the circumstances surrounding the Standedge Incident, and the status of the investigation into what happened to the missing young people that the community and media have come to call the Standedge Five. Please refrain from asking questions, as I am not taking any at this time.

'In the early hours of yesterday morning, we received an anonymous phone call that led police to discover an alternative entrance to the disused railway tunnels that run parallel, and are explicitly connected to, Standedge canal tunnel. The caller stated that they saw a dishevelled man leaving by a crack in the side of the tunnel in distress. Police found what can only be described as

a shelter of sorts inside the railway tunnel. It was suf-
ficiently hidden by rocks, but the man seemed to have
abandoned it, leaving in a hurry, and had not replaced
them properly on this occasion. This is how he was able
to evade the initial search.

'It appears that the shelter had been lived in for a
long time, leading us to believe that this confirms the
rumours of the individual colloquially referred to as the
Standedge Monster. The tunnels will remain monitored,
although we are mostly sure that he has abandoned his
makeshift home for good. We are working hard to locate
this individual as well as ascertain his actual identity.
Who knows how long the man has actually called the
tunnel his home or how well he knows the surrounding areas, but every hour we get closer to establishing
the facts of this man's life. If anyone believes they have
sighted the Standedge Monster please contact your local
law enforcement. The anonymous call described him as
a thin man of average height with unkempt long black
hair and a long black beard. He is dressed in a ragged
and dirty white T-shirt and muddy grey tracksuit trousers. I know that isn't exactly a lot to go on, but when
we have an official picture of the man, we will circulate
it to all news outlets.

'This comes to the subject of Matthew McConnell, and
his current situation. It is clear now that law enforcement, guided by myself, have been too hasty in wanting
to resolve this investigation due to public interest and
. . . personal emotion, not only from myself but from the
squad. This has been a misstep. I am by no means saying

that McConnell is not involved in the disappearance of the Standedge Five. He is still heavily a suspect in this investigation. But it is clear circumstances yesterday, as is sometimes the case, are not the same as circumstances today.

'Therefore, the court session that was set for this week, regarding Matthew McConnell's ongoing incarceration has been postponed. Given that we now have an alternative timeline of what could have occurred in the tunnel on 26 June 2018, we have decided to release Matthew McConnell pending further investigation. I must stress that this is not because he is innocent. There are still many questions to be answered about what happened on that fateful journey, and McConnell is still heavily embroiled.

'Matthew McConnell will be released later today, but placed under house arrest. He will also have a police presence outside his house until further notice. I must stress that this is not only for his own protection, but very possibly for the people of Marsden as well.

'Thank you for your time. We will be providing regular updates as the investigation into this man progresses.' Claypath stepped away, out of frame. And the television cut to a wide shot as the thrall of reporters followed him as he bypassed them as he went down the steps. There were shouts from various journalists.

'Would you say that the arrest of Matthew McConnell was premature?' one asked.

'Was the judgement in any way influenced by your personal stake in this case?' another asked.

'Is this grounds for resignation?' yet another said.

But Claypath did not respond. He didn't even acknowledge the questions had been asked. He just made his way down the steps and into the back of a black car. As it pulled out, the reporters swarmed behind it and kept shouting.

Robin picked up his phone, bewildered. He couldn't think. Matthew McConnell was going free. The court hearing was cancelled.

'So it was you, right?' Loamfield said, as though the conversation had never stopped. 'You called in the anonymous tip?'

'No.'

'Yeah whatever – wink, wink and all that. You've been a busy boy. You and this Red Door thing.'

'What?'

'There's an article about the Monster blowing up on social media. You are named.'

Robin got up, pulled his laptop out of the desk drawer and opened it, navigating to The Red Door through his history. The main page flashed up and Robin read the name of the latest post: 'The Standedge Monster Is Real (PROOF!!). There was another article under it: There Is Another Way Into Standedge! They were both posted in the early hours of the morning.

Robin didn't need to read the articles. He had lived them. But he did skim them to try and find his name. It didn't take long. It was at the bottom of the first one:

Writer Robin Ferringham, who is known for hard-hitting memoir *Without Her* about coping with the disappearance of his wife and who has recently been seen around Marsden expressing interest in the Standedge Five case aided The Red Door in their investigation. He proved invaluable in the search.

'Your name is attached to this thing now,' Loamfield was saying in his ear. 'Hope you don't mind. Seems to be the thing most people are latching on to. People love a celebrity, no matter how big or small. Hell, even if it's one they've never bloody heard of.'

'I'm not a celebrity,' Robin said.

'Oh, Robin,' Loamfield laughed, 'we all are now. We just played a part in what will be the sinking of Roger Claypath. I think that's grounds for celebration.'

'The man is just trying to find his kids,' Robin said, and to reinforce that being the end of it he changed the subject. 'Claypath said Matthew is going home. When?'

'That was a recording that you just saw. McConnell's being released in an hour. I'm on my way there now.'

Robin jumped up, spun around, finally eyeing what he needed to find. His car keys on the desk. He snatched them up.

'So am I.'

37

Robin tried to reach Sally on the way to the prison. He wanted to thank her – thank her for getting him back to The Hamlet, thank her for getting the word out, thank her for everything. He still didn't know how to react to her putting his name in the article but if it meant it got more attention, then he didn't blame her for doing it. She didn't pick up. So he called again. Nothing. She was probably busy managing the undoubtably inordinately high amount of website traffic. Robin had images of one of the computer towers sparking and hissing with activity and Sally running around it trying to repair it. He smiled as he pulled into New Hall and parked.

Reporters were still crowding the steps of New Hall. Robin walked up and slowed as he saw them. He had to get inside, and this wasn't likely to be pretty. He thought maybe there was a chance the reporters wouldn't have read The Red Door article, and even if they had, there was an even better chance they had no idea what Robin Ferringham looked like. But as he made his way towards the thrall, one reporter looked around and noticed him.

'Mr Ferringham . . .' he shouted. And then the thrall was upon him, lurching forward in a collective swarm.

He ran up the steps, barely keeping ahead of them, ready to be swallowed up.

Sporadic shouts followed him, over the steady thrum of chatter.

'Mr Ferringham, why are you here?'

'Mr Ferringham, is it true that you are writing a book about the Standedge Five?'

'Mr Ferringham, what is your opinion of the way the police investigation into the disappearances has been handled?'

'Mr Ferringham, do you think Roger Claypath should resign?'

He didn't look back, or engage at all. He actually copied Claypath, and as he got to the main door and went inside the building he felt a sense of relief.

The hall was quiet and bright, just as it had been before. Guards stood at the entrance, no doubt to keep reporters out. Robin didn't think he'd ever been so happy to see an armed man.

He went through security and spotted a familiar terracotta-coloured suit standing by the reception desk. Loamfield looked as squirrelly as ever, although this time he had a huge smile painted on his face. He was wearing a bafflingly ugly blue tie with little yellow stars on it. He was chatting cheerily to the officer behind the desk.

Robin made his way over and before he could announce his arrival, Loamfield clapped eyes on him. 'Robin Ferringham, the man of the hour.' Loamfield seized his hand and pulled him up to the desk. 'Must say, you look dreadful. But that's what happens sometimes.

You've got to get hurt to make something of yourself.'

'Hello, Mr Loamfield,' Robin said, feeling the familiar pang of disgust towards the man. 'Where is Matthew?'

'Guards gone to get him. Been about half an hour. Paperwork, you know.'

'Isn't that your job?' Robin said.

Loamfield beamed, but didn't answer the question. 'How did you do it? Just between us? How did you find that crack in the tunnel?'

Robin repaid him by not answering that either.

Loamfield seemed satisfied. 'I know, I know, it'll ruin the magic of it. Truth be told, I don't really give a stuff how you did what you did. I just know I'm ready to reap the rewards. If you catch my drift.'

'I'm afraid I don't think I do.'

Loamfield leaned in, and whispered in a harsh gush that seemed louder than his normal speaking voice. 'Me, Terrance Loamfield, defence lawyer extraordinaire is front and centre for the acquitting of Matthew McConnell, in a crime that was pretty much an open and shut case. I won't ever have to worry about work again.

'Par example – double, triple, hell, quadruple murder, perp caught bang to rights. Witnesses out the wazoo. What's that guy gonna want – a lawyer who can do the impossible. Enter me. I'll be the guy they all want, and it doesn't even matter if I get them off, because there will always be more and more silly pricks doing stupid things and needing a guy like me.'

Robin raised his eyebrows. 'Do you care about your clients at all?'

'Caring never got anyone anywhere in life,' Loamfield said.

Robin disputed that but didn't want to talk about it anymore. 'What's going to happen when they bring Matthew out?'

Loamfield shrugged. 'He gets entrusted into my care for a short time. I am to take him straight home and wait for the police tech team to come and install his bracelet that won't let him leave the house.'

'Can I not take him home?' Robin found himself saying.

Loamfield shook his head. 'In the eyes of the law, you are an unsuitable guardian. You're too close to this case. They're only allowing me to take him because I'm his representation and . . .'

'And what?'

'And if I run off with him they know where to find me,' Loamfield laughed.

Robin surprised himself by smiling too. He nodded. It made sense.

'Mr Ferringham,' a voice called. 'I mean, Robin.'

Robin and Loamfield looked around. The small frame of Matthew McConnell was standing at the entrance to the corridor Robin had previously gone down to meet with him. The familiar face of Stanton the guard was standing with him. When Robin met Matthew's eyes, the young man rushed forward. Stanton hurried to keep up as he ran across the hall, clattering on the marble floor.

Matthew got to Robin and launched himself at him,

enveloping him in a hug. 'Thank you, Mr Ferrin—Robin. Thank you, thank you, thank you.' The young man started to cry.

Stanton caught up and he, Robin and Loamfield exchanged awkward glances as Matthew cried into Robin's jacket. After what seemed like a long moment, Matthew relinquished his grip.

'Thank you,' he said, rubbing his eyes and looking up at Robin. He looked shocked. 'What happened to you?'

Did his forehead really look that bad? He should have at least looked in the mirror when he was back in the room.

'I . . . ran into a few things,' Robin said.

'Like a truck?' Stanton said gruffly, and they all looked at the guard. It could talk.

'You ready to go home, Matthew?' Loamfield said, smiling, although the smile was far less excited than it had been when the man had been thinking about himself.

Matthew looked from Loamfield to Robin. 'Are you coming?'

Robin couldn't help but smile, hopefully more genuinely than Loamfield. The lad seemed to need him, to want him around. 'Of course. I'll follow behind you.'

'You kept your end,' Matthew said, 'and I'll keep mine. I'll tell you everything.' He meant it too.

Robin nodded.

'Just one small thing,' Matthew said to him, and seeing his expression, added 'Don't worry, this one's easy.'

'Okay, what?'

'Can you get me a pizza?' Matthew said.

Robin laughed, and nodded. 'Yes, I can get you a pizza. What type of pizza do you want?'

'Literally anything,' Matthew said, and laughed too.

Loamfield said something under his breath to Stanton and turned to them. 'We have to go out the back. Try and minimise the risk of any of the vultures outside seeing us.'

Robin nodded. 'What's the address?'

'Nineteen Parkfield, Marsden,' Matthew said.

'Okay,' Robin said, 'I'll see you soon.'

Matthew looked at him. 'Yes, you will.'

38

Robin found a supermarket just before the dual carriageway that led back to Marsden. He got a frozen pepperoni pizza and, on the spur of the moment, three bottles of beer too. If anyone needed a drink, it was Matthew McConnell.

He got back in his car and started along the dual carriageway. It was deathly quiet – everyone was at work or having lunch, so the roads were clear. He saw less than ten cars in about twenty minutes. His eyes wandered to the edge of the dual carriageway, trying to find some stimulation. He felt calm for the first time since starting this whole crazy journey – since Matthew called him. It was hard to believe that was only a week ago. It felt like a year.

The roadside was short. The hard shoulder was really all there was as past it, a steady hill dipped down into a forest. He wondered what forest it was. Did every forest have a name?

There was something draped at the top of the hill coming up on his right. It was blue and snaking. Robin didn't think anyone else passing would have noticed it, so it was odd that he did. Wasn't it?

It was coming up. A small thin piece of shiny blue fabric lying in the grass. It had yellow stars on it.

He passed it, mulling it over in his mind. And then his eyes widened. He hit the brake and the clutch the hardest he ever had – the car seemed to almost lurch upward before being held back in a stop.

His breath came short and fast as he parked on the hard shoulder and got out. He looked up the hard shoulder, the way he'd come. He saw it. And he started to run.

He got to it, grabbed it and turned it over in his hand. A tie. A blue tie with yellow stars, ugly as sin. The same tie he'd seen around Loamfield's neck not half an hour before.

He looked around where he picked up the tie. The shoulder didn't have a barrier protecting the road from the forest below. It was very muddy but Robin thought he could see two very ill-defined tyre tracks, veering off the road and going down the hill.

He couldn't understand what he was seeing until he looked down the hill to the tree line. A car, wrecked – the bonnet wrapped around a tree.

No. No, this wasn't happening. This couldn't be happening. It wasn't supposed to go this way. But what he was seeing wasn't a lie, and he didn't have to guess that this was Loamfield's car.

He didn't even think. He launched himself down the embankment towards the car. He couldn't see inside it from his viewpoint. The roof was bent in the middle, warped by the impact. The back of the car looked almost fine, but the front looked like some kind of metal concertina. There was smoke rising from the crushed bonnet, and there was some kind of hissing sound he couldn't quite understand.

He got to the bottom of the hill, sliding on the mud, and got to the car. He looked inside. Loamfield was in the driver's seat, his head limp against the seat. His face was drenched in blood but Robin couldn't see from where. The passenger's side was empty – and what was more, the door was open.

Robin looked around desperately, into the trees. He couldn't hear anything except the hiss of the engine. But then – a crunch of leaves and twigs nearby. And he thought he saw a figure through the trees.

He instinctually stepped forward, ready to run. But a spluttering behind him stopped him. He turned to see that Loamfield was coughing up blood. Robin had to think – he didn't know what to do, he didn't want to be in this situation. To have to make this call. But –

A small sound answered him. The sound of something igniting. A flame curled out of the crack in the bonnet. And Robin didn't have a choice anymore.

He pulled open the driver's side door – it was difficult as the car's frame was so badly misshapen but he managed. Loamfield looked like he'd lost consciousness again. Probably best. Robin looked down at the footwell to see a mess of Loamfield's limbs and warped machinery. There didn't seem to be anything wedging him in, which was good for both of them. They had to get away from the car, now.

Robin unclicked Loamfield's seatbelt and gripped him by the shoulders, wrenching him out of the car. Loamfield was obviously back with him as he screamed out in pain. So did Robin – the small man was a dead weight and it was taking every ounce of strength he had to get him out.

He got Loamfield out and he flopped onto the ground. His legs were bloody, his expensive trousers ripped and soaked. There seemed to be something sticking out of his lower left leg – a small piece of metal.

Robin quickly took a few breaths, and looked up to see the small flame had been joined by three more. He wiped his brow and took Loamfield's shoulders again, pulling him from the vicinity of the car. He was the one who screamed this time – in anger, in pain, in simple white hot emotion. He got Loamfield ten metres away, then twenty, then thirty – all the time thinking he was going to pull so hard his arms would dislocate from his elbows. He stopped at the base of the embankment and looked at the car, as it became ablaze.

He looked down at Loamfield – there was phlegm frothing from his mouth and suddenly his eyes flickered open. He instantly howled in pain. His eyes flicked around and fell on Robin. He looked, seeming to recognise him. 'He . . .' he wheezed.

'Don't talk,' Robin said, 'you're going to be okay.' He got his phone, dialled 999. As he did, there was a creaking sound from the car. He looked up.

The car exploded, the sound and the heat working together to frighten the hell out of Robin. Robin dived over Loamfield, shielding him. His ears rang and he felt as though his face was on fire. And in a second, it was over.

Robin looked around. The car wreck was still flaming.

And then a voice. On the phone that had slipped out of his hand. He picked it up. Didn't even wait for the person on the other end to speak. 'We . . . we need an ambulance. There's been a car wreck, on the dual carriageway between New Hall and Marsden. I don't know the road, sorry. There's . . . I've got the driver out – he's bleeding badly, he's in and out of consciousness. Please just send somebody.'

The person on the other end said something. But he didn't know what. He just ended the call and knelt over Loamfield.

The man was out again. Robin ripped open his shirt to see an open wound the size of his hand in his stomach. Must have been from the collision – it was oozing blood and some other substance. He got a better look at the man's legs – they had no definition to them at all. He suspected they were both broken. Robin looked back at his face, and almost jumped when he saw Loamfield staring at him. His right eye was bloodshot and his stare was askew. He kept fluttering his eyelids and Robin could tell he was holding on to reality.

Loamfield wheezed.

'Help is coming, I've called them,' Robin said, hoping he was providing some comfort. But truth was, he didn't even know if Loamfield was understanding him.

'Where is he . . .' Loamfield started and trailed off – the

rest of the sentence a whisper. Robin bent down and put his ear to Loamfield's mouth. 'Matthew. Matthew . . ran me off the road.'

Robin looked at him. And his eyes closed again.

An intense anger swelled in him, and he looked around himself, into the forest. He staggered up and into the trees, the sounds of the smouldering car skeleton behind him. Matthew McConnell was here. He was somewhere nearby.

Had he planned this? Had he planned it all? Robin looked through the trees and started to run, dodging in between them.

'Where are you?' he said.

Had Matthew chosen Robin specifically? To get him out of prison? How had he done it – found out what he had about Sam? Was he really lying about all of it?

He pulled himself through an outcrop and just kept going. The figure he'd seen couldn't have gotten far.

'Where are you?' he shouted, and it seemed to bounce off the trees. A bird fluttered out of a tree and startled him, but he just kept going.

Sam had been leading him here? Of course not. How could he have been so gullible, so profoundly stupid? And he had believed in Matthew – seen some kind of good in him.

'Where are you, you son of a bitch?' Louder. His voice cracking.

But there was no good in the world. Only different shades of bad. He wasn't chasing Sam. He was chasing a murderer. Through the woods.

217

He emerged into a clearing, turned in a circle. No sign of anyone – 360 degrees and nothing.

He breathed in and at the top of his lungs –

'Where are you?'

39

Robin had lost the concept of time which was ironic seeing as the only thing to focus on was the ticking of the insanely loud clock on the wall. The four walls surrounding him made him feel like it was where he'd always been – this were his home now. He prayed for something – anything – to occupy his mind. Anything other than the image of McConnell getting further and further away.

The door opened and a different man came in. No doubt to ask the same questions he'd been asked three times before. This man was young, scrappy, and he sat down with a manner that hadn't quite matured. He placed a device on the desk in between them – a dictaphone. He went to press it and paused.

The door opened again, behind him, and Robin watched as a familiarly imposing figure came in. Roger Claypath. He stood behind the young man, who pressed the button on the dictaphone and introduced himself as Fields.

He did indeed ask the same questions. How long was Robin at the supermarket? What attracted his attention to the crash site? Was there any indication that anyone else was watching? Had any other cars stopped to help? What happened when Robin got to the scene of the crash? What was Loamfield's condition – was there any evidence of a struggle? How long did it take to rescue Loamfield? And how far did he pursue the figure into the woods?

Loamfield was in the hospital, he'd sustained a severe injury to the head. He hadn't woken up yet.

Robin answered all the questions flatly, reciting them as if they were lines in a script. They might as well have been. They didn't feel real.

This wasn't happening. This kind of thing didn't happen to him.

Fields stopped the recorder and left, but Claypath didn't. Robin couldn't meet his eyes, and only heard the scrape of the chair as Claypath sat down. They sat in silence for a while, Robin wilting under the gaze of the Chief.

'It's a pity you didn't take me up on that offer of a chat,' Claypath said and Robin looked up for the first time. Claypath didn't look angry, or sad, or disappointed – he was a blank slate. And why was that even more scary? 'Things could have been different.' Claypath interlocked his fingers. 'Shame.'

'Am I free to go?' Robin said.

'Of course,' Claypath said. 'Unless you've done something unlawful?'

'Unlawful?' Robin said, 'No. I helped you. I saved a man's life.'

Claypath nodded. 'Yes, you're a regular superhero.'

'Do you have people looking for him?'

Claypath chuckled. 'Of course we bloody do. I have the whole force combing the entire county looking for him. And what you've done, what has happened, has made national news. I can't keep the Standedge Incident contained anymore. We have to find him.' But he didn't look confident. In fact, in that moment, Robin saw a chink in Claypath's armour. The part where the sternness subsided into uncertainty. Claypath liked everything to go his way, and as Chief of Police it almost always did. But this – this situation – worried him. No – more than that – he was afraid.

'Do you have people looking for the Monster?'

Claypath didn't say anything. His eyes were a fire that had just been lit.

'Do you . . .' Robin started again.

But Claypath interrupted. 'This is a police matter.'

'But I deserve to . . .'

'This. Is. A. Police. Matter.' Louder.

'But I might . . .'

'Mr Ferringham . . .' Louder.

'But . . .'

'Don't you think you've done enough?' he bellowed at Robin, making him shrink away. His face had gone red, a vein pulsing in his forehead. If looks could kill, Robin wouldn't just be dead – his headstone would be cracked down the middle.

'I'm sorry,' Robin said in a small voice.

'So you should be,' Claypath said. Having reached the summit of his anger, he was making his way down the other side. 'We have two suspects in this case, and you have managed to chase them both away. You're lucky I haven't arrested you for obstructing police business.'

'With all due respect, you wouldn't have a second suspect if it wasn't for me.'

Claypath did the unthinkable – he laughed and turned his nose up. 'McConnell ran that car off the road – if that isn't an admission of guilt then what is? And the Monster? – you didn't exactly serve him up to us on a platter, did you? You've done far more harm than good. And if McConnell really killed my children like I think he did, like he seems to be confirming through his actions, then your direct involvement has let a killer go free.'

'You are the ones who let him go.' Robin said.

'YOU GAVE US NO CHOICE!' Claypath shouted, a vein popping in his forehead. 'I tried to warn you but you didn't listen. And your bullheadedness has now cost my children justice. Their killer is out there, running, and now we have to try and catch him. And that will always be on you. That will always be on the shoulders of Robin Ferringham and I swear to God, I will have everyone know that fact.'

'I wanted to find out what happened. To your children. And the others.'

'Did we ask for your help? I don't recall calling you to enquire about your opinion. You are nothing, Ferringham. And you never will be again. I have had enough of you. Marsden has had enough of you. Huddersfield has had enough of you. Get the hell out of my county. Go home. And never come back. And if you don't, you may start to find Marsden can be a very dangerous place to be.' Claypath got up, his anger presented to Robin in a clearly laid out threat. 'I don't suppose we'll be meeting again,' he said.

Robin opened his mouth to say something – an apology, a plea, just something – but the door shut.

Claypath was gone.

40

A uniformed officer dropped Robin back at his car. She didn't offer her name, and Robin didn't ask. When they got to the scene, Robin saw that there had been police tape placed around the edge of the dual carriageway. Police cars were lining the hard shoulder and the officer dropped Robin off then added her car to the line.

Robin paused at his vehicle. Traffic had slowed down on the road – everyone slowing down to see what was going on, and as he looked across the barrier, he saw a van parked up – a man with a beefy-looking camera pointed at the scene.

Robin started towards the scene himself and then thought better of it. What else could he possibly do here?

He got in the car, and with one look in the wing mirror, took off to Marsden. He didn't look when he returned down the other side of the dual carriageway.

Roger Claypath was right.

He had done enough.

He went back to Marsden. He parked at the station and walked through the town. Every step he took, he thought he felt a new pair of eyes on him – watching his every move. The man who let the bogeyman get away

– that's what they'd think of him as, and they were right, weren't they?

He'd been there. In the forest. He'd been right there.

Sam's voice plucked up in his mind, *But then, a man would be dead. You saved the lawyer's life. You did the right thing.*

His phone rang. It was Emma. He didn't want to think of all the people watching him anymore so he picked up.

'Robin. What's happening?' She sounded more worried than he'd ever heard her before. 'Is the news true? This McConnell guy, and something about a monster, and there was a car crash? Are you alright?'

'I'm fine,' he said, in a tone that didn't even convince himself, so had no chance of convincing his sister. 'I just . . . I messed up, Em.' And it all came out – everything. Everything that had happened ever since he came to Marsden, a story full of sheep, canals, underground websites and too many pubs. And when he was at the end of it, she was silent, so he just said again, 'I messed up. You were right. I should never have come here. I have no business being in Marsden. Matthew McConnell played me. He used Sam against me, and now he's got what he wanted.'

There was silence on the other end of the phone for so long that Robin thought the connection may have cut off. But finally Emma said, 'Robin, why don't I come and get you and you can come back to London.'

Robin opened his mouth, all ready to say yes, to beg 'yes' but he couldn't. This was his mess – he had made it and he had to get himself out. He owed something to this

225

town, and he didn't know how yet but he was going to at least take a step towards making amends.

'I'll be home soon,' he said, and hung up before Emma could say anything else.

41

He quickened his step as he got to the duo of pubs marking the start of the town. As he started up the street, he saw a group of people crowding around a uniformed police officer, asking questions in hushed tones. The group was between him and The Hamlet, so he took a left at the clock tower and found himself on the street that Sally had led him through the day he met her.

He found himself gravitating to a bench next to the quaint little church. His feelings were conflicted – he didn't exactly want to be out in the open for people to gawk at him, but he didn't want to be in his room alone either. It was funny how the mind worked sometimes.

Seeing no one around, he sat down on the hard bench. The light breeze felt nice against his face, and even seemed to soothe his cut forehead. He had been running around so much chasing phantoms and crawling into tunnels and rescuing people from car wrecks, he couldn't remember the last time he'd just sat still.

He wondered what Sam would say if she could see him now.

'This seat taken?'

He jumped and looked up to see Sally standing there. She was being trailed by the two sheep, who were obviously hoping for some kind of food offering. Sally looked deflated – her hands tucked inside her hoody pockets, her hood up. She looked like she was in mourning.

Robin shifted to the side of the bench so Sally could sit.

'Heard what you did,' Sally said. 'So are you like Superman now?'

Robin started to respond and then realised she was joking. He looked at her. She didn't really seem to be enjoying it either. 'I'm not really in the mood, Sally.'

'You mad at me because I put your name in the article?'

He shook his head. 'No, I'm not mad at you. You did good work. Thank you for getting me back to The Hamlet.'

She smiled. 'Believe me, I'd love to take all the credit but your little friend helped me.'

'What friend?'

'Polly Pocket. From The Hamlet.'

'Do you mean Amber?'

'Yeah, that's her name. I got you to the Marsden side of Standedge and she was there walking so she helped me carry you back.'

Amber? 'What was she doing around Standedge?'

'I don't know, walking. You better be thankful she was there or you'd have woken up in a bush. You should really do some cardio,' Sally said, eyeing his stomach. He had a feeling she was attempting humour again.

Robin opened his mouth to say something, and

realised he had no idea what, so closed it again. They sat in silence for a moment.

'Is there any news?' he said finally. 'Anything at all?'

'What do you mean?'

'You run a news website, you must have sources – is there any news on Matthew McConnell?'

'I run an underground website that no one had ever heard of before today,' Sally corrected him, 'I don't have any sources. I don't know any more than you do. Unfortunately. We're both civvies.'

Robin looked around the street. It was empty, apart from an old couple walking down the other side. The woman was glancing at them, and the man was mumbling something at her, no doubt telling her to stop staring. 'We're not civilians though, are we? We did it. We went into that tunnel, we chased the Monster away, we got McConnell out of that place. It's our fault . . . It's . . . *my* . . . fault.'

Sally put a hand on Robin's shoulder, a gesture that seemed alien to her, judging by her expression. 'What we did . . . was nothing more than the police should have done in their initial investigation. Claypath got so blindsided by wanting Matthew to be guilty that he rushed the search of the tunnels, even though he didn't (and still doesn't) have a clear timeline of what happened. We just did his job for him. We have nothing to feel guilty about.'

Robin looked at her, and knew she really believed that. And maybe she was right. But it wouldn't stop him feeling guilty. And it wouldn't stop the rest of

Marsden blaming him. He wasn't going to hold that against anyone.

'Look, Robin,' Sally said, 'you just saved someone's life. You ran after two suspects, one when you were incredibly spaced out. You deserve to feel better about yourself right now.'

'And yet I don't,' Robin said.

'I know,' Sally said, standing up, 'and that's because you're a good guy. Samantha was a lucky woman.' She smiled sadly.

'What do I do now?'

She shrugged. 'The same thing everyone does. You wing it.' And with a nod, she turned and started to walk away.

Robin watched her go for a few steps and then said, 'Your name's not Sally, is it?'

She turned. 'No. It's not.' And that was that. She left, and Robin just watched as she disappeared down the road. Robin smiled – he guessed she was 'winging it'.

Where had 'winging it' gotten him? It got his forehead cut open, running hot with a probable fever, and got him questioned for five hours by the police. Maybe he was the planning type.

When Sally disappeared down the road, he looked around. The old couple across the street had gone as well. The town seemed oddly silent but then he guessed he would prefer that than it being crowded. Maybe they were all just avoiding him.

He was startled then when he looked to the church and saw a woman standing there, appearing seemingly

230

from nowhere. She was walking down the side of the church. She looked like she was crying. She paused and reached up to the noticeboard on the side of the church. Robin watched as she painstakingly took the pins from one of the posters. It was a 'MISSING' poster with a picture of a cat. Mittons.

She took it down and turned around, finally seeing Robin. She avoided his gaze, looking down at the picture of the cat with a longing that would never be satisfied again. She balled up the poster and threw it in the bin beside Robin.

Robin watched her sadly. She glanced momentarily at him, with nothing in her face but sorrow and walked away. He looked at the noticeboard now with an open spot. Maybe he should make a 'MISSING' poster for Matthew M —

Wait.

Robin stood up. The Mittons poster had been half covering up another one. It was a poster of a blue sky with clouds. He stepped forward to the noticeboard, reached out for the poster reading the small print.

It was a poster for a gathering at the church dated three months before. A Church Counselling Group. The name was at the top in big gold lettering.

ASCEND.

He ripped the poster off the board and stared at it.

Maybe it was time to wing it some more?

It was time to go to church.

42

The church of Marsden was much as it was at the vigil – modern, all pine and light. But now it was empty and when Robin entered into the small hall area, then through a set of double doors was the church proper, with pews running up to the altar he could look around a bit more. There was no one around, and the place was so silent, he would guess that there was no one else in the building.

He looked around the entrance area, which didn't look unlike a doctor's waiting room. There were two stands full of pamphlets, all about a various aspect of religious life. Robin stepped forward and picked one up, absent-mindedly. Grief and God. He slotted it back in to the stand. Even the big man upstairs couldn't help him there.

There were posters on the wall, but from a quick scan, Robin couldn't see any others for the Ascend group. He wasn't surprised seeing as the group meeting had passed and the posters inside were probably changed quicker than the ones outside.

He reached into his pocket and pulled the poster out again.

Ascend. A journey of Acceptance – learning to live with the path God has set you on. Location just said 'the church'. He looked around again – didn't even know what he was looking for.

'A lost soul,' a kindly voice said, and Robin wheeled around.

A man, tall but not imposing, was standing in the double doorway into the church. He was watching Robin with kind eyes. For some reason, Robin suddenly realised what a state he must be. He hadn't showered, or cleaned at all, since pulling Loamfield out of his car, since being just outside of the blast radius of an explosion. He still felt singed, and his clothes were covered in dirt. He must've been sweating profusely as he felt constantly damp.

The man's eyes moved from Robin's face to the poster in his hands and back. 'I have never seen a man so in need of a cup of tea.' He smiled.

And Robin did too.

43

Robin sat in the front row of the pews, staring at the altar and behind it, a stained glass window depicting Jesus feeding the five thousand, while the Father, who'd introduced himself as Michaels, went to make a cup of tea. Robin looked at the image in the glass for a long time, thinking the congregation of the church must stare at this window for hours on end. He wondered what they saw, what they felt, when they looked at it. Did they feel some kind of overwhelming salvation? Because all he saw was a nice piece of art.

Sometimes he wished he saw more.

The Father came out of a side room, carrying two novelty mugs full of piping hot tea. He sat down next to Robin and handed him one – a white mug with 'You don't have to be religious to work here, but it helps!' on it. Robin gave his thanks.

He sipped at the tea, finding it way too hot, and lowered the mug. The Father, on the other hand, took a deep sip and smiled. 'What brings you here, my friend?'

Robin felt the poster that he had replaced in his pocket, and decided that if there was ever a time to be truthful, it was now, under the watchful eye of the saviour of the world. 'I came here following a lead.'

The Father regarded him. 'A lead? A lead for what?'

'I'm sorry, but, don't you know who I am? I'm pretty much the talk of the town and I must have been on the news, and . . .'

'I know who you are, Mr Ferringham. I want to know what brought you here.'

'I just said . . . it was . . .'

'What really brought you here?' the Father insisted.

Robin shut his mouth. And thought about the question, really thought about it. What really made him come to Marsden? 'I'm chasing someone. A ghost. My wife. I kept kidding myself that she was leading me here, that if I came here I would find her, or at least find what happened to her.'

'You had faith?' the Father said.

Robin looked at him and after a moment nodded. 'I suppose I did.'

'You thought that you were part of some design. A design that she made.'

'Yes. But now I realise that I was just used, that my blind faith made me a tool in someone else's plan. That maybe my love, for her, is a weakness.'

The Father didn't comfort him. Instead he took another swig of scalding tea, and looked up at the altar. 'If you believe that she is leading you somewhere, how do you know that this is not part of the design? Maybe this was always part of the journey?'

'I don't understand.'

'The long dark night of the soul,' the Father said, and offered no further explanation.

'You're saying,' Robin said, trying to see if he got what the Father was trying to say right, 'that Sam wanted me to play a major role in freeing a prisoner, you're saying she wanted me to nearly get blown up saving someone, that her design got me this cut on my forehead?'

The Father drained his tea, and looked at Robin simply. 'I'm saying that things are rarely easy. And you must keep your Faith. If not Faith in God, then Faith in her.'

He didn't want to talk about this anymore, he swallowed half of his tea in one gulp. 'What is this?' Robin said, pulling out the poster for the group. He handed it to the Father.

The man looked at it for a second. 'Ascend was one of the groups designed to bring the community together through the power of the church.' He folded it up and gave it back. 'It didn't really take off.'

'Were the Standedge Five involved?'

'What?' Father Michaels seemed genuinely confused. 'No. I mean, I suppose I can't say for sure. I didn't run the group.'

'Who did?' Robin said, pretty sure he already knew the answer.

'That would have been Amber Crusher.'

44

He walked down the road, back to The Hamlet, mulling over what he had learned. He needed to talk to Amber again – she knew something. She had to, she was obviously closer to Tim than she had let on, and now she may know something about the Five's Ascend tattoos. He couldn't go back to London with this looming over him. He needed answers. And who knew? Amber might know what forced Matthew out of the friendship group, and turned him murderous.

He needed to get back. If Amber wasn't at the bar, he'd wait. He could have a drink, regroup, and then talk to her.

He cut through the alley to get back to the main road. He was about halfway before he looked up.

His heart skipped a beat. There was a figure standing at the end of the alley illuminated just as Ethan Pack had been a few days before. But this wasn't Pack. At least he didn't think it was. The figure seemed tall, and whoever it was standing there wore a black jumper with the hood up. He didn't know exactly why at first but he felt deeply unsettled. And then he realised, he felt another set of eyes on him. He turned back to look where he'd come from. There was another figure at the end. Exactly the same. A tall foreboding presence in a black hooded sweater.

They were blocking him in.

Robin looked between the two figures, finally realising what was happening. The figures started advancing, a step at a time – every time he looked they seemed to be closer. He looked around him, scrabbling amongst the bins as if he could magically find a way out, some concealed exit or something or at least find something to defend himself with. He tried both the back doors to the butchers' and the café but they were locked. When he looked up, the figures were nearly on him. For some stupid reason he looked up again, as if asking for help from the divine, as though he was going to find a magical ladder to carry him out of this situation.

Instead, when Robin looked down, he found a fist sailing towards his face. He turned his head just in time so that it went smashing into his cheek. Pain exploded in his brain, as his head was propelled backwards guiding his body. He was caught from falling, and for a second he was glad, until he realised that it was the other figure who had stopped his descent. He dragged Robin back to standing and whispered in his ear, 'Shoulda gone home, city boy.'

The figure in front of Robin brought its knee up to his crotch so fast he couldn't prepare. His groin erupted in pain – his world spinning from the impact. He let out a wheezing shrieking sound that sounded like a small animal in panic.

He fell before he could even try to struggle. He was vaguely aware he was thrashing out with his arms – a reflex action, and incredibly useless, but he felt all the better for trying to fight back. Not that it would make the slightest bit of difference.

One moment he was freefalling and the next he was on the cold alley, with his cheek pressed against the rough granite. He tried to call out for someone, any-one, but as soon as he'd opened his mouth, he realised he'd made a grave mistake as a boot came up to meet it. His vision squirted red and somewhere, not here, not where he was, he realised it was blood. It splattered over the ground in front of him becoming real in his mind. His mouth flared with pain, and as he was processing it, the boot kicked him square in the forehead. His cut sang and the rest of his forehead felt like it had cracked open.

He made a pathetic scream, choking on his own blood before he could get any volume and he spat something tangible out. It flung out in front of him and clattered away – a tooth.

Robin found himself curling up – retreating into himself – into the foetal position as a barrage of kicks cracked at his back. The figure in front of him started kicking him in the chest, finding an opening between his legs and chin. He tried to curl up more to close the gap, but the attack of kicks was so strong he couldn't. Pain became a constant, punctuated only with peaks of it. The figures showed no signs of letting up, and con-sciousness was a thing he had to work to keep.

Kick, kick, kick. And he squirmed on the floor of the alleyway.

He lived a lifetime of anguish.

And then, letting the darkness in, he let go. His final thought before he lost the world was not one of pain, or suffering. It was one of anger. Anger at the person who had done this to him. Neither of the people kicking the life out of him.

No.

Anger at Matthew McConnell.

45

He didn't know how long he was out. But his first thought was that he was making a habit of this.

He surfaced gradually, coming back into the world, with slight indifference. He opened his eyes – his left one was back to being glued shut. No doubt the figure's barrages had reopened his cut. He felt the rough ground on his cheek and saw a canal of blood flowing from his face down the alley. He jerked his head up, a rock clanking around inside it every time he moved even ever so slightly. Of course, he was alone – the figures were long gone.

He got up – his body shifted around him before his mind caught up. He had a sharp pain in his chest – a biting, grating feeling, as though something was out of place and rubbing up against something else. His legs ached and a certain point in his spine, about halfway down at the bottom of his ribcage, was on fire.

He tripped – reached out for one of the wheelie bins and used it to steady himself. He sniffed blood and was sent into uncontrollable splutters as it flowed into his mouth. He tasted pure iron.

He brought a sleeve up and ran it under his nose to

try and quell the constant bleeding. It didn't work. His sleeve just came away drenched in his own blood.

Shoulda gone home, city boy.

That gruff voice. He didn't recognise it. Could have been anyone. Literally anyone in Marsden. After all, why shouldn't he be public enemy number one now. After what had happened. Maybe he deserved it.

No, Sam said strongly in his head, *you don't get to feel sorry for yourself.*

'You're right, Sam,' he said, and then realised he was talking to no one. He needed rest – he needed to try and clean up. The Hamlet. It wasn't far. Even he, in his broken state, could get there.

He started to walk down the alley. When he stepped on his left leg, a spike of white hot fire shot up to his brain. He tried to ignore it, skating the wall of the butchers with his hand. It took longer than he would care to admit to get to the opening of the alley. When he did, he looked around, hoping against hope no one was there to see him.

No one was.

Small mercies.

He left a trail of nose blood from the alley to The Hamlet and he crashed through the doors trying to block his nose with his sleeve. He kept his head down, not wanting to see the life of the pub and any reaction to his entrance, but he couldn't help noting the deathly silence as he entered the scene.

And then a voice, familiar. 'Robin.' It was Amber.

Robin looked up to see her rush over to him.

'Robin, what happened?'

He grunted something, didn't even know what it was meant to mean himself.

'Come on, sit down.'

The scene was fluid, pulsing. He couldn't concentrate on it. Behind Amber, people were looking now. There was a family sitting at the table by the window, the table where Ethan Pack had attacked him. The Golden Retriever was there, looking at him.

'Not here,' Robin said, in a voice he didn't recognise.

'Okay.' Amber put an arm around him. 'There's no one downstairs. We'll go there.' She led him downstairs to the basement, helping him with every step. Soon, they were down, and she was helping him into a chair. Amber disappeared and Robin slid back on his chair. He lifted up his shirt to see where one of the figures had kicked him and saw that a small amount of blood was rising up under his skin. He had never been great at anatomy but he knew that that wasn't supposed to happen.

Amber came back with a bowl full of water and a cloth. She put it down on the table and pulled up a chair. 'What happened?' she said, as she dipped the cloth in the bowl.

'Couple of guys, in the alley,' Robin muttered.

'Jesus,' she said, as she put the wet cloth to Robin's forehead. It stung and he let out a gruff gasp. 'Sorry, I should have warned you.'

'Do you know what Ascend is?' Robin said.

Amber dipped the cloth back in the water. It became pink instantly. 'What?'

243

'Ascend. A church group called Ascend.'

'Yeah,' Amber said, continuing to clean him up. 'I used to run it. But that was like two years ago.'

'Were the Five there? Were they at the meetings?'

Amber put the cloth down, and looked confused. 'Yeah, they were. Now how would you know that?'

'Because each of the Five had the word Ascend tattooed on their wrists.'

Amber looked lost, utterly and genuinely lost. 'They . . . what?'

'Their wrists. Do you know why they would do that?'

'No,' Amber said, 'they would come to the meetings but they would just sit there in silence. They would never even say a word. They would just sit there and then when it was over they would leave. Sometimes they were the only people who would turn up and I would just have to sit there with them. It was bizarre, so in the end I cancelled the groups, because I didn't want to do it anymore. I didn't want to be around them. I didn't want to be around him.'

'Tim?' Robin said.

'Yeah, Tim. We . . . we didn't get on. After we . . . I didn't tell you the whole truth that first night, when we talked. Tim and I were a couple for a while. But it didn't work out. It's rather sad really. First love. You start to realise that love actually isn't the whole world, you know.'

'The cat,' Robin said. 'Was it true what he did?'

Amber's brow creased. 'Where did you hear that?'

'Benny Masterson and . . . your mother.'

244

Amber looked away, around at the room, as though she couldn't look at him. And then finally she did again. 'You talked to my mother? My mother is a fickle bitch who would say anything to make herself the victim.' Amber got up and picked up the bowl with a force that made some water splash onto the table. Amber sniffed, she was almost crying. 'When you're doing your investigating, Robin, remember that you're not just hearing stories, you're seeing into other people's lives.'

'She's your mother,' Robin said.

Amber scoffed, 'My mother can burn in hell.'

46

Amber helped him back upstairs, although he felt better from the rest. There was still an incredible pain in his ribs, and his head felt like it was pulsating up to three times it's normal size.

He hadn't known what exhaustion was until now. Every sap of energy had been kicked out of him, and every second he remained standing up seemed like a triumph.

Robin left Amber without a word, and clattered up the stairs as fast as he could, getting to his door.

He dug into his pockets, not at all surprised to find everything still there. Phone. Keys. Wallet. Of course they hadn't taken anything. That hadn't been the point. They had beaten him for Standedge. They had beaten him because he hadn't left yet. They had beaten him to send a message. He pulled out his keys and took one jab at the lock, thanking God he got the key in the lock. He was seeing about five versions of it.

He entered his room, staggering a few steps and then slipping on something on the carpet. He was momentarily airborne, before his arse connected with the floor with a sharp *whack*.

'Arrrggh,' he managed. He scooted around on the floor to see what he had slipped on. At first, he thought that someone had posted about ten paper notes under his door. No, hundreds of them – uneven and ripped. And then he saw a coloured page. It was one he knew well and he picked it up to make sure. A picture. It wasn't paper – it was stronger, and it was ripped in half. He took the two pieces and held them up next to each other. The blue cover with the pictures of her. *Without Her* by Robin Ferringham. Someone had ripped up an entire copy of his book and posted it under his door.

It was a slightly vaguer message than the beating, but still undoubtedly nothing good. Robin laughed at that, despite himself – despite everything

He got up and went into the bathroom. He didn't want to, but he forced himself to look in the mirror. He understood why Amber had winced when she looked at him. He looked like a Picasso painting – his left eye was not just stuck shut, it was swollen shut. The cut on his forehead had expanded. His cheek was scratched and bloody from where he'd scraped the ground, and his nose was a sickly kind of purple and twice its normal size. He snarled at the mirror to see that the tooth he'd lost had been one of his molars.

Not getting that back.

He laughed again, before realising nothing was funny.

He picked up the roll of toilet paper by the toilet and unrolled it about five times, until he got enough paper to last him for hours, and he balled up two bits and shoved them into his nose.

He walked out of the bathroom.

What was the time? It didn't matter.

Who were the people in the hoodies? It didn't matter.

Who ripped up a copy of his book and stuffed it under his door? It didn't matter.

What was he going to do? It didn't matter.

All that mattered now was sleep, and Robin was fast asleep before he hit the pillow.

47

He woke up, felt something hot and pleasing on his forehead. A warm flannel. He opened his eyes to see someone sitting by the bed. He jumped up and made his way to the other side of the bed before he realised who it was. It was Emma. In her smart GP suit. In his room in The Hamlet.

'Sorry,' she said, 'your friend Amber let me in. She didn't believe I was your sister at first, but when I said I was a doctor, she gave in. She said you needed one. You do need one.'

Robin breathed out, still recovering from the shock. 'What are you doing here?'

'I've come to take you home.'

'I told you I would be home soon.'

'Do you want to come back, Robin?' Emma said. 'There's nothing left for you here. You have to start to think about what you want to do with the rest of your life. You have to move on. You have to . . . let her go. You have to let Sam go.'

Robin said nothing.

'You think this is what she wants for you?' Emma said. 'You've half killed yourself. How much have you slept in the last few days?'

'Does being unconscious count?' Robin said, and absent-mindedly smiled.

'That's not funny.'

Robin got up and slid his legs over the bed. He chuckled. 'It's a little funny.'

Emma just looked at him, evidently lost for words. She looked away as though she didn't really see him anymore. She saw someone new – a stranger. 'Are you coming home?'

Robin wheezed – his breath still hitching on something in his chest. He thought of Standedge, he thought of the Five, of Sally and of Matthew, and Claypath and Amber. Could he just leave? Turn his back on all this and just return to how things were? He didn't know if he could, let alone wanted to. But then he thought of the warnings. Of the beating and of the book. And he knew what he wanted didn't really matter.

'Okay,' he said slowly and softly. 'Let's go home.'

Emma's face lit up although she was obviously trying to hide it. She got up. 'I'll get us something to eat, and then we'll go.'

Robin nodded.

She left and was back in ten minutes with two bags of chips and two bottles of water. As soon as he smelled the food, he realised he was desperately hungry. When Emma handed him a bag, he ripped into it and started eating.

Emma just watched him, barely touching hers. 'I took a look at your injuries while you were sleeping. You got beaten up pretty good. Your eye is fine, it looks worse than it is. It looks like you have swelling around your ribs, but from what I could see, I don't think they're broken. You were lucky.' Emma sighed. 'But you're fighting off a fever. That cut on your forehead's deep. Should have had stitches straight away. It might be infected.'

Robin said nothing, just unscrewed the top of the water bottle and upended the whole thing into his mouth.

Emma said nothing else, picking at her own bag of chips.

Over the next few hours, Robin finished his – lunch? dinner? – and he packed up his things. Emma helped him as much as she could, but it was still slow going. His body was seizing up, and every movement seemed to be in slow motion. Every movement seemed to require a build-up and a cooldown, as though running on a motor.

Emma seemed shocked by every move.

He didn't have much scattered around the room but he wanted to make sure he had everything. There were the important things – his notebook, his laptop. The things he could use to carry on searching for an answer. An answer to what happened to the Standedge Five. Because going home wasn't a sign of defeat. It was a tactical retreat.

'Are you ready?' Emma said, as he finished up and put his bag and backpack on the bed.

Robin slowly nodded.

This wasn't the end. Because Matthew McConnell was going to pay for how he used him. Robin Ferringham was once a man who would roll over and admit defeat, but not anymore. He swore to himself, to Sam, he was going to find that son of a bitch.

He was going to find Matthew McConnell.

48

Two months later . . .

Robin got home, anticipating the usual evening of a Pot Noodle, a television boxset and some quiet. Maybe he would spend some time in the study if he felt like it. Not that he'd felt like it in about two weeks now.

As soon as he was through the door, he threw off his company branded T-shirt. The clucking chicken on his breast always burned his skin, some kind of rash brought on by the material used, like some kind of religious torment. It symbolised his hatred well.

He'd had multiple conversations with Stan, until eventually he just stopped answering his calls. For the first few weeks, it was multiple times a day. Then it became once. Then it became a few times a week. A letter came in the post saying that he had terminated their arrangement, he couldn't represent him anymore for circumstances beyond her control. He knew what she really meant. Standedge – and his actions in Marsden. Whereas before no one had heard of the Standedge Incident, now you would be hard pressed to find a person in the whole of the British Isles who hadn't. And with the details of the Incident there was always Robin's name and how Matthew McConnell came to disappear. No one in publishing was interested in Robin Ferringham anymore, and he couldn't exactly blame them.

He kept track of the news. Loamfield was finally out of hospital, Claypath was still hanging onto his job by a thread, the Monster and McConnell were still at large. People were apparently flooding Marsden just as the locals didn't want – taking pictures by the tunnel and wanting to see the place where they disappeared into thin air.

Every day, hell, every hour practically, there was a new theory about how it had been done. There were websites dedicated to it, forums with strings of millions of comments. Some theories were outlandish – tales of lizard people and *Star Trek* beaming (stuff the Ghosts of Marsden could barely dream of), and some theories were less so – puzzles of body doubles and secret hatches. Robin let it wash over him, he couldn't avoid it but he didn't engage in it.

There was only one thing he was looking for.

He turned the kettle on for his Pot Noodle, switched on the television and used the bathroom. He surfed the channels for something to watch that definitely would not be about Standedge. He settled on an episode of *Most Haunted*, narrowly winning out to an episode of *Resident Detective*.

He started back towards the kitchen, and passed the door. He saw it out of the corner of his eye, felt the weight of the key in his pocket. He could always work instead. He turned to the door and nodded.

He made his meal, then unlocked the door, reaching in to turn on the light. The small box room lit up. This was his work, the real work, not serving stupid chicken.

The walls of the room were plastered in newspaper articles, printouts, images. All about the Standedge Five. All about Matthew McConnell. The articles about the Incident were on the right-hand wall – the things he had amassed while he was in Marsden, coupled with what had come out since. He'd cut out all the national newspapers' articles that reported on the Incident, even if they did all basically say the same thing. On the left wall, was information about the Five – social media page printouts, details of their university courses, any concrete information about where they lived and how they spent their time. Matthew McConnell took up the far wall – the wall above his desk. He had done a deep dive on the guy – found his birth certificate, school grades, property details, things like that – things that couldn't possibly be relevant, but all helped to make up a picture of the young man who used him. Robin also kept track of potential sightings – anyone who spied someone matching his description (and had something written about it online) Robin found and stuck on the wall.

He thought that doing all this would somehow un-lock something, like he was putting together pieces of a puzzle, and once he'd found them all they would all make the big picture – and that big picture would make perfect sense.

But in reality . . . it just looked like a mess – an

impressive mess. But then an impressive mess is just a bigger mess. Robin smiled at that.

He sat down at the desk, and opened his laptop. His notebook was next to it – the notebook he had used in Marsden. He hadn't touched it since leaving. He reached under the desk into a drawer and brought out a folder which was full of the information on Sam's disappearance. He hadn't been able to bring himself to put that stuff up on the wall – probably wouldn't have been able to come into this room if he did.

He opened the folder. On the first page, he'd just written – BLACK HOUND, HORSE HEAD. How many times had he searched these terms online? How many internet rabbit holes had he gone down? Were they names of pubs? Were they images, maybe pictures? Were they passcodes to something or even someone? He'd spent hours upon hours with four little words and he'd always came to the same old distressing conclusion.

It wasn't enough.

And in all probability it wasn't even real.

Matthew had made the call up. He had found out the information on Sam and he had used it to get Robin to help. Why him? Maybe because it was easy. Maybe because he had the opportunity so he took it. But after all the anger (and there was plenty) Robin came back to a couple of questions: how did Matthew know that Robin would be able to get him out of prison? And how did he know that he would be able to escape?

And that only added to even more questions – why were the Standedge Five attending the Ascend group at the church? What were they hiding from Matthew, forcing him to feel dangerously exiled? And the big one, the glorious one-million-pound question, how did he do it?

Robin closed Sam's folder and settled into the chair. He opened his Web browser and made the scan of all the usual news outlets, conspiracy sites and forums. Nothing new of note, just another ridiculous theory about mirrors and refracting light. A load of rubbish.

He rubbed his eyes and made the rounds again, looking at all the sites that even slightly referenced the Standedge Five and then looking at all the records of the sightings of Matthew McConnell scanning all the comments sections to see if anyone had any new information. This process was absolutely exhausting and he wasn't surprised when he looked at the clock and saw that three hours had gone by.

Three hours and nothing.

Zero.

Zilch.

Just the same old shit. Over and over again. Robin ate his long cold Pot Noodle and looked around the room. This was insanity – he had found absolutely nothing. Maybe it was time to give up. Maybe it was time to lock the door on this room for good.

Maybe Emma was right. He had to start to move on.

Let them go.

Let her go.

Robin found himself going to the Fives' Facebook pages. They were still up and running, basically a digital memorial at this point. He went to their 'About' pages and went down to quotes. Maybe one of the Five had something inspirational to say to send him on their way.

All Robin found were cheesy one-liners, in the vein of 'Every cloud has a silver lining.' Quotes that a teenager – someone who saw the world and thought they understood it perfectly – would find deep and poetic. But really they were just awful.

Robin stopped at Tim Claypath's page last, and his eyes wandered to the box that showed his friends. He had comparatively fewer friends than the other members of the Five. Robin had just chalked that up to Tim liking to pick and choose, but it could have been what Benny had said – he was weird. Whatever it was, it didn't really matter anymore.

But something did catch Robin's eye. A small picture in Tim's friend box, accompanied by a name he knew. Amber Crusher. She smiled out of the picture, and Robin clicked on it.

Her profile picture was just Amber's face, doing some kind of half-smile that was obviously a pose. Her profile opened on the 'About' page, although her profile was totally public so he could see her feed too. He looked down her page not really knowing what he was looking for. Nothing stood out. So he clicked on to her feed.

She hadn't used the page in a while and he wasn't surprised. The kids had deemed Facebook 'uncool' now after all – probably something to do with the fact their parents had decided it was 'cool'. The latest post was from June 2018, and was about some TV show or something. He scrolled down to see a few more posts in a similar vein, until he stopped on a picture.

His stomach dropped out of the world. His cold Pot Noodle dropped out of his hands and synthetic chicken and mushroom splashed onto the floor. He didn't hear it. He just shuffled his chair as close to the desk as he could.

Amber's picture was labelled 'NEW TATTOOS :)'. It was picture of her holding up both wrists.

She had sweatbands on. Whenever he saw her, whenever he talked to her, she had sweatbands on her wrists. Obviously, he had thought nothing of it. No reason to.

He looked at the picture, unable to wrench his eyes from it. Unable to think. His pulse was hammering his temples.

He reached out with a shaking hand and found his phone, dialling a number he didn't know he'd call again. And the images in front of him burned into his eyes.

Amber was smiling, her two wrists held up. On the left, she had a small tattoo of a dog, coloured in black. On the right, she had a silhouette of a horse from the shoulders up.

The phone kept ringing and Robin willed her to pick up.

He kept looking. Knowing what he was seeing.

Her.

A black hound.

And a horse head.

259

49

She dusted off the record player, moving all the junk off the top. Circuit boards, frayed wires, hard drives – all stuff she thought she would need but knew, in her heart of hearts, she actually wouldn't. She opened the record player lid, slipped in the Stones greatest hits, and pressed play. 'Not Fade Away' started playing and she smiled.

She cleared all the junk off the desk, just letting it fall to the floor in disgrace. One of these days she'd have to tidy up the place, but it wasn't going to be today.

The sheep announced their arrival and she went to feed them. After that she came back, and checked all the connections on her computer towers. Everything was fine, as it always was, but you had to maintain these things. One connection slides just out of place, one fuse goes, and that would be a fifth of her income gone. Some guy in Iowa mining his Bitcoin would have fallen off the drill – metaphorical drill anyhow.

She sat down at her desk, checked her email. There were more sponsorship offers – would The Red Door be interested in running banner ads for a festival in Guernsey? Would it like pop-ups for a Bingo app? An energy drink, titled simply ENERGY JUICE wanted to become the official drink of The Red Door.

She moved all the emails to the trash folder. Not interested.

The site had received an insane amount of attention since the whole 'McConnell' thing. For a news site, all news was good news, even if that did mean a possible – no, probable, killer was on the loose. Did she feel bad for her part in getting that dick out? Sure, of course, absolutely. But she also couldn't help but reap the benefits of what may have occurred now could she?

She flicked her mouse, clicking on the site stats. Still going up and up. Every outlet on this big stupid island was reporting about the Standedge Five now, but she was still the original, the OG. You couldn't pay for that kind of luck.

Her phone started to ring, the tone layering over 'Get Off Of My Cloud' in a not displeasing way. It could make for a nice remix even. She looked around herself. She couldn't see it. She listened, trying to pinpoint it.

It was somewhere in the pile of junk under the record player. She cursed – of course. She bent down and started rummaging through the pile of broken hardware. Until she finally found her phone lighting up with a call. It was Robin.

She picked it up. She hadn't talked to Robin since that day on the bench. In all reality, she didn't think she would ever hear from him again. She went to press the green button.

'I wouldn't do that if I were you.'

She looked around. There was someone standing in the doorway. She could only see the figure through the filing shelf. She put the phone in her pocket and walked out from behind the shelf, to see a girl, a familiar girl with something shiny in her hand.

'Well, hello there.' The ringing stopped in her pocket. She put up her hands. 'Did you knock? I'm pretty sure my front door was locked. Usually that's a pretty clear indication that . . .'

'Who was it? On the phone,' Amber said, thrusting the barrel of the thing at her. She wasn't exactly holding the gun like she knew how to use it. She wondered where the barmaid had got it – it looked like an old revolver, probably took standard bullets. Probably plucked from the Deep Web. 'Was it Ferringham?'

'I don't think I have to answer that.'

'Just answer the question. Can't you see I have a gun?'

She smiled. 'Pretty hard to miss, Polly. But you're holding it like they do in the movies, not like real life. You need to move your bottom two fingers otherwise they might get broken when that bastard recoils. Did you even check the safety's off? This is all presuming that you are actually intending to fire it, of course.'

'Shut up,' Amber shouted but looked uncertainly at the gun in her hand. She didn't have a clue. 'He wants to see you. I have to take you to him.'

'Why don't you just put down the gun? And I promise, I'll come voluntarily.'

'I know who you are,' Amber said, far from putting down the gun. 'I know who you really are.'

262

'Well, you could have just asked,' she said, waving her hands. 'Not like I'm trying to hide it. I mean, God, there's been plenty of hints.' She looked in her periphery. There was a spanner on the desk by her – wouldn't do much – but next to it, yes, next to it was a hammer. That would do nicely. She took a miniscule step towards it – a few more and she'd be able to make a grab for it. Amber would hesitate at pulling the trigger, weighing up the ramifications of what she was about to do. But she eventually would pull it, because she wouldn't be able to deal with what would happen if she didn't pull it.

Amber didn't seem to notice the move. 'You're going to have to come with me now, "Sally".' She said it all twee-like, like she was a character in some kids show. She was most definitely not.

'Where are we going?' Another. Little. Step. 'Who is "he"?'

'What does it matter to you?' Amber said, brandishing the gun.

She smiled. Another step. 'Just want to know if I should pack a picnic.'

Amber didn't smile. But her eyes alighted on something. She had seen. Damn it – she had seen the hammer. 'Back up. Don't you dare move for that hammer. I will shoot you.'

She waved her hands airily. 'You're not going to shoot me, Polly Pocket. Now why don't we . . .'

Amber shot her.

She looked down to see blood blossoming on her stomach through her white tank top.

'I really didn't want to do that,' Amber said plainly, her demeanour changing as easily as putting on a hat. 'You're such a stubborn bitch.'

She sank to her knees in front of Amber, clutching her stomach.

'No, no, no, I'm afraid you can't rest. We have a walk ahead of us.' Amber put the gun in her wasitband, and hoisted her up.

'Where are we going?' she said through the pain.

Amber smiled. 'We're going to the end.'

50

Robin tried Sally again and again but she wasn't answering. It rang and rang, and then one time when he tried it went straight to voicemail, and did that every time after. Where was she? He had to tell her about Amber, he had to do something . . . and being in London wasn't going to help anything.

Amber was with Sam when she had called Matthew? What did that mean? He knew what he thought it meant but didn't want to glorify it by thinking it.

He quickly made a decision. He had to go back. He stumbled out of the room, grabbing his empty backpack and shoving in only the essentials. A change of clothes. A jacket. After a moment's thought, he also shoved in his laptop and his notebook. And then the folder he had on Sam.

Thoughts rushed his head – none making any real sense. Amber hurt Sam? Matthew found out? Was Matthew helping Amber, or was Amber helping Matthew? The phone call was a great way to get Robin to help. But why would Matthew enlist Robin, if he knew he could find out what happened? And where did the disappearance of the Standedge Five fit into any of that?

It didn't fit together. He felt like he was mashing together two puzzle pieces that had no business being together. He needed more pieces, and he wasn't going to find them in London. He needed to be in Marsden five minutes ago.

He practically flew out of his flat and onto the street. He started walking towards the bus stop to get to the station but it was all too slow. The bus would take half an hour, the train would take three hours with the change he'd have to make. It wasn't fast enough. No way. But what was the alternative?

He reached into his pocket and brought out his bunch of keys. He settled on a car key. Could he –? Emma had given him a spare to her car. It'd be at the surgery about fifteen minutes' walk away.

He started off towards the centre of Islington, dialling Emma's number. He knew she wouldn't pick up – she had surgery until late on a Thursday – but knew it would make him feel better to try.

He got to the surgery ten minutes later, walking so fast that his legs were aching and the healing cut on his forehead was throbbing as hard as it had when he was in Standedge, just after the attack. The car park was small, and he located Emma's Subaru easily. He'd only driven it once, but knew he'd be fine once he got the hang of it.

He unlocked it and slung his bag inside, slinging himself in after it. He turned the keys and the engine roared into life. He put it in reverse and the car lurched backwards. He pulled away and into the busy London street, the car buckling somewhat under his quick gear changes.

But it didn't matter.

He was on his way.

51

He got to Marsden just before nightfall, lurching into the station car park and shutting off the engine. He'd just had a very heated conversation with Emma, who, upon finding her car missing had checked the CCTV and seen him take it. Robin didn't tell her much, knowing she wouldn't understand, he just told her that he was sorry for taking the car without asking and that he would be home soon. Emma was no less angry with this assurance, but he thought, somewhat funnily, that she couldn't really do much to stop him. She couldn't exactly come get him again, not without a car.

Robin ended up hanging up, knowing that when everything was said and done Emma would understand and forgive him. And she would also understand that right at this moment, she was not Robin's biggest worry.

He put his backpack on and started down the road to The Hamlet. Then he stopped. He could go and confront Amber with what he knew and make a big mess of it, or he could be more tactical about it. He needed backup, and didn't Sally fit the bill perfectly?

He cut down the houses on the road to the woods,

and The Red Door, going as fast as his aching legs would carry him. He was through the treeline before he knew it, and was instantly surprised by a duet of 'baa's. The two sheep were standing by a tree watching him, greeting him as though he'd never left. He ignored them and kept going until he found the hill at which Sally's shack was at the bottom.

He ran down the hill and rounded the mound of bushes and leaves to enter The Red Door. He stopped, confronted by the imposing door. But something was wrong. The door stood ajar. He knew Sally would never leave it like that, not with her attitude let alone how much expensive hardware there was in there.

He pushed open the door, bypassing the kitchen and entering the hallway. There was the familiar blue glow of the screens emanating from the door.

'Sally,' he called, but no one answered, unless the distant 'baa' of the sheep who had followed him closely on his journey counted. 'Sally.'

Nothing, but the low hum of electronics.

He pushed open the door to her office. The shelving unit in the centre of the room had fallen down spilling everything out onto the floor on top of the bundles of cables. The result looked like a recycling tip. He would've said it was signs of a struggle – if he didn't know Sally, and know that she could've easily just done that herself in a fit of rage.

He picked his way through the crap as best as he could towards the monitors. The Red Door was there, five times all over the wall. It looked like Sally was working on a new article – 'THE BEST STANDEDGE THEORY SO FAR' was the title. But there was no text to the article – not yet anyhow. There was just a photo – an incredibly low quality and bright snap of something he couldn't really comprehend. Something up against rock and damp – it looked like the inside of the tunnel. The subject of the photo was a red sheet of metal, with holes in the . . .

The Monster's hideaway. It was a photo of the 'doors' from the Monster's hideaway. But what did it mean? And how could that possibly . . .

He started to think – yes, but no, but *yes*. Maybe . . .

He waved away what he was thinking. It wasn't the most pressing thing right now. The most pressing thing was finding Sally.

He stepped towards the desk again, and his foot clunked against something. He looked down to see a hammer lying on the floor. He picked it up, turning it over in his hands. Wasn't exactly out of place. He put it down on the desk and . . . Saw it.

There was a bloody handprint on the desk. It was fresh, still glistening. Was this Sally's blood?

He looked down at the floor, and this time saw a small trickle of blood going across the wires, leading to the door. Like someone had been moved across them. He jumped across all the rubbish to the door again.

If this was Sally's blood, that meant she was hurt. That meant she was very, very hurt. And if she was hurt, did that mean someone else had been here? Someone who had attacked her? Maybe. He wondered if that person was still around, or if they had taken Sally somewhere? That seemed more likely. How was he going to find out where? Did it have something to do with the article Sally was writing?

He couldn't know for sure.

He followed the trail of blood into the hall. It was so slight he wasn't surprised he missed it when he had first come through here. It led into the kitchen, and then . . .

It stopped. The trail completely stopped, went cold. With one final outburst of blood, a bigger splat than the rest, it was gone. Like someone had noticed the trail and stopped it.

Robin kicked the fridge in anger.

What if Sally needed him? What if she was really hurt? And he was standing here, not knowing what the hell to do.

Calm down, Sam said, in his head, soothingly. *Keep your head now. You're going to need it.*

'I can't do this,' he said, 'I'm not some kind of action hero. I'm not some kind of detective.'

Suck it up, pard'ner. Doubt isn't sexy. Self-doubt even less so.

Robin nodded. He knew he had to. No one else was going to do it for him. 'Where are you, Sally?' he said, to Sam, to Sally, but mostly to himself. 'Where are you? Just tell me where you are.' He turned round and round in the room, until his eyes fell beside the eponymous red door.

There was something there. Something etched there. In red.

271

Well, would you look at that? Sam said. *Looks like you have somewhere to be.*

Robin stepped towards the door, got out his phone and shone a light on the marking there. Sally was sending him a message.

A long vertical line in blood. And at the top, a crude M.

In the same style as the map.

Sally was being taken to the Marsden side of Standedge.

52

Robin got to Standedge just as the sun disappeared. He crossed the bridge so he was on the opposite side to the Visitor Centre, and without thinking, hopped the fence into the field that ran parallel. He turned his torch on and looked around, making his way across the field.

Sally and whoever had Sally were in the disused railway tunnels. And the only way to get inside would be the hole. He had a long walk ahead of him. There was a 'baa' behind him, and he turned to see that inexplicably the sheep had followed him.

'Shoo,' he said.

They looked at each other and took more steps towards him.

He cursed at them, and then turned his back on them, walking across the field and cresting another waist-high fence emerging from the trees that lined the field.

His feet crunched on gravel and he looked up to see that he was standing next to the Marsden entrance of the disused railway tunnels. It looked almost identical to the Diggle end, with the two tunnels fenced off, a camera looking down at him and a concrete floor running along the fence.

He pointed his torch through the mouth of the right tunnel but saw nothing in the immediate vicinity. He walked adjacent to the tunnels, skimming the fence and started to crunch through the undergrowth that ran alongside it.

Another 'baa' came out.

He whirled around, unreasonably angry. The two sheep were standing in front of the right tunnel, looking through the fence. 'Please, just go home. Go back to The Red Door.' The sheep looked at him, blankly. 'Go back to The Red Door. The. Red. Door.' And then he caught himself, 'Jesus Christ, I'm talking to sheep.'

One of the sheep responded by taking a hoof and patting the fence. It squealed open.

Robin was taken aback. He crunched out of the undergrowth and up to the sheep. The fence's padlock was lying on the ground, and there was a mound of something – dead leaves and wheat and other things. The sheep bent down and ate some.

That's why the sheep had been following. Sally had been scattering food along the path. 'Just in case I didn't get the message, huh?' Robin said, and the sheep 'baa'd in agreement. 'Who do you think she has more faith in?' he asked them.

The sheep looked at him. They all knew the answer.

Robin patted the sheep, stepping through the fence into the railway tunnel, shutting it tight so they couldn't follow. They gave out their call again and Robin nodded, before turning into the tunnel and walking into darkness.

53

He trudged up the tunnel, trying to make as little sound as possible. He listened out for anything, but there was nothing particularly to note. Nothing to tell him that there was anyone else in the tunnel with him. Again, there was the soft thumping sounds of something he couldn't quite pinpoint. There was the dripping of water into more water – the dampness of the tunnel was just as off-putting as he remembered it.

As before, he followed the railway tracks as best as he could, stepping over the old sleepers with care.

He kept the torch in front of him, trying to shake the feeling that he was willingly walking into the lion's den. Maybe that feeling would have been easier to deal with if it was accompanied by a rather sizable one of being watched.

He thought he heard something crunch behind him and wheeled around to see . . . nothing. Sound was so odd in the tunnel, he felt like he could have been hearing something a mile away or something right behind him.

He turned back, finding he had to brace himself before he held the torch up again. Nothing in front of him, nothing behind.

Just a lovely walk inside a creepy old tunnel.

He moved forward again wondering if he should call out for Sally. He couldn't bring himself to. So he just walked.

It was another ten minutes before his light fell on something. There was a mass in the middle of the tunnel, lying across the train tracks. He started forward, before a figure appeared in his torchlight. A man – it had to be him. It had to be Matthew. He wasn't looking at Robin – hadn't even noticed the torchlight. He seemed to be operating in complete darkness. He turned the mass over and pressed a towel to its stomach.

It was Sally.

Suddenly Robin couldn't control himself. He saw red. 'McConnell?' he shouted, all the rage in his body in his voice.

Matthew turned around. But as he walked into the torchlight, Robin saw that it wasn't Matthew.

But – no . . .

That was impossible.

The figure smiled. And Robin shone his torch at the figure. The face of a bearded Tim Claypath.

'What?' Robin said, and suddenly heard someone behind him. There was an explosion of pain in the back of his head.

The last thing he remembered was Tim Claypath's laugh.

Everything else was lost to the white.

54

Three years ago . . .

T. CLAYPATH – Okay, you lot, the basement of The Hamlet tonight. I fancy getting plastered!

E. SUNDERLAND – Count me in. I haven't gotten plastered since I did up the guest room.

P. PACK – The fabulous Edmund Sunderland at the London Palladium everyone! He's a laugh a fortnight. (Also, I'm in! ☺)

T. CLAYPATH – Then we can always move on to Hudders if we fancy a dance??

P. PACK – Oh dear, is it dance time???

T. CLAYPATH – It's always dance time!!! Am I right??

R. CLAYPATH – Well, I'm sat next to Tim but for the benefit of everyone else, I have graciously accepted his invitation.

R. FROST – Let's go! I need to blow some steam off, trying to get this uni application sorted. Anyone know the difference between City University London and the City of London University?

T. CLAYPATH – Okay 5/6, what'd you say, Matt? Wanna make it a full house?

M. McCONNELL – I can't. I have the Canals Trust

interview tomorrow, and I've got a ton of facts to memorise.

R. CLAYPATH – Oh I forgot . . .

E. SUNDERLAND – Seconded.

T. CLAYPATH – No way you can get out of it?

T. CLAYPATH – Jk. Knock 'em dead, man.

T. CLAYPATH – We'll have to drink your share.

R. CLAYPATH – Good luck, Matt!

E. SUNDERLAND – Seconded.

P. PACK – GL

R. FROST – You've got this!

M. McCONNELL – Thanks, guys :)

M. McCONNELL – Have a good night!

55

Three years ago . . .

Samantha Ferringham got off the train, trailing her case behind her. She checked her watch, thought about getting a taxi to her hotel, and then decided she would walk. Despite requesting a table seat on the train, she had found she had been given a squished up seat next to the window, and when she had work to do, it wasn't ideal. She had to balance her laptop on the small tray table and strain down to see the screen. Therefore, she felt the walk would probably do her good, allowing her to stretch her aching legs. And besides, her phone said the hotel was only a mile away from the station, even if it did look to be out in the sticks a little.

Before she set off, she tried to call Robin. It went to voicemail. He was probably still agonising over his article, so she decided to try again when she got to the hotel.

She started walking away from the centre of Huddersfield, following the blue line on the map on her phone. She checked her watch – it had got dark a lot quicker than she had expected and she didn't really have anything to make her visible on the narrow winding roads she was going to have to traverse. She pressed on though, deciding that if it got too dark she would turn on the torch on the back of her phone.

Her thoughts were awash with things she had to do. With the restricted words per minute achieved from awkwardly placed limbs on the train, she still had to finish the worksheets she was compiling for the seminar. But then that was why she had padded out the trip with an extra day. Tomorrow, she planned to go to the University to talk with the staff there and the rest of the day would be free for work. She always liked to go in to introduce herself early, to observe where she was going to be lecturing and to get the lay of the land. She had never been to Huddersfield Uni before, and she didn't want to do something stupid like turn up late to her own seminar.

It started to get darker, and she checked her phone. She would call Robin when she got to the hotel – he worried if she didn't. When you met someone like Robin – someone who was so completely what you wanted – you wanted to share everything with them. When she and Robin married it wasn't only the happiest day of her life, but she knew it would be the happiest she would ever be.

But if all one strived for in life was love, then the world would only be half of what it was. It'd be filled with sonatas and films and books and plays, with little innovation, little consequence, little conquest. Beings were made to multiply, humans were made to thrive. Sam loved being a travelling professor, lecturing up and down the country – meeting people and teaching them about Psychology. Maybe it was because she learned from the best herself, and maybe it was because the subject fascinated her – and the more she worked, the more she studied, the more she found out, she just grew more and more curious. Human behaviour was so incredibly complex, and it was different for everyone. Sometimes, in her most academic moments, she thought of the seven billion case studies walking around out there – each totally different, each forever changing. By the time you'd have finished a case study, it would be outdated. 'A person going to bed wasn't the same person who woke up,' her mentor had said – a warm and brilliant old man called Simon Winter. That quote was what had drawn her in further to Psychology, and cemented the fact that she was going to dedicate her life to it. 'Always look close enough to examine a subject,' Dr Winter had said, 'but never look too close to fall in.' She supposed that was what happened with her and Robin. She had fallen in to him – and she wasn't coming out, not that she wanted to.

She got to the end of the street lights – the roads she was going to have to traverse from here on would be pitch black. The winding narrow road she was going to have to take seemed a little narrower and winding than she seemed happy about. She wondered whether she should turn back and get a taxi, but there were no taxis on the street she was on, and she'd have to retrace her steps. That seemed a little bit too much like admitting defeat, so she pressed on.

A little hiking wouldn't kill her.

56

Three years ago . . .

They went dancing. Well, that was kind of an oversimplification. Tim had somehow convinced them all that dancing was in their futures, that dancing was inevitable, that going to the Huddersfield Brickwork was destiny. What's more – it was their destiny for Edmund to drive because he had only had two pints and Tim didn't want to wait around for a taxi.

So Edmund drove and he didn't drink too much more at the Brickwork and walking back to the car at thirteen minutes past one in the morning, Edmund assessed how drunk he was. He'd had three pints (including the two at The Hamlet) and three shots that Tim had practically forced down his throat. He was over the limit, there was zero doubt about that and even zero-er (was that a word?) chance that if he got caught, he would get his licence taken away from him, but he thought he could manage getting the five of them home. Putting on the blowers in the car and playing some loud music would do wonders. He wasn't a big drinker usually so he was feeling the effects a bit more than a heavy drinker would have. It was the shots that were getting at him. He was halfway drunk. Every time he turned his head, it took a few seconds for his eyes to catch up. But you didn't really whirl your head round when you were driving, and Edmund was a damn good driver.

This would be his first real foray into the criminal circle. But then if no one knew, then no one knew. Who was to say he was over the limit, when no one was around to clarify. Maybe he somehow wasn't over the limit – there was no way he could know for sure. And it wasn't as if there'd be any police around anyway. The stretch between Marsden and Huddersfield was practically a ghost town. Sections of it didn't even have street lights, for God's sake, let alone cameras. They would be absolutely fine.

His skills whilst drunk, playing video games anyway, were unparalleled. One time, the group had got themselves shitfaced and challenged each other to competitive *Surgeon Simulator* – basically a motion controlled digital game of *Operation*. Edmund had won comfortably and he'd been way further gone than he was now. He got the ruptured spleen out and the funny bone without even breaking a sweat. Super chill-like! He was going to do it – had to really, if he backed down the five of them would be stranded in Huddersfield, and Tim would never let him hear the end of it.

Edmund picked up the pace and caught up with the others. None of them would have any objection to Edmund driving. They were all too far along to voice any kind of issue. Tim had bought even more shots for them, as if he was at least trying to keep Edmund in an acceptable frame of mind.

Edmund thought that the flashing lights and the loud music had probably affected him more than the drink. He was brewing a hell of a migraine, and wanted to get home and to bed as quickly as possible. And the car was the best way to make that happen.

The five of them rounded the corner to the car park and at the sight of the car, Robert and Tim cheered. 'Shotguns,' Tim said and laughed, even though no one would have ever attempted to take the passenger seat. It seemed to be an unwritten rule that it belonged to Tim, and if Tim was driving, it belonged to Edmund.

Tim broke out in a haphazard run to the car, while the others laughed at his jerky movements. Robert and Pru were having a hushed conversation to each other, and Rachel was busy fiddling with something in her bag. No one saw Edmund stop and take a set of slow deep breaths.

He could do this, he'd driven for hundreds of hours in his life and never got so much as a speeding ticket. He didn't even think anyone had ever beeped him.

He started towards the car.

What was the worst that could happen?

57

Three years ago . . .

The future was dictated by an infinite number of variables. You could never predict the future because of this. And that was why the future was exciting. That was why people went on living – went outside and just didn't give up and stay in bed. No one could even start to list the variables that led her, Samantha Ferringham, to that winding road that night.

Who knew when it was decided that she'd be here? Firstly, it was her decision to walk to the hotel. Then, it was her decision to get the late train. Then, it was her decision to come to Huddersfield a day early. Before it was her decision to take the job lecturing at Huddersfield Uni. Going further back, she had to travel to Huddersfield because of her decision to live in London. And that was because of her decision to say 'yes' to marrying Robin. And she met Robin because she decided to go to Emma Ferringham's party at her house. There, the celestial red thread split even more – what possessed Emma Ferringham (her GP) to invite her to that party? What drove her to that meeting with Emma in that hardware store, where they struck up an unlikely friendship?

These strands wove a tapestry of a life. A tapestry no one would see. It would hang in the Museum of the Higher-Ups, the destiny makers – if there was such a thing. She didn't believe in that – of course she didn't. She was a psychologist. But sometimes, when her mind wandered, and she was over-worked, it was warm to feel that everything was mapped out.

She guided her torchlight down the road. The blue line of Google Maps said she was almost there, maybe one more hill and she'd be able to see the hotel. The road she was walking on was very remote – there were no signs of life anywhere. Looking back, she could see the sprawling lights of Huddersfield, but they were far enough away to feel like they were in a different world.

Variables. A game of dominoes. Not always a game you wanted to win. And as she started to see the failing light of her torch, and wondered which variable was responsible for her forgetting to charge her phone before she had embarked on her trip. If she knew which one it was, she would curse it until she ran out of curses. Because her phone died and she was plunged into darkness.

Obviously running the torch and the Google Maps app at the same time was too much for her phone. The blue line had been following the road, so all she had to do was continue onwards. Soon enough, she would be at the hotel, with light, comfortable beds and, most importantly, wi-fi and power outlets. She would be able to sleep, plan her lecture and charge her phone all at the same time. This was what compelled her forward. That and the fact that turning back now would take twice as long.

In the pitch black she felt comfort in feeling the road beneath her feet. The silence of the surroundings also. She heard some chirping of birds who should almost definitely be asleep by now, and some rustling of leaves as though the night-time creatures were waking up.

She continued walking, with only the light of the moon to guide her, thinking that she had almost definitely walked as far as the Maps had told her it was to the hotel. And then she heard another sound. The sound of a motor growing louder and louder. She couldn't tell if it was just some joyrider in Huddersfield gunning it way too hard, or if it was a vehicle actually approaching. A few seconds more and she decided it was the latter.

Okay, Google Maps screwed her over. She would flag down the car and ask if they knew where the hotel was and if she could get dropped off there. She stuck her thumb out in the direction she thought was the road, because she had only seen hitchhiking in films and that was how you did it, right?

The motor sound grew louder and she looked for the car's lights, but there were no lights. Still the sound grew louder and louder. And eventually, she felt the presence of something – something coming at her fast and strong. She realised what was happening a second too late.

An indescribable pain in her side. She was whisked off her feet. And then her forehead crunched against something sharp and spiky. She felt her forehead glisten with running liquid.

And then she was flung. The world turned over like she was in a washing machine. Over and over and over and over. It was as if she was spiralling forever – and she wondered what was happening. What had hit her? And what was she doing? Where was she? Who was she? There was only one constant – the face of a kind and sheepish man, with dots of stubble and electric eyes who had once came up to her at a party and asked her to dance. His name was –

The ground – which somehow was above her – came to meet her. And the last thing she heard was a phenomenal crunch before the pain sent her under.

58

Three years earlier . . .

They sat there, not believing what had just happened. It couldn't have, right? This was fantasy. Things like this didn't happen in real life. Things like this didn't happen to them. Edmund was visibly shaking, and gagging on his tongue. Tim sat as still as he ever had in the passenger seat, shaken. In the back seat, Pru had buried herself in Rachel's shoulder, silently sobbing. Robert was speechless and had closed his eyes as if that would help.

The windscreen was smeared with blood.

They sat there, staring out of the cracked windscreen, seeing only the ground in the path of the car headlights. All of their thoughts were muddled, indecipherable – but the one thing they were all thinking – 'I hope it was a deer.'

'Oh God.' Pru gave a muffled wail into Rachel's shoulder.

They had all sobered up in an instant. They had never felt less drunk.

'It was an animal. Don't worry,' Tim said, 'It was an animal, right?' To Edmund.

Edmund didn't respond. He just kept looking ahead.

He knew it wasn't an animal. He was going too fast. He had just wanted to get home, go to sleep, carry on his life. He wanted to go to university, find a girl, get married, have kids. And now all that was gone. Because he had been going about twenty miles an hour too fast. And he hadn't seen her. She had pretty much been invisible – no light, no sound, no sense she was there. She hadn't even screamed when he'd hit her. She was mute, and now she had landed behind the car, ten or twenty metres behind them. And it was his fault.

His future evaporated in front of his eyes. He almost reached out for it, trying to grab it, but it disappeared like breath on a mirror.

'Holy shit, Ed,' Robert said, opening his eyes. He sounded smaller than he ever had. 'What the hell have you done?'

'Hey, shut up,' Tim said, 'it was an animal. Okay? We're fine.'

'No, but shit,' Robert said, and he opened his door. And went out into the night.

Edmund was roused by the sound. They couldn't see it – her – not before him anyway. He needed that, to see her. Edmund took a shaky hand and fumbled with the car door handle. Tim reached out to put a hand on his shoulder but Edmund was out of the car before he made contact.

The night whipped around him, the wind icy cold. He knew he was crying because two tracks down his face felt freezing. On legs far more uncertain than before he had got in the car, he ran after Robert. Somewhere, he still hoped that he had mistaken an animal for a person, but as soon as he found his phone in his pocket, pulled it out and turned the torch on, that thought was dashed.

Robert saw her, and started to gag.

Edmund beat him to it, rushing over to the grass verge and throwing up the contents of his stomach, which at this point was mostly liquid. He forced himself to look at her. A woman lay there in the wake of his car. She was in a dark blue raincoat, her head to the side, bleeding onto the road. Her limbs were all strangely placed as though she were a marionette puppet someone had put down carelessly. Her left leg was jutting out at an angle that couldn't be possible.

'We're screwed,' Robert said, his eyes clapped on her. 'We're shitting screwed. Look at it. I mean. Look at her. It's over. We're screwed.'

Edmund suddenly felt white hot anger, and launched himself at Robert. Robert was taken unawares and went sprawling on the road. Edmund scrambled after him and knelt over him. He got Robert by the scruff of the neck and pulled his face to his. 'You're thinking about us? You slimy little shit. We just ran someone over and you're thinking about us?'

'From where I was sitting,' Robert spat, 'I think it was you who ran her over.'

Edmund saw red, and raised a fist to him, fully intending to bring it down with as much force as he could. But then Tim was grasping him by the shoulders, and pulling him up off Robert.

'Oh my God.' Rachel.

'What have we done?' Pru.

Edmund looked around. They were all there, standing far enough from the woman to accept it may be a mirage, but close enough to really know that it wasn't. Edmund couldn't think. It was as if his mind had seized up and thoughts actively hurt.

'Is she dead?' Someone. Pru, he thought. He couldn't look away from the woman.

'She has a suitcase,' Rachel said, gesturing with an uncertain hand past the body. A suitcase was lying, slightly exploded, leaking clothes onto the ground.

Tim stepped forward, closer to her.

'What are you doing?' Robert said, who was awkwardly getting up from the road.

'Someone has to check,' Tim said, almost calmly. 'If she's still alive, we have to get her to a hospital.' Tim walked to her, crossing the scene into reality. The woman's face was mercifully pointed away from them, but now Tim's eyes lit up (not in a good way) as he rounded her and looked down upon her in all her rotten glory. 'Jesus,' he muttered. He crouched down and took a finger and placed it on her neck.

That moment seemed to last forever. Edmund watched as Tim waited, his finger perched under her chin. Edmund hoped against hope. This couldn't be happening. He had so much he was going to achieve. He would lose the world and the world would lose him.

Tim withdrew his hand and stood up. 'She's dead.'

A fresh sob escaped Pru, Robert let out a distinct moan, and Edmund's world started to spin. Only Tim and Rachel remained totally silent, regarding each other in the way they often did. They were having a silent conversation, communicating in the way only twins could do.

Edmund's legs failed him, and he fell backwards onto his arse with a *whump*. Dead. She was dead. He had run over someone and she was dead. He was a murderer. He clawed his way to the roadside and threw up again. There was nothing anymore. What happened in that split second would define him forever. A slight slip in concentration and a life was gone, and another life was ruined. What was he going to do now? Wherever could he go? He would forever be the man who killed a woman while he was drunk.

'Get up,' Tim said, and Edmund looked up. Tim was standing over him with his hand outstretched. The same hand he had used to touch the woman. Edmund shook his head, so Tim reached out and grabbed him by the wrist and pulled him to a standing position again. 'Keep it together.'

Edmund scoffed. 'Keep it together? Don't you get what's just happened? Or are you still five parts pissed?'

Tim breathed in and out. He exuded a sense of silence and calmness that was almost infectious. 'I know what happened. And I'm sorry it did. But we need to think about what happens now? And we need to think quickly. This road is hardly the busiest ever, but someone'll be along sooner or later.'

'What the hell are you talking about?' Robert said.

'What happens now?' Pru said, breaking away from

Rachel. 'What happens now? Edmund just ran someone over. He's like three times over the limit, and we let him drive. We're all culpable. What happens now is we all go to prison for a very long time.'

'What?' Robert said. 'It was Edmund driving, not us.'

'Shut up, you idiot,' Edmund said.

'Yeah, you're right, Robert,' Pru said. 'But you didn't exactly stop him driving, did you? You were happy to let him drive when you just wanted to get home.'

'We're all in this together,' Rachel said.

'Yes,' Robert said, rounding on Edmund, 'but some of us are more in it than others.'

Tim stepped between them, and shoved Robert away. 'We can't start turning on each other. We all wanted Ed to drive us, which means we all . . . have blood on our hands. What we need to think about is how we want this to play out. Do we really want this to be the end? Because it will be. This will be the end for all of us. Whatever our hopes, whatever our dreams, none of that matters anymore. Because a woman thought it was wise to walk on a narrow country road without any light or distinction as to where she was placed. You understand?'

Rachel nodded. But she seemed the only one who got it.

'What the hell are you talking about, Tim?' Pru said, throwing her hands towards the woman on the ground. She wasn't a person anymore, she was a dead body. 'Don't you understand the shit that's coming out of your mouth? This is serious.'

Tim looked around at her. 'I know it's serious. And

I promise you I'm meeting it with an equal amount of sincerity.'

'Sincerity,' Robert said, 'or insanity?'

Tim wheeled around to him. 'I've found that sometimes they're the same thing.'

Edmund stepped forward to meet Tim. 'Tim, I understand what you're trying to say, but this happened. And we're not criminals – at least not deliberate ones. I don't know what you're planning, but I don't think we can ignore this – I can't ignore this. I killed that woman, and that's going to be with me forever. I have to turn myself in, and I have to face the consequences. And even then, I don't know how I'm going to live with myself.'

Tim looked at them all in turn, stopping on Rachel. Rachel went to Edmund and took him aside. Tim gathered the other two together and started talking in a hushed tone that Edmund couldn't hear.

Rachel hugged him tight. And Edmund thought he could live within that embrace forever. But it was over all too soon. 'Ed,' she said, keeping hold of his arms so they were still close. 'You're one of the kindest and softest people I've ever met. You're not a killer. What happened here was an accident – a phenomenally tragic accident. But is it really worth ruining our lives over?'

Edmund couldn't believe what she was saying. 'You're mad. Both of you. You and Tim. Someone just died. I killed them. And you were there, too. You saw it, you felt it. You felt our hearts break. There's no way back from this. There's no way back from what we did.'

'But what if there was?' Rachel said. 'Would you take it?'

'I already said,' Edmund replied. '*No!* We need to call the police.'

'Ed, think about your life. Think about our lives. Think of all we could attain, think of all the good we could do. We can be assets to society. I'm going to be a psychologist because I want to help people. You and Tim are going to be physicists, running intellectual rings around all of us. Pru's going to build things we could never dream of and Robert's going to write things we could never fathom. We will be citizens who give so much.

'And this, this was a terrible thing. But is it really enough to throw that all away? It'd be the world's loss, her and us.' Hadn't he thought that exact thing a few minutes ago? 'Only one person needs to die out of this, not all of us. And it'll be hard, it'll be so hard, Ed, but then what isn't? We can still rebuild something for ourselves out of this, and I'm so sorry for her, that she died, but Tim's right, she was walking along this road without any reflective gear or lights on her. Not all the blame is on you, on us. Some of it lies with her too. And don't forget about it just because she's not here to face the music.'

Edmund felt tears gush down his cheeks. And Rachel hugged him again, even harder this time. 'You're one of the greatest people I know, Edmund Sunderland,' she whispered in his ear. 'Please, don't leave me.' And she shifted in his embrace, before kissing him on the lips. And that was that. Edmund was lost to her. She pulled away, and ran a finger across Edmund's cheeks, wiping away the tears. 'Okay?'

Edmund still couldn't speak. He was concentrating on trying not to cry anymore in front of her. He couldn't understand how she wasn't. But that's because she was stronger than him – they always had been, the Claypath twins. They were always people to look up to. And now they were offering a version of the future that didn't completely unravel. Who would say no? He slowly nodded.

Rachel smiled, against all of the odds. And she held his hand and guided him back to the others. Tim was looking at the woman, and Pru and Robert seemed to be quietly squabbling. They hushed as they saw Rachel and Edmund rejoin them.

'So what's the plan?' Rachel said.

'He's nuts,' Pru said, gesturing to Tim. 'He's stark raving mad.'

'So, the plan?' Rachel said.

'I agree, an absolute idiot,' said Robert.

'Shut up,' Rachel said, letting go of Edmund's hand and holding her own up to silence Pru and Robert. 'Now, what is the plan?'

'The Hamlet,' Tim said, walking up to them. 'We need somewhere to take her, to think about what we are going to do, make a more final decision.'

'How are we going to get into The Hamlet, Einstein?' Robert said, a little too loudly.

'Amber,' Tim said, softly.

'What?' said about three of them at once. It didn't really matter which ones.

Tim just looked at them all in turn.

Robert threw up his hands. 'That's pretty bloody psycho, Tim.'

'Is it?' Tim said.

'Yes, it is,' Robert said, finally.

'Let's just hear him out, okay,' Rachel said, 'Tim, please, what's your plan?'

Tim nodded, grateful that she was there and then feeling guilty about it. 'Amber's staying at The Hamlet. The Acker family are away and entrusted the keys to her so she could feed the hamster. She decided she might as well just stay there instead. She'll help us. She'll give us shelter, give us a place to hide the body, until we figure this out together. Because right now, that's all we have.'

'We really want to bring her into this?' Robert said. 'I mean, I know we're not the Scooby Doo gang, but she isn't exactly part of the group, is she? How do we know that bitch won't turn us in the first chance she gets?'

'Because she's obsessed with me,' Tim said bluntly. 'And, I'm sorry, but right now, we have to use that.'

Pru scoffed. 'Taking Little Miss Loved Up out of the equation, are we really going to reward The Hamlet — our favourite place in the entire world — by bringing a dead body into it?'

'Does anyone have a better idea?' Tim said, and they all shook their heads in turn – even Pru. 'Right, she has a suitcase so we can assume that she was coming from the station. That means she doesn't live here. So that means no one's going to be looking for her, at least not for a while. We have time to breathe and figure this whole thing out. We can do this, okay. Now, Edmund, go and get the suitcase – make sure you get everything that fell out and put it back in. It's really important we get all of it. Rachel and Pru, go and look in the car. First, for stuff you can line the boot with. Blankets, plastic bags, papers, whatever. And secondly, look for bottles of water or any liquid – anything we can use to wash away the blood on the road. We don't need to get every drop but we have to make it so it's not so obvious. If we can just make it so no one really notices, the cars in the coming days will do the rest and hell, it might even rain. Robert,' he turned to the poet, 'you and I have to move the body to the boot of the car.'

Robert looked mortified and angry. He opened his mouth, but Tim reached out and covered his mouth with a palm. 'We're in this together, Rob. All of us. We always have been, and we always will be. We need everyone, here. All of us. Where we're at our best. There's no weak links here. We're all as great as each other. And you know what that means? It means, when it's your turn, you get the shit jobs. Are you still with us?'

Robert seemed to think about it for a moment, and then nodded.

'Good,' Tim said smiling. Edmund didn't know how he managed a smile at a time like this, but he couldn't deny it made him feel better. Tim nodded to them all, and they split up. Edmund was incredibly thankful to Tim for not making him carry the body – body . . . it seemed real now. That was the thing about dealing with a problem; how to accept that there was a problem to deal with in the first place. Was that what the woman was now – a problem? No, Edmund would never forget she was a human being, and she was real. She was someone's sweetheart, someone's daughter, maybe even someone's mother (his stomach churned at this). She was just in the wrong place at the wrong time – just like he was. If it was the other way around, and he was dead, would he want that woman's life to be ruined because of a little slip-up? He didn't think he would – it wasn't going to turn back time, bring him back to life, so no, he'd want her to live on and be amazing.

He got to the suitcase, to find the retractible handle was broken in two, but the case was only halfway open and didn't seem as devastated as first thought. He unzipped the case and started dumping in the clothes from the road. He picked up some flimsy underwear, and felt utterly ashamed at touching a dead woman's delicates. In the grand scheme of things though, it wasn't the worst thing he'd done tonight. He finished putting the clothes in and put the broken handle in and zipped it up. He stood up with it in his arms and walked a few paces back, scanning each side of the road. He saw nothing else, but he walked them both just to make sure nothing had been thrown further.

He looked back towards the car and wished he hadn't. Tim and Robert were carrying the woman – Tim at her shoulders, Robert at her legs. Her head lolled lifelessly on her chest, her forehead leaking with blood, but it was splattering on her chest. Tim and Robert obviously wanted to do it as quickly as possible, so were almost running to the car. Rachel stood at the open boot, having covered it with a few blankets which were some of Edmund's mother's favourites. He didn't care.

Once Tim and Robert had hoisted her into the boot, Pru came jogging over with bottles of water, Lucozade and Coke. Edmund was glad he was terrible at cleaning the car out and even worse at finishing bottles of drink. She stopped at every drop of blood and poured a little liquid on it. The biggest amount of blood – where the woman had lain to rest – took a whole large bottle of water and a half empty bottle of Coke for good measure. With the empty bottles under her arms, Pru used a rag to slosh around the water and scrub some of the blood away. The resulting effect were wet patches that did seem red, but looked more like some kind of dark drink spillage than blood. And luckily there weren't enough spatters to draw attention – the only one that might being the main one. Edmund looked at them and couldn't see anything but blood, but he supposed that a member of the public wouldn't even bat an eye, especially when they were going forty miles an hour just interested in getting where they were going. And if they thought it was blood, they'd probably just think it was a badger or a rabbit that had got clipped by a car. That happened a lot out here in the country. It might just work.

Edmund started walking towards the car. Pru was just rejoining the others, who were huddled around the open car boot. They all seemed to be looking in at the body. Edmund didn't understand why. Other than to say sorry, he wanted nothing to do with the body. And that made him feel even more guilty. Tim and Robert had had to touch her – clean up his mess.

We're in this together. All of us. We always have been, and we always will be. We need everyone, here. All of us. Where we're at our best. There's no weak links here. We're all as great as each other.

That was what Tim had said to Robert, and he had to believe that. It was true that everyone was in trouble. Maybe not equal to him, but trouble nonetheless. Letting someone operate a vehicle who you know is drunk is just as illegal as driving it yourself. But Edmund still felt an immense amount of gratitude to everyone. This would never not feel like his crime – at least not to him – but everyone was helping him.

Edmund heard a rustling in a lone bush on the roadside. It was bush which had fought its way through a stone slab wall, and provided a hole into the farmer's field next door. Edmund looked to see a brown rabbit watching him from the cover of the bush. Its nose was bobbing up and down, sniffing out what was happening, while it watched Edmund with black shiny marbles for eyes. A witness – although Edmund didn't think they had to worry about this one.

But under the rabbit's gaze, the lone surveyor, the utter shame began to sink in. It burst inside him and filled him from head to toe. What had he done? Really? What had he done?

'Sorry,' he said pathetically to the rabbit. He didn't even know why. And when he started moving to the car again, the bush made a great shush and the rabbit was away, back into the farmer's field, and back into a brighter future. It wanted no part in this scene, and who could blame it? This darkness was his, and it was theirs, and they would live with it forever. Edmund got to the car, and the others looked around. Even Tim's optimism had gone from his face. Pru and Rachel looked like they were on the verge of tears, and Robert looked like he was on the verge of mania.

'What?' Edmund said, a new coldness working into his brain. The wind whipping around them seemed to pick up. They parted so that he could see inside the car boot.

The woman lay there in her raincoat, her limbs barely more organised than before. Blood was matting her hair, but the movement had shifted the hair from her face, so he could see her now. It was suddenly a different situation.

They all looked down at her in the cramped car boot. A real woman, battered and bleeding from cuts on her face. Her limbs were limp and at odd angles. This was real. This was happening.

'Okay then,' Tim said. 'Looks like we're going to The Hamlet.'

He shut the boot.

59

Three years earlier . . .

They parked behind The Hamlet, as close as they possibly could. Marsden was sleeping, totally silent and dark,
with no one around to witness them. Thankfully. If this
had happened during the day, they would already be in
prison cells. Tim had said that Edmund shouldn't drive
because of the shock, but through a quick look around, it
seemed Edmund was still the best choice. Everyone else
was still over the limit – somehow, Edmund thought he'd
never been more sober, and he was going to drive at least
ten miles under the speed limit anyway. So, he drove.

In contrast to what had just happened, the drive was
uneventful.

That sound. When she hit the road.

Edmund tried not to think about it. Tim said that he
would go in and talk to Amber, that he would explain
the situation to her and make her see reason. He seemed
confident, deflecting any 'What if you can't?' comments
from Robert and any 'What if she calls the police?'
questions from Pru. He just said that he could and that
she wouldn't. He got out of the passenger side door and
disappeared into the dark.

He was gone for a long time. Edmund kept his hands on the steering wheel, knowing that if he stopped his grip, they would just shake uncontrollably. Even as it was, his hands were twitching.

He felt like he was dead – like he had somehow been the person that had died at the side of the road. And then he realised he didn't feel like he'd died. He just wished he had.

No one talked in the car. No one even breathed loudly. Edmund shut his eyes and felt like he was alone – because in many ways he was. He should have felt love for the others. The others who were standing with him through this ordeal. But for some reason, he didn't feel love. He felt afraid of them. All of them. And maybe Tim most of all.

The radio clicked into life and Edmund opened his eyes. Robert had reached from the back and turned it on. Rock music blared out for a couple of bars before Pru reached forward and wordlessly and mercifully shut it off. Robert didn't protest. The entire exchange was mute, but meant more words than they could ever speak.

After what seemed like hours, Tim came out of the night and opened the passenger door. 'Let's go.'

They all got out the car, Edmund last, and he looked up to see another figure emerging from the darkness.

Amber.

She didn't look scared. She didn't look apprehensive. She looked positively indifferent. She said nothing, just joined them.

Tim opened the car boot, giving a slight grimace at the

scene he was presented with. Like Edmund, maybe he was hoping that the woman would evaporate, become a collected hallucination. But no, she was still there.

Amber took out her keys and unlocked The Hamlet's doors – in the side where they received their deliveries. She propped the large door open as Tim and Robert carried the woman inside, draped over with blankets, so it was impossible to discern what they were carrying. They carried her through, Amber and Rachel flicking on light switches in front of them. Just as Rachel was about to flick the lights on in the main bar, Amber barked, 'No,' furiously. Rachel recoiled slightly. 'We'll take her to the basement. We can put on all the lights down there, and not worry. Maybe even get the fire on.' Rachel nodded, but still seemed fazed at the instruction from a relative outsider. Edmund, trailing behind with the suitcase in his arms and Pru muttering behind him under her breath, had never seen anyone snap at Rachel before, had never even seen a bad word said to her, so seeing this was a shock.

Instead of turning on the light, Rachel fumbled with her phone torch and pointed it down the sharp staircase. Tim and Robert slowly picked their way down, Tim having to go down backwards. Edmund didn't know how many times all of them had drunkenly slipped up or down the stairs, so he couldn't help admire how assuredly he did it. Soon enough Tim was at the bottom and Robert followed, and then the rest of them. Amber followed last making sure the basement door was shut and secure.

Rachel turned on the lights in the basement. Tim and Robert scrabbled around the tables (someone had re-organised the basement since they had left, so the tables were separated again) and placed the body in front of the fireplace on the rug. The two of them straightened up, and Robert yelped. There was a large blood stain on his coat. He struggled to get it off and threw it on the floor next to her.

'Jesus,' Robert said.

Amber got to the bottom of the stairs and saw the woman for the first time. Edmund watched her, curiously. At the sight of the woman, anyone else would've recoiled, thrown up, fainted. But Amber didn't do that. Amber just looked with curiosity, her eyes flickering in the light. And then, the strangest thing, she smiled.

Edmund looked away in disgust.

'Can we get the fire on?' Tim said, ignoring him. 'I'm freezing.'

'I'll do it,' Rachel said, fiddling with the fire. Soon flames were starting up.

They all just stood around the body, not knowing what to really do. Blood was already soaking through the blankets onto the rug, but stopped there. The rug was incredibly thick, so would stop any leakage.

Amber had retreated to the far corner, watching as if she were a curious bystander. It was clear she was going to offer nothing to the conversation, but she wasn't going to put up any roadblocks either.

'Right,' Pru said, 'So what the hell do we do now?'

'We need to find some way of, um, disposing of her,' Tim said unassuredly.

Edmund thought once again about how simply these phrases were coming to his friend's mouth. Maybe there was another side to Tim that no one ever saw. Yes, he always liked a problem to solve but could that really apply to this incredibly morbid situation too? How bad did the problems have to get before he tapped out?

'Christ, Tim,' Pru said, obviously agreeing with Edmund, 'can you say that any less creepily? Like get rid of her, or make her disappear, or . . . No, you know what, they're all equally bad.'

Tim didn't react. 'I'm just being real,' he said, in that same cold voice he'd adopted since the crash. 'I'm seeing what is in front of us, and I'm thinking about how we can resolve the situation. We can't turn back the clock, we can't undo this. It happened and as a result of our actions –' despite his fear, Edmund felt a kinship to him when he said 'our', '– this woman is dead. This woman, who happened to be alive and be on that road at the time our car was too. Our world has changed, whatever happens now. We can never go back to a time before it happened. Nothing we ever do is ever going to make this different. Our world has changed. I'm just trying to make it a little brighter.'

'But what can we do?' Edmund said, 'how can we ever be the same again? Because – she's dead. She's bloody dead. I did that.' Edmund started to sob again.

'No,' Robert said, his face stony. 'We did that. We all did.'

'Let's go upstairs,' Tim said, 'we'll go in one of the back rooms, get Edmund a drink, and we'll talk about what happens next.'

Rachel nodded. 'We're not going to get very far when our eyes will always go to her – the body, I mean.'

'This is so crazy,' Pru said, 'I'm dreaming, right. This is some messed up nightmare.'

Edmund was staring at the woman. This picture – the one he was seeing – would be imprinted on his mind forever. Her lying there in front of the fire. Blood starting to clot from the wound on her forehead. Her legs bent out of shape.

'Edmund,' someone was saying. Tim.

He looked around. Everyone was staring at him, looking concerned. They should be bloody concerned. He had – oh God.

'Edmund,' Tim said again, 'let's go upstairs. Away from all this. And let's think.'

All he wanted to do was to get away from the body. So he nodded. But some part of him wanted to stay too. This is what you did, a voice inside him chirped. This is what you did, and you want to run away? What gives you the right?

Edmund ignored the voice, and let himself be led upstairs by Tim. Pru, Robert and Rachel followed behind. Amber was the last to go up. She heard the door close behind the others and she went to the body. She looked at the woman with something like admiration. 'How does it feel?' she whispered, wishing the woman could answer. 'How does it feel to be broken? How does it feel

309

to be without hope?' She reached over and threw another log on the fire, replacing the fireguard in front. As she passed she drew her wrists over the woman's eyes, which flickered in a small and imperceptible motion. 'How does it feel to be dead?'

Amber shrugged. 'Sucks to be you.' And smiled.

She took the stairs two at a time, and paused at the door at the top – the basement was laid out so when you were at the very top, you couldn't see down into it anymore.

A rustle. Amber listened, not even sure if she had heard it, or if it was just another noise made by the crackling fire. She waited a few more moments, heard nothing else and shut the door.

In front of the fire, no one noticed that the woman's eyes had opened.

Her right index finger twitched.

60

Three years ago . . .

The last person. A black hound and a horse head. Why did she remember that?

Because there was only . . . Darkness.

Pain. Everywhere. Arms. She couldn't feel her arms. She tried to move them. Left twitched, but her right wasn't there. Or rather it was, but it wouldn't move. Her legs – there was nothing, no movement.

She felt hot, blazing hot. That kind of whole searing hot, that came with a bonfire. Or a fireplace. She tried to open her eyes. Her left opened but her right stung with something, a red liquid that came pouring in. She smelled it – blood. Her left eye was fuzzy, couldn't focus on anything. But as she blinked, things started to come into focus.

Confusion. What happened? Where was she? The last thing she remembered? Train. A train – she was on a train. But she got off the train, didn't she? Yes, she had been walking somewhere. It was dark. Something ran out of battery, and it had got darker. Her phone. And then, a sound. The sound of a . . . car. Oh God, it had hit her . . . and then . . . she had hit the ground.

She had thought she had died, but . . . then here.

A few more blinks and a scene presented itself. A basement – tables, a fireplace, chairs, a rug she was lying on.

Everything hurt. Existence felt like something she had to fight for. She reached out with her hand, and felt the perimeter of where she could reach. Hard, cold floor but then something else. Something swishy. She grasped it and pulled whatever it was into her vision.

A coat. Nothing that would help.

She felt an overwhelming sadness. 'Help,' she tried, but found the word quiet and gargled. Then she clamped her mouth shut.

Why wasn't she in a hospital? Why hadn't someone found her? Unless – whoever had hit her had brought her here. And if that was the case, then she didn't want to alert them.

How was she going to get out of this? She couldn't feel her legs – let alone walk, let alone run. She shifted her head to try and see around the room. Stairs. Stairs – she couldn't get upstairs. She was stuck.

Call for help? Not call out, but maybe there was something she could find to get a message out to people. Maybe . . . what was one of those things called? A phone, yes, a phone.

The coat.

She reached her hand out again and pulled the coat even closer. She patted it down, fully expecting to find nothing. But there was something – in a pocket. Something rectangular and solid. She tried the zip but every time she pulled, the coat went with it. It wasn't going to work when she had no way to stop it.

A phone. She knew, in her mind, that it was a phone. And she couldn't get to it because of a bloody zip. To her, the phone meant instant salvation – as though she'd use it and instantly the police would come and the doctors would come and the paramedics would come and scoop her up and fix her.

She tried pulling on the zip again to the same result.

How was she going to—? She thought of something. She pulled the coat over, so it was in front of her face, blocking the room out of view entirely. She moved the fabric as close as she could, and then bit down on the corner. She pulled the zip, and the fabric held. The pocket opened. She put her hand in and brought out a phone.

Relief plunged into her like a wave. This was it. All she needed.

She tapped it. Thank god it wasn't password protected. She tapped the phone symbol and then tried dialling 999. But her fingers weren't working very well. At least one of the nines always came out as an eight or a six. She kept trying – over and over and over to the same result. She tried one last time and that was the worst of the lot – 856.

Something shifted upstairs. A creak in the building. Almost like someone was up there. Waiting for her. A monster, just biding its time, coming to gobble her up. She thought back to all the monsters she had been scared of when she was a child. The monster under the bed, the monster in the closet, the ghost in the basement of the hotel they used to stay in in Skegness. The monster above her now, in her mind, was all those combined.

She didn't have time to waste not tapping three numbers. And that meant she definitely couldn't tap out Robin's number . . . Robin . . . Robin was . . .? So she just tapped the phone button and saw a name at the top of the recent calls.

Matthew McConnell.

Just a name. She managed to press it. Someone. Anyone. To get help.

She propped the phone against her ear.

Dialling. Dialling for a long time. Crackling. White noise. Of course, she was in a basement. No signal, or very little. And then, '. . . Hello . . .'

'Hello,' she whispered harshly.

'. . . who . . . this . . .'

'Matthew . . . McConnell?'

'. . . yes, who is . . .'

'It's me, Sam.'

'Sam . . .?'

'Sam Ferringham. Please help me. Oh god.'

'. . . who . . .'

She could barely hear him. She needed to tell him where she was. She strained her head up to see any landmarks. Then she remembered she was inside. So, anything that could tell him where she was. But she couldn't move her head far, before something in her neck cracked. She screamed in pain and stopped. She was looking above the fireplace, as far as she could go, and two monsters looked down at her.

'There's . . . a black hound . . .'

'What are you . . . about?'

'A black hound . . . and a horse head.'

'A black . . . and . . . horse . . . what?'

'The . . . whoever is up there . . . the horse head . . . is coming back,' she mangled the sentence but didn't have the strength to put it back together.

'Are you in danger?'

'Find him . . . find Robert Ferringham . . . if . . . ever . . .'

'What?'

'In trouble.' She meant to say, *I'm in trouble.* She wanted Robin. She needed Robin. Now, she knew. Robin was her love. Why had she ever left him, to go away and work? Why hadn't she spent more time with him? That was what she would truly come to regret.

She couldn't focus on the conversation. Didn't even know if it was going the way she was thinking. '*Wait*, Clatter . . . Clatteridges, 7.30 p.m. 18 August 1996!' Why did she say that? What did that have to do with anything? It was like she had split into two different people. The one acting and the one thinking. And the one acting was operating at double the speed of the one thinking.

Wait!

'Hello?'

The voice at the other end. But she heard something. A new sound from above. A door opening.

She ended the call.

Door. And then creaking. Staircase. She pressed the phone into her hand so it wasn't visible.

She strained her head to look around, wanting to at least look her monster in the eye. It wasn't what she expected it to look like. A young girl. Pretty. They locked eyes. As the pain became too much, she closed her eyes.

'Shit,' the girl said, running back upstairs.

Door again. She shifted again so she could see the phone. Had to get rid of it. But then . . . She quickly and painfully put it to her ear. And made another call. When she was done, she stabbed at the red button and without thinking, tossed the phone as far as she could. She heard it skittering across the floor and colliding with something. One of the last sounds she ever heard.

61

Three years ago . . .

'She's still alive.' Amber rushed into the back room, and slammed her hands down on the table everyone was sitting at. 'She's still bloody alive.'

'What?' Edmund said, his heart leaping.

'Barely, but she's there. I heard her muttering to herself.'

Edmund stood up. 'Well, we need to call an ambulance. Quickly.'

They had been talking about how to hide the body. And they had all come to the same conclusion thanks to Amber's insight. The floorboards in the basement were loose. They would take them up, dig a hole, place the body inside within the suitcase, fill the hole in and replace the floorboards, making sure they were more secure. A body under The Hamlet. It would ruin their favourite spot, but they couldn't risk going outside with the body again. And even if it was found, which it never would be, who was to say it was them who killed her? Suspicion would fall on the owners. Done and dusted – the group didn't have a key. It was regrettable others would fall under suspicion because of them, but that's all it would be. There'd be no evidence to hold them. And that was if the body was ever found – which was very unlikely.

Amber didn't seem to worry about the fact that suspicion might eventually roll around to her in such a scenario. She just seemed to be happy to be along for the ride, truth be told. Edmund watched her with a kind of disgusted fascination. She was taking it all incredibly well. Far too well. She really was so obsessed with Tim that she would do anything for him. She was the kind of sure deal that would have been great for a guy, until she turned around and killed him. Edmund had no doubt that she had that in her heart.

But now the woman was alive. That changed everything. Edmund got his phone out, but Tim snatched it away.

'What are you doing?' Edmund said, not understanding. He swiped at his phone but Tim moved his hand. 'She's alive. It's over. We don't need to be in this nightmare anymore.'

'It's not as simple as that,' Tim said. 'I wish it was, but it's not.'

'You said she was dead?' Robert said to Tim.

Tim looked at him, angrily. 'I'm a goddamn physicist, not a doctor.'

'She's seen my face,' Amber said, 'She looked straight at me, and who's to say who else she's seen, while we've been piddling about here.'

'Tim,' Rachel said softly.

Tim snapped at her. 'I'm thinking.' He started pacing

around the room, every step he took appearing to be a struggle.

'I don't understand what there is to think about?' Edmund shouted. 'She is down there alive.'

'Yes,' Tim said, stopping, 'but who knows for how long. She was messed up pretty bad. Who's to say she won't die in the ambulance, or in the hospital, and we're all still up for murder. Or death by dangerous driving. Or whatever. It's still prison time. And what if she lives? Grievous bodily harm. Prison. Drink driving resulting in injury. Prison. And then we tried to cover it up. Prison. We're all staring down the barrel of a boatload of shit however you look at it.'

'But, she's alive,' Edmund said.

'Yes,' Tim said, 'and unfortunately at this point, that's a problem.'

'What are you saying?' Robert said.

'Yes, what are you saying?' Edmund stressed.

'I'm saying,' Tim picked his words, 'she's alive. But for us to continue our plan, she has to . . . not be.'

Amber stepped forward. 'We have to kill her.'

The group of them stared at Amber for a long time – Edmund didn't know if it was more for the sudden outburst or for what that sudden outburst entailed.

Edmund scoffed. 'What?'

'No,' Pru said, 'Tim's right. Amber is right.'

'Are you all utterly insane?' Edmund shouted. He turned to Rachel, whose warm eyes had cooled. 'Rachel, please . . . we can't . . .'

She shook her head. 'I'm sorry, Ed,' she said, 'there

is no other way from here. We set off on a path and we can't turn around now. We have to go the distance.'

Edmund looked round. No one was looking happy, but they weren't denying what had to be done either. 'I don't believe this. I can't . . . I won't . . .' He pointed at Amber. 'Don't listen to her. She's crazy. She's insane. I can't stand by . . . I can't kill someone.'

'You don't have to,' Tim said, to Edmund first and then to Pru, Robert and Rachel. Amber stood by him. 'I'll do it.'

'You can't . . .' Edmund said.

'Yes, I can,' Tim said quietly, 'there's nothing more in this world I love than the people standing in front of me right now. I would do anything for you, and sometimes that phrase requires some physical clarification.' He slowly unbuttoned his cuffs and started rolling up his sleeves.

'Oh, Jesus.' Edmund looked away and gagged, feeling as though he was going to throw up again.

'No,' he heard Amber say, and he clung onto one last hope that she would stop this. But she said, 'You don't do this alone. We do it together.'

Tim nodded.

'Are you kidding?' Edmund said. 'Have you all lost your minds? Who is this girl? We don't know her. What the hell is going on?'

But by the time Edmund looked around, all he saw was them disappearing through the doorway.

62

Three years ago . . .

They went down the staircase, Tim first, Amber second. Hand in hand. The mass, the body, was still there in front of the fire. Her eyes were closed. She looked dead. The blood from her forehead had clotted, mostly in her hair, the spindly fibres matting and creating a sort of gauze. It was hard to imagine that she was still alive. At this point, they were hoping against it. But as they looked, a finger twitched.

'Maybe a reflex action,' Amber said, 'dead bodies do that.'

But then the woman gave a long and incredibly laboured breath.

'Shit,' Tim said. 'What do we do?'

'We kill her,' Amber said. 'It's as simple as that.'

'What do you mean, simple?' Tim said.

'Do you remember the cat I told you to kill? My cat,' Amber said rolling up her sleeves. 'Piece of shit yowled all night, you remember? Basically woke up the whole street. The vets said he was in heat or something stupid like that. And my bitch of a mother wouldn't take him to get his balls chopped off.'

'I remember,' Tim said. 'I remember that day.'

'So do I. Luring that cat out there like some stupid horny piece of shit. Remember when it came to it?' Amber said, looking at him.

Tim looked away, at the crackling fire.

'You couldn't do it,' Amber said.

'You didn't have to skin it,' Tim barked, so loud that he paused to make sure no one upstairs heard him. After a creaking from above them, there was nothing.

'No, I didn't,' Amber said, 'I just got a little carried away. Shoot me. Then as I recall you got a little carried away with me in the bushes. Some may say that you got carried away a little prematurely.' She beamed. 'I became something else that day. Something new. Maybe today's the day you become new too.'

Tim sighed, went to her. 'I brought you in on this because I know you're good with this kind of stuff.'

'Hence the cat,' Amber laughed.

'Hence the cat,' Tim agreed, with far less aplomb. 'Look, are you going to help or not?'

'Of course,' Amber said, her eyes on fire with possibility, 'what's the plan, Mr Claypath?'

Tim looked around, for anything to end it quickly. But he found nothing. It was just the basement of a pub. Plastic menus and beer mats. Nothing for a quick departure. Upstairs, there were knives and things like that. But that would make a mess.

Tim sighed and then suddenly knew what they had to do. And he didn't want to do it. Dear god, he didn't want to do it. But they had to. He had to.

'You have to hold her limbs down,' Tim said.

Amber looked at him. 'How is that going to . . .' she trailed off and then it clicked in her head. 'Oooh, what are you going to do with her? Are you going to smother her? Strangle her? Maybe you should just throw her in the fire, or . . .'

Tim couldn't meet her eyes. 'Just bloody do it, okay.'

Amber let go of Tim's hand, and approached the woman. She was incredibly calm – maybe bringing her in had been a terrible idea. She was crazy, Edmund was right. But then this whole situation was crazy. And it was going to get a lot worse before it got better.

Tim thought of the group. He pictured them in his mind. He had to do this for them. Or it was over. They'd never see one another again. All get shipped off to different pens, prodded and poked, and made to eat sludge, and told when to piss and shit. That wasn't any destiny for any of them. And this insipid imbecile, this stupid bitch, had threatened to take that all away, because of her blundering incompetence. She deserved it.

Amber crouched down over the woman's legs, even though they looked like they were never going to move again, and gripped her wrists. The woman made no sign of recognition of this. She was so far under she wouldn't know what was happening.

Bitch.

He went to her, knelt down, one leg either side of her torso, his face looking down at her battered, broken one. This bitch, walking along some road in the dead of night, without any sign she was there. Just there to make them all suffer.

What a silly little bitch.

He reached out with his hands, and clutched her throat in his palms.

They were going to achieve so much before she came along. Now they had to fight to survive. Because of her.

An anger flared up inside him.

He pressed down. Hard. He felt the muscles in her throat, felt them tighten and then constrict. And he carried on. He watched her face and saw that her one visible eye was fluttering open. Good – he wanted her to feel it. He wanted her to know what it felt like, to have your life flash before your eyes.

Her whole body started to shake, as he pressed down even harder. It was easy, this. Just grip down and watch a soul disappear, a life force fade away. Her eye rolled back in her head, and a frothy spit started coming out of her mouth.

Amber was making some kind of sound behind him – something between a laugh and a cry, holding the woman's shaking limbs down. But Tim wasn't laughing. But he wasn't crying either.

He was in the moment, existing faster and stronger than he ever had before. What a feeling – to have a life in your grip. And to be allowed to be the one to decide that it was over. He pressed even harder just for the hell of it, and a little laugh escaped him.

Such . . . fun.

And then she gave one final choke, a wheeze. And her

body stilled. Her eye rolled back. And she stared at him, would forever. He knew she was dead.

But he carried on, squeezing her neck.

For how long – he didn't know? But soon enough, Amber was forcing him upright and pulling him into a hug. She was laughing, and he did too. And then she cried, and so did he. But for him – for both of them – they weren't tears of pain, they were tears of joy.

At becoming something new.

63

Three years ago . . .

They were all sitting around the table in the basement. Except Edmund, who couldn't seem to sit, as though sitting was too much of a normal action for this crazy night. They had been meaning to get to work – they got the shovels from The Hamlet shed that was never locked. And they found a tool box with a crowbar that could be used to prise up the floorboards – although it wouldn't take much prising.

No one was talking, no one was looking at each other – except Amber and Tim. They were having a hushed conversation at the head of the table, sitting as close to each other as if they were lovers. Edmund watched them out of the corner of his eye, and saw that Rachel was watching them too.

The woman hadn't moved for almost twenty minutes. She was really dead this time. The subject was now going to be how the group could live on? Not Tim, he would be fine, Amber had shown him the way.

But for the rest of them. They all felt it. They all felt bad. And they would make this ruin their lives. They would constantly be haunted by the woman's bent form, lying there on the road. They didn't feel any excitement over it, they felt regret. And regret was like a wave eroding a cliff – it was only a matter of time before it collapsed. In saving their own lives, they had also condemned themselves. He needed a fix. He needed some way of convincing the group that they would be absolved of this crime altogether, so they could continue to cover it all up – dot the 'i's cross the 't's – and then they had to go on living without this shadow over them.

He had to find a way for them to see that they could have a life beyond this. That they could still be together. And together was all that mattered. Tim looked around. Everyone was staring at the table. This wasn't right – they should be alive, more than alive. They had just overstepped a line the majority of humans never would. They, collectively, had killed someone. And that was awful. But also kind of beautiful. They always said their friendship was strong. But now they were bound in ways they could have never hoped. So he stood up, and Amber stood up next to him. 'I know what we need to do.'

The rest of them looked at him, expectantly, hopefully. Hoping that he would be able to fix it all. And maybe he could.

Tim smiled, a warm hearty smile that he truly meant, looking into the faces of the people he loved.

'We have to die.'

64

The present . . .

'Robin. Robin . . .' A girl's voice. Familiar.

Someone splashed water over his face.

He opened his eyes. He was resting against the wall of the tunnel. His head ached, and something was dripping down his forehead. Back to Marsden and back to frequently getting knocked unconscious. Against everything, he almost laughed.

The abandoned tunnel looked a little different from before. The tunnel was lit – lit by a small battery-powered light. The same one he had seen in the Monster's hideaway all those months ago. Now he could see the tracks running through the centre of the tunnel clearly, and see that the floor was dusty, cluttered with rock debris and pockets of pooled water. The light did not reach to the other side of the width of the tunnel, so he could not see the other wall, but he knew it was there. He wondered where exactly in the tunnel they were, and if the wall he was resting on had the canal on the other side of it, or his freedom.

He tried to move but his body wouldn't respond. There was something resting on his shoulder. Someone.

Sally. She was taking shallow breaths and her eyes were half open. 'Hey,' she said, 'I guess I don't need to tell you that you probably shouldn't have come.' She gave a chuckle that turned into a splutter. She spat out a mouthful of blood. Robin looked down to see her arms were wrapped around her midriff – they were covered in blood. 'It's not as bad as it looks.'

'What happened?' Robin whispered.

'Well, the damnedest thing happened. I got shot and now I'm bleeding to death,' Sally said, somehow making it sound like a minor affliction. 'What the hell are you doing here?'

'It was Amber,' Robin said, 'Sam saw Amber that day. That's what Sam meant when she talked to Matthew. A black hound and a horse head. Amber has those symbols, tattoos, on her wrist. Amber's behind this.'

'Bit late on the newsflash there,' Sally said. 'She was the one who shot me. Got any theories about Tim Claypath?'

'No,' Robin said, 'how can he be here?'

'I'm just glad you saw him too,' Sally said, taking a rasping breath. 'I thought I'd started to see things. Was he riding a pink crocodile for you too?'

'What?' Robin said.

'Joking,' Sally said. 'At least have the decency to laugh, I'm dying here.'

As if to cement his existence, there was a sound of footsteps crunching up the tunnel. And Robin looked up to see Tim Claypath towering over them. He was an imposing figure – he felt like a fictional character that had leaped off the page. Because he shouldn't be here, he couldn't be here.

'How?' Robin said. 'How the hell are you here?'

'That's really the least interesting question you could be asking right now,' Tim said. 'Probably the most relevant would be what is going to happen to you and your little friend here. Although you might not like the answer.'

'Don't give him the satisfaction,' Sally said.

'What are you going to do?' Robin said anyway.

'Well,' Tim said, crouching down in front of him, 'you, Mr Robin Ferringham, came to Marsden chasing ghosts and monsters and your lovely wife, and just couldn't bring yourself to fail once again. So you lured Ms Morgan here out to Standedge, and you horrifically drowned her, before shooting yourself. Really is a nasty business. You must be really messed up in the head to do that.'

'But I'm not going to do any such thing,' Robin said.

Tim put his head in his hands and screamed. 'Yeah, dipshit, I know you're not. We're gonna drown the bitch, and then shoot you making it look like a suicide. I thought you were meant to be smart. But we've been watching you throughout all this, and the whole thing has been an incredibly poor showing on your part.'

Robin didn't have time to process it, and even if he did, he didn't want to, so he moved on. 'What do you mean, "we"?'

And then suddenly, another figure came into view, carrying the two bits of metal sheeting that had been the doors to the Monster's lair. 'Got the evidence.' Amber. It was Amber. But she was almost a different person from the one he knew. Her voice seemed different and she held herself differently. She propped the two sheets against the far side of the tunnel and Robin saw that she was carrying a gun.

'Is that everything?'

'I don't know. Looks like it.'

'Can you be sure?'

'I think so. Take them back to the engineer.'

Robin looked from Amber to Tim. Tim didn't react to that. 'Prudence?' Tim wheeled around to him, at the mention of her name. 'She's alive too?'

Tim looked unstable, like he was battling with himself. 'They all are.'

'But how did you do it?'

'Well,' Tim said, 'we didn't use the opening in this tunnel you happened to find. If we'd known about that, we wouldn't have had to go through all the pomp and circumstance. We really were kicking ourselves when we heard about it.'

'If you didn't use the opening, the crack in the tunnel, what did you do? How did you do it? Don't you at least owe me that?'

Tim laughed, looked at Amber and she laughed too. 'We don't owe you shit. You have been an incredible pain in the arse to us. You and your oozing friend.'

Robin changed tact. He just wanted to keep Tim talking, because he didn't want to get to what was next. Maybe if he had time to think, he could think of a way out of this, but right now, he couldn't see any. Tim would be a lot faster than him, and that wasn't even taking into account that he'd have to carry Sally. And Amber had a gun.

'You got Matthew too, didn't you?' Robin said, 'Loam-field said. I thought he was saying that Matthew caused the crash. But he meant you, didn't he?'

Tim didn't say anything.

'And your sister? Where's your sister, Tim?'

Tim grabbed Robin by the neck in a swift motion. He gripped hard so all the air left Robin's throat. He choked. 'Shut up.'

'*Tim!*' Amber shouted, and Tim let go. Robin slid back down the wall, gasping. 'We stick to the plan. We have the evidence. We stage the crime scene. You know that.'

'Why are you doing this?' Robin said, still gasping. 'Why did you do all this?'

Tim laughed again. 'Well, it all started very simply really. You see, Robin, you're staring at the two people who just happened to kill your wife.'

65

Robin couldn't feel anymore. The life went out of his body, replaced with an inconceivable sorrow. Sam. His Sam . . . was dead. She wasn't here anymore, not here in this world. And the worst thing about it was that he had known. He had felt it that first day she was gone, three years ago in their flat. He had known that she wasn't coming back. And three years of unchecked grief fell on him in one instant.

As he listened to Tim's story, he didn't cry. He didn't squirm. He didn't try to run away. His voice was distorted, like he was underwater, like he was drowning.

'Robin, you still with us?'

Robin looked at Tim, through misty eyes. He didn't even notice he'd stopped talking. 'You killed her?'

'Yes, that's what the story was about,' Tim said.

'She was alive. She was still alive, and you . . . Why didn't you help her? Why wouldn't you just take her to the hospital? You didn't have to . . .'

Tim looked at him, almost looking like he pitied Robin. 'You clearly don't understand. She was on that road, in the dead of night. She was invisible. We would have run her down if we'd been stone cold sober. Anyone would have. So what happened to your wife – she brought it upon herself.'

Robin felt his blood boil up. He wanted to lunge at Tim, but his body still didn't work. All he managed was a small dip forward and back.

Sally's head lolled on his shoulder. She had gone quiet and he couldn't see if her eyes were open. Please, Robin thought, don't let her be dead. But then she made a noise and Robin knew she was still there. At least for now.

'Why did you tell me?' Robin said.

'What?' That wasn't Tim. It was Amber. She walked into his line of sight, and stood next to Tim.

'Let's just get it over with,' Tim said.

'No.' Amber held up a hand. 'What did you say Robin?'

Robin looked at her, and sniffed. 'I said "Why did you tell me?" Why did you tell me about Sam? You could have just killed me, you could have just got it over with and I would never have had to know.'

'Oh, Robin,' Amber said, crouching down in front of him. She took one hand and rubbed his tears away. 'I read your book. *Without Her*. And I understood. I understood something that I don't think you even knew yourself. But it was obvious to me. I had to make you see. And now you do – you feel it.'

'What are you talking about?' Robin said, more tears coming to take the place of the ones wiped away.

'Look at all this,' Amber said, standing up again, stretching out her arms to indicate the whole scene. 'Look at everything you've been through. All to find out

334

what happened to Samantha Ferringham, your doting little wife. You've been running towards the truth for so long that you didn't stop to realise that you don't want to know it. You never actually wanted to find out what happened. Because then there would be nothing left – other than to have to face up to actually having to let her go.'

Robin said nothing. The tears were a steady stream now. And he gasped. He couldn't believe it – but she was right. Sam's story was over. And soon, his would be too. That was what Amber and Tim had wanted. They had wanted to break him. And he was broken.

There was just one thing he wanted to know.

'How are you here, Tim?' His voice was tiny now. 'How can you be here?'

Amber looked at Tim and shrugged.

Tim sighed. 'Fine. I'll tell you. But you have to act impressed.'

66

Three days before the Incident . . .

'Can you believe how many texts Matt has sent?' Edmund said, laughing as he placed his phone on the table. 'I mean, Jesus Christ, have some self-worth.'

They were in their usual place – the basement. The body beneath their feet had been there for just shy of three years. It remained unfound. The police had never come, never even so much as asked a single question. It was as if she just disappeared, and the world shrugged. But even so, their plan was not changing.

Robert finished his game of Solitaire by sweeping all the cards into his outstretched hand. 'I'm starting to think he's just doing it to piss us off.'

Sometimes Edmund caught himself. Sometimes he remembered that Matt used to be one of his best friends. But Matt had not been there that night, and Edmund had come to resent him for that. Even though it wasn't Matt's fault, everyone had come to resent him for that. What had first been protecting him from the truth had soon soured – he didn't need protecting from anything. They did.

Amber was sitting in her usual seat at the back of the

room, not engaging with any of them, except Tim. Over the years she hadn't become any less crazy, and somehow she seemed to be able to sway Tim

'We all know the plan, right?' Tim said.

Rachel put her hand up, 'I am still a little fuzzy on the whole disappearing act we're doing?'

Pru jumped up, running up the stairs with glee. Robert looked after her with a playful disgust, then he turned that disgust on Rachel. 'Did you just ask that so Pru could do her little demonstration? We've said – we shouldn't enable her.'

Pru came back down the stairs with a bowl full of water. There was a model boat bobbing around on the top of the bowl. She placed it in the centre of the table. 'Here's one I made earlier. Now this is all very simple. It all has to do with swimming pools.'

'Swimming pools?' Rachel said, feigning confusion and ignoring a side glance from Robert.

'Yes. Interning for a spa company I was able to learn certain tricks. And while I was there they were perfecting something, something which is pretty commonplace now, the invisible pool. My company was trying to figure out how to make swimming pools a little less . . . roomy. You got a whole room for a swimming pool and not much else. You can't entertain in that room, especially if you don't want to go swimming. So, they had the idea – what if you could have a swimming pool that's not so permanently on display all the time. What if it was invisible, hidden, and could just become a swimming pool when needed. Right? You have a swimming pool under the

337

floor, then the floor lowers, leaving pockets where the water can flow through. The floor goes down and down revealing the pool. When you're done swimming or sitting or peeing in the pool, whatever, you press a button, and the floor comes back up. Same thing happens, but in reverse. The floor has enough drainage to let the water pass through it. The floor rises and the water goes from on top to underneath.

'I wondered if maybe I could do the same thing but in reverse. I wondered if I could create something, suck the water out, and create . . . let's say, a room. Then we could get rid of it at a moment's notice. Flip a switch and the room is gone.' Pru picked up the little toy boat, it had an extension on it, that didn't match the main boat's colour. It created an extra part of the boat.

'Roomy,' said Rachel.

'So,' Pru said, holding up a hand to silence Rachel, 'we're all going to be in this secret room, right. Matt's out there, making a mess on deck. We hear a guy spot the boat. The guy runs off to go call the police. We sit tight. And we may have to sit tight for bloody hours. We wait for a window. The police or ambulance or whatever will take Matt away, and then they'll be back soon enough to set up a crime scene. That is the window.

'Matt gets taken, and by the time police realise that six people had gone in and only one has come out, and what's more two of those missing are bloody Claypaths, we'll have scarpered. We have to be very careful there are no witnesses when we finally come out of the boat, and we all know there's no cameras or anything round

338

there. We pop out and I flick my switch. And the extra rooms disappears, and what's more the hatch we use to get to the secret room is closed up.'

'Okay. All joking aside, I don't actually get that bit,' Rachel said.

Pru smiled like she knew something no one else did, and she was very clearly relishing that fact. 'I've made it so the hatch is the same dimensions as the underbed cupboard in Edmund's uncle's narrowboat so if any joint is visible then it'll look natural.'

'Okay. That is clever,' Rachel said. 'You've earned your demonstration.'

'Thank you,' Pru said dutifully. 'Check this out. She held up a switch, and gestured down to the boat. Everyone watched it. It had settled on top of the water. The 'secret' room underwater. Pru pressed the button. 'Watch carefully,' she said. 'Now you see me . . .' The secret room started to shrink – the water flowing out of it, spurting back into the wider body of water. When it was impossibly small, they saw the pieces of metal that were the walls and floor break off and sink to the bottom of the bucket. What was left was the original narrowboat. '. . . Now you don't.' Pru smiled, clearly happy with herself. 'The bits of metal float to the bottom of the canal, and seem just like some leftover rubbish. Boo-yaa!'

There was a curt applause and Pru took her bowl of water and put it on the floor.

'Great,' Tim said, 'so we're all okay with the plan.'

'I will stay behind,' Amber said, 'someone needs to be

your eyes and ears in Marsden. Someone needs to guard The Hamlet. I am honoured to do this for you.'

'Us or just Tim?' Robert mumbled.

Tim slammed his hand down on the table. 'Robert, do you have something you would like to share?'

Robert shook his head.

'Okay then. I have purchased a cottage in the middle of Sherwood Forest. It wasn't official. It was cash in hand. That is where we will go after we "die". We must stay out of sight, at least until Matthew is convicted. After our names and faces are out of the news, we can start to be a little braver. In the early stages, Amber will rendezvous with one of us, rotating, at a location, again rotating, getting us food and water, as well as letting us know of anything we should know.'

'Looks like we're in your hands,' Edmund said to Amber.

Amber said nothing, but gave a beaming smile.

That he didn't trust in the slightest.

67

The present . . .

'You happy now?' Tim said, 'I told you it wasn't important.'

'The metal sheets,' Robin said.

'They're the parts of the secret room that broke off. When we heard that the Monster had them, and that the investigation was picking back up, I decided it would be better to come back and get them.' Tim said. 'They were supposed to just sink to the bottom of the canal and stay there, until maybe someone just mistook them for rubbish. And by then, maybe they'd be all the way down the opposite end of the Narrow. But you just had to get involved and mess this whole thing up.'

'You messed it up good enough yourself,' Robin said, 'it would have only been a matter of time before someone worked out what you did.'

Tim smiled. 'You're a bad liar, Robin. Anyone ever tell you that? No one would have known a thing. We would have disappeared. Matthew would have been convicted. And your wife would stay right where she is. Right under people's feet while they get pissed and eat food and warm themselves by the fire.'

'Why go through all this?' Robin said, 'All this stuff that you've done. If you were going to betray Matthew, why not just frame him for Sam . . .' his breath hitched and he let out a sob at her name. He tried to carry on but couldn't.

'We thought of that,' Tim said, 'but we couldn't have done it well enough. Matt was in his house when all this was happening, and his aunt would provide an alibi. And Matt didn't drive or have a car, so how could he run someone over? And besides, back then, we still wanted to protect that smug bastard. We didn't want to frame him. That only came later, when our desire to protect him evolved into something else.'

'He's your friend,' Robin said. 'How could someone – How could you do that to a friend?'

'He's not my friend,' Tim said. 'Not anymore.'

Amber stepped forward. 'Okay, enough stalling. Time for the main event, buddy.' She brought the gun up, holding it at Robin's head. 'You ready to drown Ms Morgan here? Or whatever she's called.'

Sally grunted. Robin couldn't believe she was still conscious. 'You'll have to come and get me, bitch.' But Sally didn't move – she couldn't. She was bleeding from a gunshot wound from her stomach after all. And she had lost a lot of blood. Even in the bad light, Robin could tell she was sickly pale colour. All that and Sally was still trying to fight back, even if it was just with words.

And then Sally surprised him and the two captors in equal measure. She must have used the last of her strength to lurch forward. She connected with Amber's torso,

342

head-butting her. Amber was propelled backwards. The gun flew out of her hand and clattered somewhere off down the tunnel.

Robin took this as his only chance – for Sally's sake, if not for his own. He felt angry, murderous, and Tim had paused in front of him, wide-eyed and off guard. As Amber and Sally collapsed in a heap, Robin pushed himself off the wall and charged into Tim, He collided with him, sending himself and the young man tumbling into the back of the tunnel.

They kept going, Tim being pushed and Robin doing the pushing.

Robin expected to hit the opposite wall, but instead they both went sailing even further, colliding with metal railings. The railing gave way and Robin realised his mistake too late. They had been next to a cut-through and Robin had sent them into the canal tunnel.

Robin and Tim went plunging head-first into the ice cold water of Standedge.

68

During . . .

The service station near Sherwood Forest was full of truckers and families on road trips. Everyone was rushing around. No one gave a toss about the man with the beard and the low cap sitting drinking a latte. Even when the hot brunette sat with him, he barely got a glance.

'There's someone poking around,' Amber said, giving him the box of supplies. 'His name is Robin Ferringham.'

Tim shook his head. 'Who's that?'

'He's a writer. He wrote this book.'

She pulled a copy of *Without Her* from under the table. Tim looked at it – looked at the pictures on the cover. It was unmistakeable.

'Her.'

'He's the husband. Don't worry, he's running around like a headless chicken at the moment.'

Tim's eyes widened and looked at her. 'How?'

'Don't know,' she said. 'Still trying to find out. But you're going to have to start to consider that you might have someone in your cottage talking.'

'A traitor?'

She nodded. 'Who else knows? No one.'

'Okay,' Tim said, 'I'll deal with it. But in the meantime, have you had any luck finding the evidence?'

Amber shook her head. 'It's probably halfway down the canal by now.'

Tim sighed. 'Okay.'

Amber got up. 'Make sure you find the traitor. And make sure to make an example of them.'

Tim grabbed Amber's arm before she could walk away. 'What would you do?'

'You want to ask The Hamlet barmaid or the cat skinner?'

'The one I fell in love with.'

Amber smiled and bent down and kissed him deeply. She pulled away before she bit his lip. 'I'd kill them.'

She walked away, leaving Tim to his latte and a little light reading.

69

During . . .

Matthew wound his window down and then the other, relishing the way the wind played on his face. Freedom – it felt so much better than he had even imagined. Mr Ferringham had done it – he'd kept his word, and now it was time for him to keep his. He thought he knew where his old phone was, all he had to do was charge it up. He knew he'd saved what he needed to find.

Loamfield undid his tie with one hand and threw it into the back next to Matthew. He was driving along the dual carriageway, back towards Marsden. They'd be at Matthew's house in no time at all.

This was really happening.

He was really going home.

'I hope whatever you've got to give Robin Ferringham is good,' Loamfield said, looking in the rearview mirror. 'That man just saved your arse. Big time. I couldn't have done anything like that. If you'd have got into a courtroom, you would have been all kinds of screwed.'

Matthew nodded, but didn't say anything. A black van came up alongside Loamfield's car. The windows were tinted and he couldn't see inside. For some reason, it made him feel incredibly uneasy.

'What's this idiot up to?' Loamfield said, as the van coasted across the lines into their lane. Loamfield hugged the hard shoulder. 'Drunk much?'

The window of the van started to roll down. Loamfield didn't see, but Matthew did. The person behind the wheel of the van.

But . . . it couldn't be . . .

'Speed up,' Matthew shouted.

The van touched the right hand side of the car, ever so gently, and then Matthew felt it push the car further over onto the hard shoulder.

'Shit,' Loamfield said, 'what the . . .'

'Mr Loamfield, speed up,' Matthew said. 'It's him.'

The van moved away quickly, swerving back into its lane. Loamfield looked at the van, must have seen who was driving. 'Wait, wha . . .'

The van swerved back into the car, slamming into it. Matthew felt himself get thrown to the left, his seatbelt cutting into his neck. Loamfield's tie hurtled out of the open window. And then the car was airborne, flying off the dual carriageway, careening down the hill into the trees below.

All Matthew knew was the tree coming towards them. And then, black.

He was out for mere seconds, but in those seconds he felt he lived another life. Pain. His arm. His left arm was on fire. He couldn't open his eyes, or maybe he just didn't want to.

The sound of a car door opening. And then hands on him, pulling him out of the car. Someone hoisted him up, and his left arm hung limp.

He opened his eyes to see a fuzzy world. Trees everywhere. He was moving. Pointed down. Looking down, he could see legs moving. Fireman's lift – he was on someone's shoulder.

Consciousness came and went. But every time he surfaced, they were still there. The trees. Going by. Whoever had him was taking him a long way.

And then eventually the trees became constant.

They had stopped.

The sound of an engine coming closer, closer, closer. And then it stopped. A sliding door.

And suddenly, he was airborne again. He had been thrown, and in a second he crumpled on a cold metal floor, with his left arm under him and howling with pain. He tried to straighten up, and saw that he was in the back of a van.

The figure who had carried him, dressed all in black, wearing a cap climbed in after him and slid the door shut. Matthew tried to look around but his neck felt stiff and unwieldy.

'Drive,' the figure said. And the metal started pulsing under Matthew as the engine started.

The figure took off his cap. And smiled. 'Hey Matt,' Tim said, 'long time no see.'

70

During . . .

Tim slammed through the cottage door, dragging Matthew by the scruff of his neck. Pru was at the kitchen sink, washing up and listening to a podcast. She looked up at the sound and her eyes widened.

'What's going on?' she said, 'Is that . . .?'

Tim threw Matthew on the floor, and the young man collapsed in a heap. Unconscious. Bleeding forehead either from the crash, or where Tim had knocked him out with the butt of the gun, Tim didn't know. 'Do we have any rope? I'm going to tie him up in the basement.'

'What have you done Tim?' Another voice. Another female voice. And then they all came in, Edmund, Robert, Rachel. Tim wondered, as he often did when he saw them all, which one it was. Which one had betrayed them? Which one was helping Ferringham? Who was the reason Matthew was on their kitchen floor right now?

I'd kill them, Amber had said.

'Shit,' Robert said.

Tim hadn't told the others what Amber had told him in the van. Ferringham had found another way into Standedge – an opening in the side of the disused railway tunnel. How was that possible? How did he know? Tim didn't want to tell the others, because if they had found the opening, it would have saved a lot of grief. Pru wouldn't have had to make her contraption – they could have disappeared far easier.

Matthew groaned on the floor – he was waking up.

'I need rope now,' Tim said to the shocked faces in front of him.

They looked down at Matthew. 'Tim,' Rachel said, 'we need you to talk to us. What is happening?'

Tim looked up at them all, angrily. Amber said that someone had sent a map to Edmund's father, James Sunderland. He looked at Edmund, saw him look away under Tim's gaze. Tim kept staring.

'Why are you acting this way?' Rachel continued. 'Why are you the only one allowed to go see Amber anymore? We just want you to talk to us.'

Tim tore his eyes from Edmund, and looked at his sister. She looked pleading, loving, pathetic. They all were. They were followers. They weren't strong enough to take the reins. To do what was necessary. 'Rope.' Tim said savagely.

Pru cursed under her breath and went into the cupboard under the sink. She pulled out a coil of rope and threw it to Tim.

'Thank you,' Tim said. He picked up Matthew by the scruff of the neck and dragged him across the kitchen floor. Matthew moaned in response. The others parted to let him through. He didn't look at them, couldn't bring himself to anymore. They made him sick.

He got to the stairs down to the basement. And made his way down. Making sure Matthew slammed on every step.

'What the hell are you doing Tim?' Edmund said, behind him.

'I'm doing what I've always been doing,' Tim said, going down the stairs and not looking back. 'I'm cleaning up your mess.'

71

During . . .

It was three months since Tim dragged Matthew through the kitchen door. And now Tim was sitting at the kitchen table, in the dark, halfway through his second bottle of vodka for the day.

Matthew was still down there, in the basement. He wanted so badly to kill him. He needed to feel that rush again – the rush he'd felt in the basement of The Hamlet as he choked the soul out of that woman.

They were in the living room. Pru, Robert and Edmund. They were playing cards or some rubbish – something inconsequential and stupid.

Amber had just called him again. He'd thought his troubles were over when Ferringham went back to London with his tail between his legs, but apparently the Morgan girl was sniffing around again. He thought that it was only a matter of time before Ferringham got back in the mix again. They both had to be dealt with.

Tim took a deep swig of vodka, and scratched his forehead with the butt of the gun.

The kitchen door opened and a figure, illuminated by

the moonlight, came in. Rachel.She turned on the light, and jumped when she saw Tim. 'Jesus.'

'Where have you been?' Tim said.

'I went for a walk,' Rachel said, still recovering.

'You go on a lot of walks these days,' Tim slurred.

Rachel's eyes flitted to the gun in his hand. 'How much have you drank, Tim? You shouldn't have a gun in your condition.'

Tim ignored her. 'Can I ask you something?'

'Just put the gun down, Tim.'

Far from what she wanted, he pointed the gun at her. 'I want to ask you a question.'

Rachel froze. 'What?' she shrieked.

'It was you, right?' he said, 'It was you.'

'What are you talking about?'

'Answer me,' Tim shouted. The noise from the other room stopped. There was a shuffling and Tim knew that soon they would have an audience. He didn't care.

'You're drunk. And you're emotional,' Rachel was saying. But she might as well have been talking a different language. Because all Tim heard were lies.

'Tim.' Edmund's voice. Then Pru's. And Robert's. All asking after him.

Tim cocked the gun – *click*. 'Tell me.'

'Yes,' Rachel shrieked. 'Yes, it was me.'

'It was all of us,' Edmund said, stepping into Tim's eyeline. 'This has gone too far, Tim.'

'Who sent the map?' Tim said.

'Me,' Pru said, 'One of the people I was on the engineering and construction course with was interning in

353

construction at the Rivers Trust. Found the opening. Put it on Facebook.'

'You sent it to James Sunderland,' Tim said, 'Why?'

'Because this needs to be over, Tim,' Robert said.

Now they were all in front of him. All in the path of the gun.

'You ungrateful pieces of shit,' Tim said. 'Everything I've done, everything I've become, has been for all of you.'

'No, Tim,' Rachel said, stepping forward from the others, 'what you've become? That was all for you.'

Tim thrust the gun forward, put his finger on the trigger, pressed it halfway. Rachel tensed but said nothing. He was going to do it, blow the bitch away. But then a single tear rolled down Rachel's cheek. And somewhere, in his vodka-addled mind, he forced himself to stop.

She was his sister. His twin sister. He couldn't do it.

'Get in the basement,' Tim said.

The four in front of him faltered. 'What?' Rachel said.

'Get in the damn basement,' Tim shouted, 'All of you. Now.'

With little more arguing, they all filed down the basement stairs. And opened the door. In they went, Robert, then Pru, then Edmund. Rachel paused at the door. Tim came up behind him. Still pointing the barrel of the gun at her. Even though it was an empty threat now. She knew it too.

'I hope you know what you're doing, Tim,' Rachel said, before going in.

Tim slammed the door behind her. He slid the lock and padlocked it.

'I've always known what I'm doing,' Tim shouted through the door. 'And now it's time to end this.'

72

The present . . .

Freezing cold.

Numb.

Blackness.

He couldn't see much – bubbles racing past. His eyes stung.

He flailed around, felt the body next to him, Tim, doing the same. He pushed up against Tim and broke the surface of the water. He saw the faint light of the railway tunnel and the lamp. Salvation.

There was a ledge, the steps – they were close. Robin tried to push himself towards them but found himself being held back. Tim crested the water, and had grabbed Robin's arm.

'You bastard,' Tim said. He pulled Robin back underwater. Robin got a mouthful of icy water and he spluttered, kicking out with his legs. They connected with Tim's stomach and he was propelled backward, letting go of Robin's arm.

Robin broke the water again. Tim came up too and grabbed at him again. Robin tried to move his arms out of the way but they were too slow. Tim got him again.

'Who the hell do you think you are?' Tim said.

Robin ignored him, pushed at Tim's face with his free hand. Tim screamed and relinquished his grip. Robin pushed off him and got an arm on the steps. Tim pulled him back into the water. Robin kicked him away and got back onto the step, onto dry land. The air was somehow colder than the water, attacking him and sending him into uncontrollable shivers.

Tim was still splashing around in the water.

He was suddenly aware that Amber was over him. And she wrenched him out of the water, so he was lying over the steps. 'You've shown great promise, Robin. Great promise.'

Robin gasped, feeling the air attack his cold drenched clothes. It was worse than being in the water. He straightened up. Tim was splashing around in the water. He was trying to grab the step.

'Kill him, Robin. He killed your wife. Become something better.' Amber's voice in his ear.

Robin grabbed Tim, a little bit of hope in the man's eyes, before he pushed him and held him underwater. Tim squirmed under his grip.

'That's right, Robin. Ascend.'

And then Robin realised what he was doing. Amber had got into his head, as easily as that. Was Tim under her spell too? 'You're insane.' He grabbed Tim and pulled him out of the water, next to him.

'What are you doing?' Amber said, exasperated. Like no one had ever defied her before. 'He killed your wife.'

Robin nodded. 'And I'm going to put him in prison. I'm not a killer. Nobody dies today.'

Amber smiled, 'I appreciate the sentiment, Robin. We've all grown as people, learned from each other, completed our arcs, but here's the rub.' She held up her left hand. She was clutching a knife. 'Somebody always has to die.' Amber advanced towards him.

Suddenly, a gunshot rang out. Robin and Amber looked at each other, sharing the same confused look. And then Amber staggered. She looked down to see a blood plume spreading from the wound in her chest. She collapsed.

Behind her, Sally stood holding the gun. 'I really bloody hate canals.'

73

The tunnel had him again, just like it did that day. But this time, he was walking towards the light, walking towards the exit. At least he thought he was, hoped he was. They had been walking for hours, days, months, years. It felt like that, anyway. And the tunnel kept going. On and on and on. Exhaustion lapped at him, just like the water had. He felt as though he were freezing to death, his limbs numb. He wouldn't have known they were there, if his right arm wasn't supporting Sally and his left wasn't dragging an unconscious Tim Claypath. And his legs were moving, almost of their own accord, trying to get out, trying to save them.

They had left Amber where she lay. She was dead. Her story was over.

Sally had stopped talking and her eyes were closed, but she still had strength in her legs to carry her so he supposed that she was still with him. Among the living.

It was hard to believe that it was over. But then it wasn't exactly. There were still things to sort out, sort through. And he silently cried to himself at the prospect.

Sam was buried under the basement of The Hamlet. He'd been right there. She'd been right under his feet.

God. He needed to retrieve the body. He needed people to get it, and then he needed to bury her properly. He needed it to be done. He needed it to be over. What Amber said had been true – he had been scared, scared to even consider the prospect of it being finished. *Her* story. But now he was ready. He was finally ready to let her go.

He pulled Tim along the tunnel and propped up Sally and staggered on and on. Every step he thought he couldn't take another one, but every step he did. And finally, he started to see light.

Light at the end of the tunnel.

He spluttered, laughed. As the pinprick of light expanded. And became the size of a postage stamp, a door and then finally the entrance.

He quickened his step, feeling energy seeping out of him. He made it to the gate, hurling Tim Claypath through with the last of his reserves. He got Sally out and she murmured something, as if in thanks.

They were okay. Everything was going to be okay.

'What the hell?' He looked up to see a man in a reflective vest. A van with the Canals and Rivers Trust logo was parked to the side of the entrance.

That was all he saw before he collapsed.

74

Two months later . . .

Robin got there first and ordered two coffees. He watched the motorway, with the cars flying past – people in a hurry to get where they were going. He remembered what it was like to be someone like that, but since Sam's funeral he had been content to sit back and let everyone else do the rushing around.

The coffees came, and he wondered if she was going to show up.

As he did, a voice said, 'This seat taken?' He looked up to see Sally there, smiling. She slid into the booth, placing a packet on the table. 'Hi, Robin.'

'Hey,' he said. She looked good, a lot better than the last time he'd seen her, when he'd visited her in the hospital. She had been impossibly pale then. Now she looked full of life. 'How are you?'

'I'm better. Still not fantastic. But better.' She smiled. 'You?'

'Same,' he said, pushing a coffee towards her.

Sally took it and took a sip. 'Have you heard the news?'

'That all the Five got arrested? Or that Matthew's free?'

'Neither. Roger Claypath resigned today. He stood up in front of the whole world and said he'd got it wrong. He offered a public apology to Matthew, and to the entire community. It must have burned him to the very core to have to do that. I heard he's going to move away with his wife. Would be just like him to run away.' Sally said, matter-of-factly. 'I have this for you.' She slid the grey packet into the centre of the table.

'What is it?' Robin said.

'It's from a friend.' Robin went to pick it up, but Sally's hand shot out and stopped him. 'Maybe open it when I've gone. I was told it's only for you.'

Robin retracted his hand. 'Okay.'

Sally smiled. 'I can't stop. I've got somewhere to be.'

Robin nodded. 'Of course. Going back to The Red Door?'

'Always,' Sally said, laughing, 'but I have a detour to make first. I'm actually working another case.'

'Even after you almost died the last time?' Robin said, only half-jokingly.

'Nothing like almost dying to make you feel alive,' Sally said. 'Besides there'll always be something crazy happening somewhere. And when it does, The Red Door should be there to cover it.'

Robin nodded.

'You never told me,' she said, 'what was Clatteridges? The thing Sam told Matthew about. The thing that convinced you to help him.'

Robin was quiet for a moment, and then told her. 'Clatteridges is a restaurant. 7.30 p.m. on 18 August

1996. It was when we first met. I was on a date, set up by some friends. It went terribly, and the girl (I can't even remember her name) left before coffee. I sat there on my own, and then this waitress comes up to me and gives me the bill. Her. Samantha. She was the most beautiful girl I'd ever seen. I knew, that moment, that I would marry her. I knew I would spend the rest of my life with her. So I did.'

'Why didn't you put that in the book?'

'Because that memory is mine.'

Sally didn't respond, she just nodded. 'You going to be okay?' Sally said, taking a swig of coffee before standing up again.

Robin smiled. 'Yes.' And he meant it. 'Goodbye Sally.'

Sally took two steps, and then came back. 'My name's not Sally. It's Rhona Michel.'

Robin nodded. 'Then, goodbye Rhona.'

She smiled. 'Open your post.' And she left.

Robin watched her go and then picked up the package. There was something rectangular inside. He opened it and tipped the insides out onto the table. An old mobile phone.

He looked inside the package to find a scrap of paper. He took it out and read it.

AS PROMISED, MATTHEW (PASSCODE 1234, CHECK SAVED VOICEMAIL)

Matthew? Matthew had sent him a phone? Why? He picked it up, turned it over in his hand until he found the power button. He turned it on, put in the passcode and then went to the voicemail. He put it to his ear tentatively.

'Robin, it's me.' Sam's voice. His eyes filled up with sorrow. Her voice. 'I want to tell you that I love you so much. And I want you to know that you made me the happiest I ever was. But I think that might be over now. I think you have to go on alone. And you have to, Robin. You have to live. And you have to be amazing. Be amazing, please. For me. I love you so much. I will always love you.'

Robin waited until the line cut out. And he waited some more, listening to the dull tone of the dead line. He sat there and he cried. He cried until he couldn't cry anymore. He cried for Sam, and for himself, and for everyone along the way.

When he was done, he wiped his eyes, and finished his coffee. And resolved to not cry about it anymore. After all, Sam had told him what to do.

He put the phone in his pocket, got up and paid the bill.

And then he went to be amazing.

Acknowledgements

Now You See Me has been a big project, and the first that I have set in a real location. Marsden is a beautiful place, and Standedge tunnel is incredibly eerie and equally stunning. I would like to thank everyone I met on my travels there, and the crew who took me through the tunnel. If you get the chance to ever visit Marsden, or take a trip through Standedge canal tunnel, I'd highly recommend it.

As always I'd like to thank my #SauvLife crew – Fran Dorricott, Jennifer Lewin and Lizzie Curle – for giving me support whenever I needed it, and a digital Whatsapp shoulder to cry on when things went wrong.

Ever since the launch of *Guess Who*, I've found a wonderful home at Waterstones Durham Crime Club and met many authors and readers who have inspired me, and I now consider firm friends. These people include the wonderful Fiona Sharp, who I met completely by chance whilst going in to buy a book – and I'm convinced has now become the reason for over 70% of my book sales – Daniel Stubbings, who beta-read this book and provided really encouraging and honest feedback when I was feeling really down on it, Claire Johnson and Dave Dawe, for words of kindness and encouragement, Liam, Not Andy, Mick, Helen, fellow authors Robert Scragg and Judith O'Reilly, and everyone else from the group, whose passion for crime fiction really inspires me to keep going and make every book the best it can be.

To my MA Creative Writing colleagues who have helped me through the early stages of my writing.

To Claire McGowan and A.K. Benedict, whom I could never have got to this stage without.

To my wonderful agent Hannah Sheppard, who is always incredibly supportive, and is always on the other end of the phone when I need to chat. To my fabulous UK editor Francesca Pathak, and to the rest of the team at Orion, and also to my US editor Peter Joseph – you're all fantastic.

Loved *Now You See Me*?

Then don't miss Chris McGeorge's
epic locked-room mystery

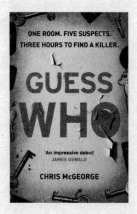

'Packed with gripping twists and turns, *Guess Who* is an
inventive, entertaining locked-room mystery that kept
me utterly hooked'   Adam Hamdy

'An ingenious twisty mystery in a totally unique setting'
Claire McGowan

Read on for an extract now.

The school is quiet by the time I get back. My mum always used to say I was scatter-brained when I forgot stuff, but she never got round to telling me exactly what it meant. Looks like I've been scatter-brained again though. I knew it the second I looked in my bag, halfway home – I'd left it in the Maths room. My jotter, with tonight's homework on it. I don't want to let Mr Jefferies down, so here I am.

I slip back across the field and into the main entrance. There's something really creepy about school after dark – when all of us have gone. Usually it's loud and busy, but now the corridors are quiet and my footsteps sound like elephants stomping because they echo up and down, up and down. I don't see anyone but a man dressed in green overalls, using that weird machine to clean the hall floor. He looks like he's the most unhappy man in the world. Dad says if I don't study, this is the kind of thing that'll happen to me. I feel sorry for the man, and then I feel sorry that I feel sorry because pity isn't nice.

I start walking quicker and get to the Maths room. The door is half open. Mum always taught me to be polite, so I knock anyway. The door squeaks like a mouse as it opens.

I don't see him straight away. The door gets stuck on the papers and exercise books all over the floor. I recognise one and bend down to pick it up. Mine. Mr Jefferies had collected them in at the end of class.

I realise that something is very wrong, and I look up to see him. Mr Jefferies, the Maths teacher, my Maths teacher. My friend. He's hanging in the centre of the room with a belt around his neck. His face looks a strange colour and his eyes look so big he looks like a cartoon.

But he's not. He's real. And it takes me too long to realise what it really is that I'm looking at – too long to see that this isn't some kind of horrible joke.

But as I look, there he is.

Mr Jefferies. Dead.

And at some point, I start to scream.

1

Twenty-five years later . . .

A sharp, undulating tone – drilling into his brain. But as he focused on it, it separated into ringing. In his head or out there – in the world, somewhere else. Somewhere that couldn't possibly be here.

Bbring, bbring, bbring.

Brring, brring, brring.

It was real – coming from beside him.

Eyes open. Everything fuzzy – dark. What was happening? The sound of heavy breathing – taking him a second longer than it should have to realise it was his own. His senses flickering on like the lights in a hospital corridor. And then, yes – he could feel his chest rising and falling, and the rush of air through his nostrils. It didn't seem to be enough. He tried to open his mouth for more, and found it to be incredibly dry – his tongue rolling round in a prison of sandpaper.

Was it silent? No, the *brring brring brring* was still there. He had just gotten used to it. A phone.

He tried to move his arms and couldn't. They were above his head – elevated – slowly vibrating with the threat of pins and needles. He could feel a ring of cold around both of his wrists – something cold and strong. Metal? Yes, it felt like it. Metal around his wrists – handcuffs? He tried to move his limp hands to see what he was attached to. A central bar running down his back. And he was handcuffed to it?

Both arms were throbbing at the elbow – both bent at odd angles as he tried to manoeuvre himself. He was sat up against this thing, whatever it was. But he was sitting on something soft – and felt his current unease was most likely because he had slipped down a bit. He was half sitting and half lying down – an uncomfortable arrangement.

He braced himself, digging his feet into the surface and pushed himself up. His foot slipped, unable to keep any type of grip (shoes, he was wearing shoes, had to remember that), but it was enough. His bottom shuffled back so the strain on his arms was released. With the lack of pain focusing his mind, the blurs around him began to come into focus.

The objects to his left were the first to appear – the closest. He saw a table, between whatever he was sitting on and a white wall. On the table, a black panelled cylinder with red digital numbers on it. A clock. Flashing 03:00:00. Three o'clock? But no – he watched it and it didn't change, illuminated by the light of a lamp next to it.

It hurt his eyes to focus on the light, making him realise the room was rather dark. He found himself blinking away sunspots and looking up at the white wall. There was a picture there, framed. A painting of a distant farmhouse across a field of corn. But that wasn't what drew him to it. The farmhouse was on fire, red paint licking at the blue sky. And in the foreground there was a crude representation of a scarecrow smiling. And the more he looked at it, the more the scarecrow's smile seemed to broaden.

He looked away, unsure why he felt so unsettled by the picture. Now, in front of him he saw his legs and feet – black trousers, black shoes – stretched out over a large bed. The plump duvet had slid down and he had been scrabbling against the bunched up sheets. Assorted dress cushions were scattered around him.

In front of him was a familiar scene – would have been to anyone. Desk, small flat-screen TV, kettle, bowl full of coffee and tea sachets, a leather menu standing open on its side. There he finally saw the phone – far and away out of reach. He moved his head slightly to see a walk-in wardrobe to the front left. To the front right, a window – curtains drawn with the ghost of light creeping through.

Unmistakeable. This was a hotel room. And he was handcuffed to the bed.

And it was all wrong.

Three sharp tones, drilling into his brain. Brring, brring, brring.

This was all wrong.

2

He didn't know how long he sat there, listening to the ringing. Forever and no time at all. But eventually there was a new sound. A voice. A female voice. Slightly robotic.

'Hello, Mr Sheppard. Welcome to the illustrious Great Hotel. For over sixty years, we have prided ourselves on our excellent hospitality and vast range of unique comforts that you can sample while staying in your luxurious surroundings. For information on our room service menu, please press 1, for information on our newly refurbished gym and spa, please press 2, for room services such as an early wake-up call, please press 3 . . .'

Mr Sheppard? Well, at least it was his name. They knew his name? Had it happened again?

'. . . information on live performances in our bar area, please press 4 . . .'

Had he had too much, *done* too much? Twenty years of using and drinking, and using *and* drinking, he had started to think that *too much* was a concept that didn't apply to him. But it had happened before. A grand blackout where he woke up somewhere else entirely. A rollercoaster of a fugue state, where he'd bought the ticket.

'. . . information on the local area, such as booking shows, and transport options, please press 5 . . .'

But he knew how those situations had felt. And this wasn't that.

Because —

It still wasn't there. Where had he been? Before. Where — the last time he remembered. Now, a hotel room, and then — a figure danced around on the edges of his memory. A woman.

He swallowed dry and ran his tongue over his teeth. There was something in them — the grey and rotting aftertaste of wine along with something chemical.

'. . . for early check-out, please press 6, if you would like to hear your options again, please press 7.'

This was wrong. He shouldn't be here.

And the phone — the phone had gone silent. For some reason, no voice felt worse. If he could hear her, could she hear him? *It's a robot, just a robot.* But the line could still be open. Worth a shot.

'If you would like to hear your options again, please press 7.'

He tried again to move his hands, to get some feeling back into them. He made quick fists with his palms. And when he had enough control, he braced himself and moved his wrists quickly against the central metal bar. The centre of the cuffs clanged against it. The sound was loud, but not loud enough. *You're wasting your time. Just a robot.*

'If you would like to hear your options again, please press 7.'

He opened his mouth, his lips ripping apart as though they hadn't been open in years. He tried to say something, not knowing what. All that came out was a hoarse grunt.

'If you would like to hear your options again, please press 7.'

Silence.

He opened his mouth. And what came out was something like a 'Help'. *Just a robot*. Still not loud enough.

Silence.

And then the robot on the phone laughed. *Not a robot*. 'Okay, Mr Sheppard, have it your way. But you're going to have to start talking soon. Can't wait to see what you do next.'

What? He didn't have to time to think about the words because there came a terrible sound. The dull tone of a dead phone line. The woman was gone.

He tried to calm down – his heart racing in his chest. This wasn't happening – couldn't be happening? And maybe it wasn't. Maybe it was just some bad dream, or some kind of new bad trip. He had been hitting it pretty hard lately. But as he thought it, he couldn't believe it.

It felt too real.

Someone would come. Someone had to come. Because the staff obviously knew he was here, which meant the whole hotel knew he was here. And he couldn't have handcuffed himself to the bed, so . . .

Can't wait to see what you do next.

What was the point of the call? That was the thing about phones – you could pretty much be whoever you wanted to be and there was no way of knowing for real. Why would this woman *robot/not a robot* be calling him? He couldn't reach the phone. So, this woman could be the one – the one who'd handcuffed him to the bed. The one who was playing some sick joke. And if she wasn't a staff member, maybe that meant no one would come.

No. This was a hotel. Of course someone would come. Eventually.

He shut his eyes. And tried to slow his breathing enough to listen for anything outside of the room. Any thundering past, any suitcases rolling. But there was nothing. Silence.

Except that wasn't quite true.

He felt it before he heard it. That prickling on the back of his neck. And then, very softly, the sound of breathing.

He wasn't alone.

**The rules are simple. The game is not.
Can you solve the mystery?**

Order now.